'......In the weekends crowds would come to have a gawp...It wasn't so nice for the children. On one occasion my daughter Hanneke came home from school quite scarlet in the face, crying her eyes out, so I asked her what was the matter. She sobbed, 'I told a lie, because they said to me, 'You live in that loony house' and I said that I didn't live in that loony house.' Something like that was very hard for a child to cope with.'

Truus Schröder-Schräder, Interview, 1982, aged 94

Architectress

Ar´chi`tec`tress

n.   1.   A female architect.

Webster's Revised Unabridged Dictionary, published 1913 by C. & G. Merriam Co.

Rietveld Schröder House, Utrecht. Built 1924

The interiors of the Schröder house are open plan, with movable walls and otherwise transformable features; the windows can be opened out completely, removing the indoor-outdoor boundary. None of this had been done before. Many contemporary architects, including Le Corbusier, were deeply influenced by the Schröder House and this influence has endured up to the present. At that time its design was an entirely free and new approach to the relationship between living and architectural form. The building has become an icon of the Modern Movement in architecture. It has been a listed monument since 1976 and UNESCO World Heritage Site since 2000.

Table of Contents

Prologue
Verdigris Copper

Utrecht, 10 July 2017

Out of the hundreds of cyclists who pass below my apartment daily, along the brick path that intersects Wilhelminapark, students and office workers snaking their way to and from the University District or the old MuseumQuarter beside the canal, there is one that I always look out for. She rides one of those old-fashioned steel framed bikes without gears, a young woman of slim build with a calico dress rising and falling below a yellow linen smock. Visible beneath its low hem and pushed through the pedals are boots laced up the front.

Her bohemian clothing might come from one of the vintage shops in the old quarter, but I prefer to think of her as a ghost riding among them as they tap their smartphones or listen to music through tiny earpieces. Some are hands-free, knees undulating to a rhythm, backs straight, expert in their casual balancing of groceries, friends, children, books, weaving in and out of each other, never colliding.

The woman has a mass of auburn curls tied loosely back. Sometimes she carries a small child on the rack behind, its arms wrapped tightly round her waist, being taken to kindergarten perhaps, and at other times the rack holds rolls of parchment held together with ribbon. Always intent, as if aware of a small window of time, vital to get to where she is going before it is lost.

One time she looked right up and seemed to catch my eye as her wheels kept turning. She smiled, then looked back to her route. Perhaps I was dozing and dreamt this, but ever since I feel we are aware of each other's presence, even when she keeps her gaze fixed ahead.

Propped up on the old chaise I gaze around at my white walls, coombed ceilings and tall oak doors. I have been thinking to take down the internal partitions and create an open loft, bringing the two rooms into one and allowing light to pass through, like the ones on *Airbnb* that Inge shows me when she is taking a holiday. I have no family to leave it to, so have bequeathed it to my beloved Centraal Museum for visiting researchers. They might prefer an open space. I'm drawn to attics. Aberdeen, London, the locked one in Glasgow. Even, technically, the upper floor of the *Schröderhuis*. With an attic comes freedom. Do we choose them, or do they choose us?

It was on this day, exactly a quarter of the way into the last century. Hotter than today. I checked. I probably waved her off, trusting that she would be back in the afternoon. Perhaps someone waited behind with me, long after all the other children had gone home, when she didn't come. I wonder if I was accepting back then, unquestioning when one of the others arrived in her place. Perhaps Binnert was sent; he'd have been old enough, at thirteen. One of them anyway, Binnert or even Marjan. Not Hanneke. She'd have only been six, nearly seven. I wonder if I sensed the seismic shift even as I was taken the few blocks from the kindergarten to Prins Hendriklaan.

From my rear window here, between the entrance door and wetroom, with its fixed glass screen and rainforest shower, I can glimpse the house at 50 Prins Hendriklaan, a sliver of white piercing the red brick mass beyond the canal on Rembrandtkade. I can see it because this apartment is on the attic floor of a neat three storey block on Koningslaan. To the front, full height windows, french doors, a set in each of the two rooms, overlook, beyond the tops of the oaks and sycamores, the little bridge that crosses the narrow cypress swamp marking the entrance to Wilhelminapark. Each has a modern take on the Juliet balcony, a ledge of thick, clear glass to waist height, simple, unadorned, no handrail, providing the *wow* factor as they say these days. It takes me back to the Seventies, the first time I saw a structural glass balustrade. To each side, copper sheet wraps around the window reveals and tucks into the slope of the tiled mansard roof, its weathered greenish verdigris patina cool and matt against the red brick façade.

My care package involves a daily visit from the essential Inge, who has promised to have my tabby Mies when the time comes. Inge prepares a light meal of my favourite *ontbijtkoek* with butter and soup or perhaps bread and cheese with fruit, then does a bit of tidying up, not that there is much of that required. The apartment is sparse. Migration allowed me to offload baggage in all its forms, later even books, once I became a *zilver surfer* for my genealogy and learned one could read electronically. In the same way that I believe a home, however frugal, should reflect the latest technology, so it goes with living. I painstakingly order groceries and prescriptions online and read journals in large print that way too. Sketching I still do by hand, though now with some difficulty.

Designers today cannot imagine life before the Internet. In our day we waited frustratedly for brochures in the post or, latterly, browsed the building library in Store Street, coveting small

perhaps a cork tile or wood veneer, an upholstery fa'

I specified a finish based on whichever arrived first

sample board to be taken hurriedly across London in a ~...

presentation. Once, in a weekly meeting with the men, trying to choose the colour a wall should be (someone had cut up the only paint chart) I remember running upstairs to grab a peach coloured toilet roll. 'THIS is it!' How they laughed. A woman's touch.

Now professionals, or indeed anyone, can find or draw or print or share any choice electronically. They can tour any home or building virtually, or any city. It must be wonderful for them. People's own homes are proudly shared by the owners with the world, to rent out, or for others to emulate. Teaching must be very different too. I hope good students still sketch ideas manually and don't rely on a computer for everything.

Mies wakes me at five every morning. Neither of us sleeps much now, happy to doze together propped up on pillows waiting for the dawn that presages birdsong. Whenever winter approaches the view changes from this summer curtain of verdant leaves, a dense green canopy that eradicates the long-distance view but offers as compensation a constant stream of small fat-bellied birds amply supplied from feeders hooked over the glass ledges, to falling gold through autumn, and finally to bare ochre branches, thin and thrashing, intertwined skeletons in the storms. A white moon blurred by cold mist then lies behind the still, black silhouette of branches, moonlight that can be as strong as day. On winter days I can again see the paid dog walkers criss-crossing the park, each with four or five energetic charges

g through crisp frosted carpets of leaves or on pathways rutted
th bike tyre tracks.

We moved from the lower wharfside conversion on the Oudegracht
six years ago, once I could no longer climb the steep steps from the
canalside to the upper wharf. Perhaps I needed one more attic. Had
this eco-loft been built even a few years earlier, it would have been the
preserve of a one-off showcase aimed at the more discerning buyer
with an interest in climate change. Now it is becoming the norm, and
for that I feel privileged to be still living. To be able to see that come to
fruition, I almost think the planet may indeed be saved. We missed the
canal activity for a while, the working barges and tourist narrowboats,
and the mice, all a source of pleasure for Mies, but here he can lie on
the oak floor stretched out in the sun. Other than a distant hum of
traffic when the windows are open, and the cyclists, there is no
indication of city dwelling, even though we are in the very heart of it.

As I sit here, I luxuriate in this frugality. The simple life always
coveted is now mine to savour, albeit made comfortable by the few
design classics and minimalist furnishings I hung onto. An Eileen Grey
table here, a Marcel Breuer chair there, the cracked and worn leather of
my Corbusier chaise by the window, the limited-edition prints. As
William Morris said, *'Have nothing in your house that you do not know to be
useful, or believe to be beautiful.'* The few items here are both. I cannot say
the same for me.

Not only have I pared down fixtures and fittings, but also people.
Most have died of course, but I was always a recluse-in-waiting, even in
the midst of a corporate gathering back in the day. Nothing worse than
receiving an invitation to some launch and agonising about how to

decline without causing offence. Such a relief to be free of that. When I first moved here, I had the company of one or two colleagues at the museum, but made a conscious choice not to generate a new social circle. It suited me to chat to tourists, American or British or those who preferred English, who came to look around the Schröder House, answering their questions as best I could. They came for an hour, for the tour with blue plastic coverings over their shoes, *please do not sit on the chairs*, then left suitably uplifted, which was enough. I was seen as an asset for the job, English being my first language, plus by then I knew the subject well, although it meant my Dutch remained limited. In such an incubated life here, I fear I have not learned the language beyond what I require to deal with deliveries, paid help, neighbours and doctors.

For the most part now, I am content in the company of BBC Radio on iPlayer or a *Nordic Noir* drama, and catch up on local gossip with Jakob the cleaner or compare the aches and pains of old women with my neighbour Tineke. Mostly I look down from the window through clouded eyes. When the weather is warm and the burgeoning leaves obscure all, like today, I go down in the lift and sit on the bench outside, sometimes with Tineke, but often alone. Now I am so very old, people do not see me, which suits me fine. I like being invisible. When I was young and flirting with what they now call anorexia, I used to think, *I won't be happy until I disappear completely.*

Moving here was a clean sheet, somewhere I could take stock. *Die before you die.* Now, thirty years later, by some miracle I am still here, and the housing world embraces warm, open plan and accessible spaces for families to dwell in, filled with light and easy communication. We senior citizens have the choice not to live in little grey boxes, those brutalist low ceilinged properties, poorly insulated, badly proportioned and weathered in a northern climate.

I sketch shakily with whatever fluidity my stiff joints allow and annotate the drawing, showing the inner partitions removed, in order to instruct the Museum, then sign it formally, *Gertrude Flora Bray, 10/7/2017*, and put down my favourite old Rotring pen, the one Richard Rogers left on the podium at a public lecture. I am tired from the effort. Still holding the sketch on blue waxed paper in my lap, I look down to the park. There she is: the young auburn-haired woman, stopped in her tracks: she is smiling and looking up from the cycle path, beckoning me with her outstretched hand.

Black Lace

Ailsa

Leith, 23 January 1901

The captain announces the decision to return in order to allow those British passengers who understandably wish to abandon their journey to disembark, sombrely reciting the official statement from the cable telegram over the loud hailer. Ailsa's hopes, that only moments before soared as she took in the vast North Sea for the first time, plummet now so rapidly that she feels unable to breathe. She has to grip the deck handrail to steady herself, its wet oily steel leaving a stain on her kid gloves.

As icy fathoms churn beneath her, inside the other passengers gasp, shuffle, rearrange themselves into positions of mourning. Women, although not her mother, wish they had thought ahead and packed their black lace for this half-expected event. In the cabins and salons, and at breakfast, women are sobbing quietly now, eyes downcast, their husbands protectively shielding them from public display or requesting urgent glasses of iced water. In the absence of her own husband, yet knowing his wishes instinctively, Flora Bray looks anxiously around for her daughter, trying to catch a glimpse of that copper hair, that pale freckled face in the throng.

Ailsa is alone with the cawing gulls. The seabirds are confused now by the slow but certain shift in direction. *So close*, she whispers into the spume that rises and splashes her face as the grinding vessel begins to yaw and roll, its course set now. In futile defiance she keeps her face anchored toward the sunrise, to the imagined windmills, the tulip fields and canals beyond the horizon that promised so much to a sheltered seventeen-year-old girl eager for the world, before she ducks back, drenched, through the hull in search of her mother.

Is Papa so powerful after all that he can command this too? Did he simply will the Monarch to die last evening to thwart his daughter's plans, and that grand old lady conveniently obliged?

12 Knowe Terrace

Pollokshields

Glasgow

21 February 1901

Arnhem

Netherlands

Dear An,

Thank you for your most welcome letter. I too regret that Mama and I were unable to complete the journey. Thank you also for your sympathy regarding the death of our Queen. It feels like our whole nation is overcome with grief and nothing will ever be the same.

I hope, like you, that we can continue to write and perhaps one day I will visit. I was so looking forward to our weeks together and remain indebted to your father for having offered this opportunity for me. I confess I am most disappointed.

Mama is unwell as a consequence of the premature return voyage, and consigned to bed most days, so perhaps God intervened in our plans and brought me back with her. Papa had been concerned for her travelling back alone once I was settled, so is pleased that I can be here to comfort her.

Please write to me again when you can. My father has written to Mr. Schräder regretting the untimely circumstances and to thank him again for the opportunity generously given for my intended stay.

Always, your Scottish friend,

Ailsa

Silver Pewter

Gertrude

Glasgow, 10 August 1940

It is early Saturday evening. Another argument. Heated words, stilted, awkward, his dominant, dictatorial, fired across the room like bullets, mine the speedy quivering retort of a frightened animal, preferring flight over fight yet unable to stop from standing my ground, albeit briefly. I always leave first. I cannot compete. These battles are more frequent and I long to get away.

As usual at the weekend Father (for I must call him *Father*, where others call theirs *Dad*) was following me through the streets, crawling at what he thinks is a suitable distance behind me in his motorcar, past the tennis club, observing me through the trees in Maxwell Park where I cut around the boating pond, checking who I am seeing and where I am going. Not believing me when I get home, thinking the worst, accusing me of seeing some boy, which I am not. This time I came back at him. I'm not sure why I said it. It came out of desperation, like saying, *I have no-one on my side*. I can hardly believe that I stood up to him; that I spoke about her out loud.

I left the study in that familiar helpless rage, ready to throw something across my room. This time though I am not in my room; I am in another room, at the top of the house, that I've never been in before. It is quiet, and the air feels dry, or perhaps that is my mouth. It is dark, the bare lightbulb hanging from the ceiling no longer works. I was told off for climbing these steep stairs as a child. No-one goes up here. The door on the top landing has been locked for as long as I can remember, as have the back stairs from the kitchen. The three arched attic windows, although a prominent feature from the street along with the ornate chimney pots, are never cleaned on the inside. When tradesmen come to fix leaks in the lead roof or glazed rooflights, they use long ladders and work only from the outside. No-one questions it. Edith has talked of mice and soot, of damp, of the floor being unsafe to walk on. I could fall between the joists and break the ornate plaster of the drawing-room ceiling. Perhaps that's what Edith has been told too, because this floor is as solid and habitable as below.

With my dress sleeve I wipe dust from the arched windows, and soft light floods across white painted floorboards, washing white wainscoting below a dado, evening sun through windows I've only ever known from outside. Unlike the two floors below, this one is not stifled by floral fabrics and mismatched tasselled lampshades, brocade chair covers and dark lacquered wood, but is simple, spare, expansive. It smells of old pine and is remarkably free from soot. The space, front to back, contains a few simple pieces of handcrafted wooden furniture, dry and quite intact beneath layers of dust: a daybed and table, two plain rustic chairs in the style of those we saw in the Arts and Crafts Exhibition on a school trip with Miss Peake. On the table is a doll's house, tall and narrow. The front opens out, the façade a single hinged piece. It is a model replica of this house, finished in the finest detail. I am astounded.

At the back windows, above what must be my bedroom, is the outline of a bulky object covered in a yellowed dust sheet, which I remove to reveal an industrial contraption of shoulder height, comprising a solid angled wooden board and tee square, below which is a series of small iron wheels painted red that must serve to adjust its angle. This is mounted on a heavy cast iron base painted bottle green. It appears to be an engineer's drafting table. It must weigh a ton. How did anyone lift it up here?

I feel cocooned, like arriving at a protected harbour having survived a raging storm. Following my trepidatious climb, compelled to go on by the promise of something (an old suitcase amongst the mice droppings?), and once I knew it was not the perilous, hostile environment I'd been led to believe, I locked the door from inside with the pewter key I'd just been thrown. I sit rather shakily in one of the chairs, the floral tea dress I wore to Margaret's now too dusty to matter, to try to make sense of his words, and how they must relate somehow to this self-contained sanctuary above our heads all these years.

Not knowing my mother, a lifetime of it being impossible to speak of her, or to ask questions, is accepted, and too much time has passed for that to change; too much precedence. Although she grew up here, the subject of her is taboo. I think I was told she died, but I don't remember and cannot possibly ask again. That would be unthinkable, too embarrassing now, too excruciating, after all this time, to ask, even about my grandparents, who presumably lived here too, if she did. As if to mention them would also sting. As if they are all to blame.

'I don't even have a mother! I know nothing about her. All I have is the black book, and one photograph!'

The black book contains notes from cookery and housekeeping classes she attended, skills which no doubt pleased my father, and at the back of the book there is a sketch of Knowe Lodge signed by her, so she must have liked to draw for pleasure. I worked out she made the sketch from the middle drawing-room window. The photograph was taken in London when she must have been in her twenties, but she is wearing a hat so I don't know what her hair is like. She looks fair skinned and any strands of hair look light. I hide these in the inner pocket of my portfolio case, ever since he said it was *macabre* to keep them on my bedside table. That makes me think she's dead.

The window to my mother's life has always been closed, and I dare not ask to open it. Father makes that very clear. Sometimes when he is drunk he will open it slightly, just a glimpse, not to let me see but to try to look back through there himself, for no more than a few minutes, and certainly not to let me go with him. I can't interject. I can't ask, *what was she like?* Then he slams the shutters and turns the topic onto me, most recently to my lack of morals, peering over his spectacles as he pours his whisky, angrily tamping down the tobacco in his pipe, the weapon he remonstrates with, pointing its stem at me. The tone is one of self-pity, rambling words about what he could have become but for the last war, lost opportunities, the lack of a *proper wife*.

Perhaps he was so shocked at her being spoken of in the sober light of day that he responded as he did. Limping away unsteadily (I remembered then that he and Edith were at a fundraising lunch today for the war effort, which would explain his verbosity so early in the day) from the other side of the study he unlocked his bureau and took an object from the inner drawer, also locked. He threw it and it thudded at my feet, a large silver pewter key with an ornate Celtic knot fashioned at the bow, and a cardboard label that read *Attic*. Groping for it on the floor through blinding tears, I took flight before he could change his mind.

If you are so keen to know your precious mother, have this to add to your collection.

Red Sandstone

Ailsa

Glasgow, April 1907

Ailsa has slept later than intended and is only wakened now by the familiar sound of iron on wood as the lion's head raps against the storm doors. She hears Bridget's brisk steps on the hall tiles, followed by the metallic slide of the bolt, then a low murmur of voices at the foot of the stairs. The gap in heavy drapes is already throwing a shaft of sunlight onto dust motes above her head, so it must be well after eight thirty. Papa will have already left and Ailsa had wanted to speak with him at breakfast and present her latest evidence.

While browsing foreign newspapers in the Mitchell Library, she found an article in a recent copy of The New York Times about a woman in America, Fay Kellogg, who has actually become an architect! The headline declared **'Woman Invades Field of Modern Architecture'** with the subtitle **'Remarkable Success of Miss Kellogg in Profession Exclusively Followed by Men Scores Triumph for Her Sex.'**

When Ailsa attended Pollokshields Ladies' School, most girls aspired to *finding a husband,* having children and running a home. She did not share such an aspiration, nor did she fit with the alternative, small academic set in her class, so found it hard to fit in with any one group. She longed for a close friend, but there seemed to be no-one like her. Not a Fay Kellogg among them.

She will ask to speak with Papa tonight. He must know that it is not enough for her to attend cookery demonstrations and talks on how to manage servants in order to run a household in some future marriage. Neither has she a spark of interest in any of the eligible sons of business associates from her father's club that he is all too often presenting as potential suitors. He tells her that she must choose a man who *puts her on a pedestal*. At such times Ailsa has an image of herself, semi-naked like the Venus de Milo. So long as she stands perfectly still, this young man that her father would wish her to find worships her from his armchair, glancing up admiringly from his newspaper when he remembers to. She is not sure what will happen when she climbs down from the podium, as she surely must eventually.

She has even thought about how she will approach the conversation. Fay Kellogg had said (in the Mitchell Ladies' Reading Room Ailsa had silently mouthed this extract in her best American drawl): *I asked father what kind of drawing he was going to put me at, and when he answered 'architectural', I fairly shouted with glee, for it was always my ambition to be able to build a nice little house which I could call my own and I am proud to say that this and a lot more has been realised.*

In fact, the article went on to say that, during her brief career thus far, Fay Kellogg has helped to design or prepare plans for the Hall of Records, the Thirteenth Regiment armour, the Monastery of the Precious Blood, and an addition to the Women's Memorial Hospital Brooklyn. Ailsa will not mention that part. Last time Papa swiftly shot down her argument by saying that he had spoken to someone at his club who confirmed there are no female lavatories in architects' offices. She had become tongue-tied as usual.

She rises and looks out. The gate to the meuse lane along the back of the terrace is ajar. Papa takes his bicycle out that way and she can see it has gone from where he leaves it in dry weather, propped against the annexe beside the fuel store below Bridget's room.

At this moment she catches sight of herself in the oval mirror over the dresser, not from vanity, for Ailsa has little interest in how she looks, but because the sun has ignited wild red curls spiralling in all directions and for a moment she is startled by the vividness. The hair of her Highland ancestors her mother says, skipped two generations, a pale complexion sprinkled with freckles and *eyes the colour of a grey Hebridean sky*; a small pert nose and wide mouth, a face that could be that of a girl far younger than her twenty-four years. So little changes, so little is allowed to change, that the marks of life which reflect maturity in a face do not apply to Ailsa. She scowls at her reflection, wraps a shawl around her thin shift, then treads barefoot across the room and turns the doorknob slowly.

Quietly, tiptoeing to avoid creaking floorboards, she crosses the first-floor landing to the front and enters the drawing room, where the familiar sight of an already crackling fire within the hearth lifts a mood which is too often low these days. She pictures Bridget in there before six this morning, while they slumbered, laying that fire in the grate on her knees, along with the two downstairs, so that they will be lit for Papa's breakfast and here for when Mama comes up from the morning-room to do whatever it is she does on the days when she doesn't have one of her heads. Do her parents think about Bridget, who rises at five o'clock in her tiny maid's room in the annexe, coming down the back stairs to the cold kitchen, when she too would rather lie in bed for another few precious hours? No, they will take her fire raking and cross stick laying for granted, as Papa reads his newspaper and Mama writes instructions for receiving her ladies for afternoon tea. Why is a household so complex, Ailsa wonders, not for the first time. She rubs her palm along the mantle's polished onyx and lingers in the warmth before moving to one of the three tall windows, their sills almost at floor level.

From here Ailsa can look down to the wide cobbled street and notices now that there is a motor car outside, that of Dr. Robertson, who regularly attends her mother. Her attention moves to two stonemasons across the road working with chisels to fashion the final alterations to the inset Greek urns on the curved sandstone wall that retains the higher ground of Knowe Lodge opposite. She has seen these men before, working some streets away on the muddy site of new red sandstone tenements on the other side of the tracks. She has watched from behind the iron railings above the railway cutting, after her daily walk through Maxwell Park, as massive blocks of stone masonry are offloaded from wagons onto the station platform, their journey from Locharbriggs Quarry complete, clouds of pink dust billowing into the air. By now most of this southside suburb of blonde sandstone has been built but, according to the local newspaper, these latest red tenement blocks on the outer edge of the village beside the cricket field seem to be affording opportunity for architects and craftsmen to try out a new style, of generous proportions and floor plan layouts, to complement the *lifestyles and aspirations of people looking for something modern in the fashionable 'Glasgow Style.'* She longs to see inside one.

Yesterday Ailsa watched from beside the fire inside the ticket office of Maxwell Park station to where an architect, or perhaps he was a draughtsman, unfolded large blueprints and could be seen discussing these with a foreman at a gap site on the new road parallel to the railway tracks. This flamboyant young man, with bold cravat and small eyeglasses, had nodded to her after alighting the train to go on site the previous week, although he was more modestly dressed that time she recalls. She watched him yesterday gesticulating rather theatrically, almost as if he were performing to an audience, towards other tenements further along as if to compare, and she dared to dream for a few moments that could be her one day. She desperately wants to learn technical drawing, to master the methods that accurately convey, to scale, the exact shape and size of stonework over an archway, the depth of a string course between floors, the raised aprons below windows.

From the drawing-room window now she sees one stonemason looking up at her but he glances quickly back to his work. She imagines him crossing the road, knocking and asking Bridget if he may speak with Miss Bray. He is shown up to the drawing room where they shake hands and consult on the best way to finish the detail on the keystone above a close entrance to the new tenements. He defers to her knowledge, as she takes out her sketchbook and provides him with a freehand drawing of a tiny quatrefoil to be carved into the stonework. He leaves with the detached sheet of paper in hand, thanking her with a slight nod. When she looks out again, the two men are laughing and smoking pipes, leaning against the wall in the sun, sharing a joke. She ducks quickly away from view.

Her little black book is lying on a side table and she glances disparagingly at last week's hastily scribbled lecture notes from the Glasgow School of Cookery and Domestic Economy, on how to successfully run a house (not how to successfully *design* a house).

Housekeeper: choice and calibre of house and furniture; manage and clean, arrange meals, buys in, keeps accounts, cooking. Good temper, early to bed and early to rise; see that she has rest and fresh air – ¼ hour rest in the middle of the day; a cup of strong beef tea a powerful stimulant.

The previous week's notes describe the phasing out of green-papered bedrooms due to deaths and illness, mainly among children, once thought to be caused by flecks of green dust detached from the wallpaper being breathed in.

We now know the cause of this illness is due to damp rooms with arsenic green wallpaper where there is a mouse-like odour and fungi living on wallpaper paste converting inorganic arsenic into a highly toxic gas.

Ailsa shudders. Why would anyone want dark green walls any more? People want lighter decoration now, and motor cars, and to show their ankles with impunity. And why does everyone need servants to run houses that are too big for them anyway?

Knowe Terrace is a short row of west facing Victorian townhouses flanked either end by a blonde sandstone tenement block, reminding Ailsa of the bookends in Papa's study. Each townhouse is bestowed with these three elegant first floor rectangular sash windows, positioned above a main door and two adjacent dining room windows, *affecting a symmetry and style reminiscent of the Georgian terraces prevalent in Edinburgh or in Glasgow's West End* (Ailsa is reading about this period currently through library books). Each house number is engraved in gold leaf on the fanlight above the etched glazed entrance behind the storm doors that Bridget opens every morning after breakfast and closes after supper. Theirs is number 12, the fourth last in the row if walking in a southerly direction.

Three smaller attic level windows sit directly above: these are the crown, the *pièce de résistance* along with tall showpiece chimney stacks that sit high up on the roof and separate each house from its neighbour. Unlike their counterparts below, the attic windows are arched, each set within triangulated stone and designed in the style of architect Alexander Thomson, whose local work Ailsa likes to sketch.

The great man himself lived with his large family a few streets away in Strathbungo, and died before Ailsa was born, having designed a number of remarkable houses, including that fine corner terraced house for himself, *resonant of classical Italian and Greek temples yet deploying the most modern of building techniques,* according to her book.

Ailsa loves his house designs with a passion. Her favourite is the small but graceful neighbouring Knowe Lodge, which sparked these later fashionable emulations of 'Greek' Thomson's unique style. The tall chimney pots on the roof of Ailsa's father's house are in the style of the gateposts of Knowe Lodge. She often draws the Lodge while seated at this window and looks across at it now, nestled there with its rusticated arches and eaves thrown into relief by the morning sun, and thinks it would be at home in any Italian landscape.

She wishes the front of her own house could open in the way her doll's house does, the entirety somehow connecting over three floors, light flooding through. Her father was so proud of the townhouse built for him that he commissioned this miniature replica for Ailsa when she managed to reach her third birthday.

She adores her home, and has read the title deeds from 1875 in Papa's study. Standard requirements of the day: *to have the property built within one year: it must be a single dwelling house with no fewer than six rooms, to include a kitchen and water closet, and to be no more than three storeys in height* (a strict stipulation in Pollokshields, Ailsa has learned, making the sightlines lower and more appealing than other parts of Glasgow where, typically, crowded four storey tenement blocks loom high on either side of dark streets.)

Charles likes to recount, in response to compliments from visitors, the day he carried his new bride over the virgin threshold to begin their life together, where they hoped to fill this house with children. He does not say this in front of Flora.

Ailsa is the only one surviving. She knows little of the babies before her who did not live long, only that her father has told her that, with her, their last hope, he *wrapped her in cotton-wool.* They named her Ailsa, meaning 'God's promise', a Gaelic name after her great-grandmother from Skye. This house is a shrine to the ghosts of those babies before her: brothers and sisters who used to whisper to her in the attic nursery, after Mama went back down, that they were here when her mother was young and energetic for life. She is the late consolation prize, the one who must not be put to risk, or upset Mama.

If Mama asks Ailsa to take tea again today she is resolved to make an excuse. She loves her soft spoken, clearly intelligent mother dearly, knowing her capable of so much more, yet such stifling activity seems to be all that she allows herself. Last time Ailsa thought she might faint with boredom. Idle gossip about who had the latest style of hat at church or whomsoever they saw last week in the Willow Tea Rooms and how stylishly or not that unsuspecting victim was turned out at the time.

Mama is too gentle to see faults in anyone, with her Highland deference, smiling along with them and trying to interject with a positive comment or two, alas never managing to steer the conversation onto the higher ground that she and her daughter would prefer. Occasionally, like the time a few years ago when the two women took an interrupted trip together by train and boat to the Netherlands, Mama seemed happier somehow, more animated when away from home.

In Ailsa's mind, her own row of houses, hopefully to remain the only row of this exact design among the wide tree-lined streets of Pollokshields, is more striking, more individual, than any other. It forms a visual bridge between the gridded rows of East Pollokshields' tenemental properties and the large ostentatious villas of meandering West Pollokshields, and this distinction pleases her. There is much snobbery and vain competition for the detached villas, especially those higher up the hill among 'the Avenues', such as who has bought or taken a tenancy on the most unusual, which one has the largest grounds and gate posts, the finest stained glass at the stair landing or cupola, a billiard room extension.

Responding to this, two speculative builders, the ones who put up the more modest villas lower down the hill, cleverly advertised each house as unique, sometimes only slightly but just enough to count. She remembers this mass building project still underway when she was a child walking home from school with Bridget, finding it far more interesting than anything she learned in lessons. Ailsa and Bridget played a game to try and spot the detail that separated one plot from another: an extra side window, a different moulding to a stone gatepost or chimney, an entrance porch, a conservatory.

What Ailsa cherishes in place of individuality is the view from the flat roof, accessed from a small winding stair on the attic floor, over the tops of spires and crescents of the West End, past the Gothic splendour of the university at Gilmorehill; the new baroque styled Art Galleries that she found so exhilarating when they opened their doors to visitors a few years ago, the pipe organ music thrilling the crowds in the Centre Hall during the 1901 International Exhibition. It offered some small compensation that year for the foreign experience she was denied.

Nestling between all of that and her own rooftop is the Clyde with its teeming noise and swirling smoke from the shipyards and engineering works, effluent spilling out towards its estuary in the west and, to the north, the undulating Campsie Fells on the horizon seeming to enfold Glasgow protectively within their southern flanks. Out on that rooftop she feels exhilarated, so much life happening all around her, that she wants to be a part of it, to grab hold of it, to fly off that roof!

Unusually, she hears Bridget, who has run upstairs, knock on her mother's bedroom door and enter, followed by the whispered tones of the two women as they descend the stairs together. Why has Dr. Robertson not come up to attend to her mother in her bed as he normally would? Back on the landing now, she hears voices downstairs more clearly. One is her mother's, the other a man's, but possibly a third? They are speaking in low urgent tones. Quickly she crosses back to her room and throws on her grey calico which has been lying in a heap on the chair, pins her hair up roughly and descends to see her mother through the open dining-room door with Dr. Robertson and a portly middle aged uniformed policeman. Flora is standing with one hand on the table as if to steady herself. Three heads turn to Ailsa. There follows a long silence. Flora's face is ashen, her other hand to her forehead, a common sight in itself, except that here it is shaking uncontrollably.

'Mama?'

"Ailsa. Sit down dear.'

The two women sit at a corner of the table, where Ailsa sees bread crumbs and used linen napkins uncleared, the glass marmalade dish uncovered, congealed egg on a plate. Bridget is nowhere to be seen. The men move nearer, too close Ailsa thinks. Her mother is now holding her hand across the tablecloth.

'Your father had an accident on his way to work.'

'What's happened? Has he come off again?'

Her mother's response is a whisper. 'This policeman says his bicycle.... collided with an electric tramcar.... on the Paisley Road.' Her words come in short bursts as she tries to breathe. 'Shortly after he left home.'

Ailsa fixes her gaze on the crumbs. Where has Bridget gone? She wants to ask this, say anything so as not to hear the next words her mother will surely speak. Should she sweep the crumbs into a napkin herself? Her mother does not speak further. There is what seems to be another endless silence, broken by her mother's doctor saying he is very sorry but her father was killed, the tram was using one of the new routes and most likely Mr. Bray was not expecting it to be there as he cycled across that familiar junction. He hit the front corner of the tramcar with full force and came off his bicycle. His head hit the edge of the kerb. He would have died instantly, which is the only mercy.

As if underwater, Ailsa hears the policeman asking do they have a male relative he can contact, someone to deal with the matter in hand. They do not. Flora will contact her husband's solicitor Robin Asher of McArthur and Murricane, who is a friend of the family and resides in The Avenues. Thank you, she says. I will send Bridget with a note. Dr. Robertson says he will return in the evening to check on the two ladies.

'My daughter and I would like to be alone now, thank you' says Flora.

Belfast Sink

Gertrude

Glasgow, 12 August 1940

He left for work earlier than usual this morning and Edith has gone into town as she always does on Mondays. Yesterday was one of those terrible, silent Sundays where the atmosphere hung oppressively over the entire day and not even the radio was on. I am determined to ask him more about the attic but not yet. I will wait until he is back to speaking to Edith at least. Meanwhile I go up to investigate further, locking myself in as before, this time with a torch.

At the back of the space, which is the full depth of this tall, narrow house, below exposed cross beams, joists and sarking boards, through a mist of newly disturbed and swirling dust particles, can be seen two plain windows, grimy with years of Scottish rain, but clearly once functional. As my eyes adjust I notice that, opposite to where I came in (I have now found the confidence to walk around), a whitewashed brick chimney breast houses a cooking range, there is a water closet and basin behind a narrow door, and an aperture through to the light well above our bathroom.

Of course: we have two areas of glass high above, skylights that are always leaking, the smaller one over the windowless bathroom off the landing, and the cupola over the main stairs and hall, which I'm used to seeing only from below. Up here those are closed off behind brick walls.

But what does this room have to do with my mother? At school we studied a nineteenth century Jesuit poet and his concept of *inscape*, or identity, the essence that is of each one of us, unique, unlike anyone else's. I had thought about this for a while and it led me to think that it doesn't matter how many photographs we see of a person, or have her or him described to us, the fact is, if we have never met that individual face to face, or heard their voice and watched them move, listened to them talking about something, seen their *personality* in other words, we cannot know them at all. Equally, it is possible that (this is my own theory) when we have not met that person, their character takes on a cloak of perfection which might not be wholly accurate. They become a paragon of grace and sophistication in our minds.

I suppose, now that there is Kodachrome, if the mother of a baby or small child knows she won't be around, she might make a *home movie* as they call it in America, a colourful moving image, something for her child to watch when she or he has grown, to be kept locked away until then by someone trustworthy. The mother in the film might do the expected thing: look into the camera and say how much she loves her child, how sorry she is that she will not be there to see her grow up, and so on. In fact, these sentiments, important though they are, would be of more value if she adds something like this:

'You will never remember me holding you, or my smell, my hair, my skin, my eyes, but I held you, like this. Look at us together here. Listen, I have a Glasgow accent like yours will be by now. I speak quietly; but here is my laugh! Here are my hands; look - my eyes are grey, like yours, and we have the same nose. I have this habit of twisting a strand of hair around my fingers when I am talking. I am reading a new book, Jacob's Room, which is 'avant garde.' I play the piano and

sing. I'm very good at dealing with servants', and so on. Views, interests, likes and dislikes. That sort of thing. It should be made law to do this. The Inscape Law they could call it.

I said to Edith last week, when I was doing my homework while we waited for Father to come home and we happened to be in the drawing room together, which was unusual without him, 'Mother, think of someone you never met, but you have wondered about, compared yourself with perhaps, even been jealous of. You've seen photographs and perhaps read something they wrote, like a postcard. You may have had them described to you. Yet the thought of them drives you insane, because you think they are special in some way, better than you. But, I wonder if, five minutes in the company of that person, one minute even, they'd be brought to life as an individual and you would then essentially *know* them. They'd become real. All the preconceptions would melt away. You'd see them now like anyone else: as an ordinary human being, with flaws, not a model of perfection. Of course, they may well be beautiful and charismatic and clever, but essentially that's all it would take. You would know their Inscape.'

I explained Gerard Manley Hopkins' theory to her. Edith is not the philosophy type. I knew I was navigating safe waters here. I could be sure that Edith would not accuse me of trying to upset her by talking about my real mother, because, as I say, in our world my mother is never spoken of directly. When Father came in that night Edith started crying as she often does when she needs to restore order, and he made me go downstairs to make her a hot chocolate before our usual night time session.

These late-night monologues are not optional. This is a routine we all three understand. My father comes in from The Star Bar at ten thirty, sits in his special chair, pours from the cut glass decanter into the crystal tumbler that Edith will have laid out for him on the silver-plated tray, and we take our places, me on the hearth rug in front of the dying fire, Edith on the settee, until he has had three more drinks. When he leans across to his decanter to pour the fourth, after perhaps an hour has passed, that is our cue to leave because then he removes his spectacles and stares unsteadily into some far-off place, no longer requiring an audience.

We dare not go to bed early. Edith and I come back together from our separate parts of the house to sit in the upstairs drawing room when we hear his key in the door, his cane on the stairs as he drags the leg up each tread, his voice already commanding attention. I could not, for instance, cross the landing and say 'Goodnight Father. I have an exam tomorrow.' Edith, his wife, could not smile and say, 'Goodnight dear, I'm turning in now.'

Before we left school, my friend Margaret knew I was tired during examinations. Why didn't I just ask my stepmother to say goodnight to my father for me and go to bed before he came home? Margaret does not understand. We may have our differences, but in this Edith and I are complicit.

His nightly sermons are mostly confined to the effect of war on morality, both this one and the one he fought in, of women having too much freedom as a result, and why Edith is not to join the WI for example. Or more recently, why *no decent man will want to marry me now*. Morality is the common theme, especially since my recent tryst and now sullied state. His current favoured expression is *now that sex has reared its ugly head*, which leads him on to something called *venereal disease* and how it will become an epidemic. He quotes the teachings of Spinoza, in Latin followed up by a translation, which I cannot at the moment recount, but by this he can demonstrate doubly superior knowledge. The theme is something called *post-coital tristesse*. He uses a quotation to let me know that men only want to satisfy an urge, that the anticipation is all, and afterwards they feel only sadness.

By this I am to know that the only way a woman can win is to snare a man into marriage while she is a virgin. I imagine he is relating this story to his own experience. I allow this torrent to flood over me most nights, without right of reply, rendered mute and, to boot, now of little worth. Meanwhile another woman sits smugly by, knitting, eyes down; nothing to do with her.

There are occasions, however, when Edith leaves first. When he starts, as he does when he's had more than usual to drink in the pub (resulting from whomsoever he had to suffer the company of), to speak of my mother, at this point Edith rises and leaves. This monologue is for me and him. The words are jumbled but the theme returns to women having too much freedom. *I was head over heels in love with your mother.* He must have said that a hundred times, as if I need to know it. I'm developing a theory on that too. He feels powerless over something. I just cannot work out what it is, or if it has anything to do with him following me.

It is after these particular sessions that I hear the bedhead banging violently off the wall in rhythm with Edith's cries, like I heard nightly as a child after Bridget left. Only when it came to a shuddering stop, and I could hear my father snoring, did I know that he had been present at all, such was his silence throughout.

Edith condones his tyranny in exchange for some small social standing and this house. She is permitted no independent life, does not socialise without him, so has no friends of her own therefore. They feed off each other, abusers buoyed one by the other, I the barely tolerated interloper in their closed world. I have no memory of being alone with Father outside the home, taken out for the day for example.

Edith is small and bird-like, sharp featured and bony, with her tightly permed curls, thin lipsticked mouth and beady eyes, in her straight skirts and peplum jackets, failing to look like Carole Lombard. She ingratiated herself by reading to me at bedtime on the first night we met, when I must have still been unable to read for myself and she was visiting us here. I remember helping Bridget put out the best tea service for the English lady, Father's friend.

Such was Edith's plan to snare him. She showed no hint then of the bully she is. That came later, after the wedding at St. Ninian's, at which I had on a pretty frock, turquoise with pink roses, that she had handsewn herself, saying I was going to be her bridesmaid. I stood proudly on the table while she took measurements or talked with pins in her mouth as she set the hem. Except I wasn't her bridesmaid. Her younger sister Janet from Shropshire was. I sat in the front pew, my hot hand holding Bridget's cold one tightly, in my stupid dress. I am not in any of the framed photographs on the piano.

After the small wedding reception here at home, they went to Loch Lomond on honeymoon, tin cans rattling along the cobbles on Knowe Terrace tied to the motorcar bumper, Bridget and I waving and smiling.

I thought they had gone forever to start their new life, and felt no concern that I can recall, but they returned a week later, and Edith was not the giggly, friendly young woman who had read to me and made me a frock. I should now please call her Mother.

She seemed preoccupied with making everything perfect for my father, and was short tempered when he was at work, apart from when Janet came to stay. They would whisper and laugh as Edith showed her the house, the piano and the books. I watched carefully to make sure they did not touch my favourite, Jacob's Room by Virginia Woolf, with *to Flora from Ailsa, Christmas 1922* inscribed on the inside cover. I have no idea who Flora is or how this gift came to be here. I'd have been three months old that Christmas. Did I merit a gift?

Then Bridget left. I was standing in the Belfast sink being washed before bed one evening, and she was telling me how she washed Miss Ailsa in here too, when Edith came in the kitchen and Bridget did not hear her. I remember shivering, as no-one was drying me, and I wanted the shouting to stop. Bridget was what I imagine a grandmother might be. I felt responsible for her going. Somehow the clash had been about me, and if I had not cried in the sink it might have been resolved.

Bridget left that night with a hard box suitcase from under her bed that had the brass letters AB on it. I often think of that suitcase, and the initials, and the hug as she left, her crying and whispering that I must be brave. I can still conjure up the warmth of her breath and its faint, sweet aroma, her piped flannel nightdress tinged with the smell of mothballs from when she would tell me stories as we cuddled up in her warm bed in the little back room up the scullery stairs on nights when I couldn't sleep.

After that, in the year before we moved to England, I remember stodgy meals, fires not lit, watching out of the window for Father coming home from work, arguments over meals or about repairs to the house, Edith calling it a *mausoleum*. I have happy memories of going to the shops on Albert Drive with Bridget, to the library in Leslie Street to change our books, up Nithsdale Road to call in at Mr. Cranston's for butcher's meat, then back home along Shields Road. We would stop and talk to people she knew, other housekeepers from neighbouring villas. I stood on Kitchin's pharmacy counter, singing a song Bridget had taught me. *In her sweet little Alice blue gown.* The women clapping and smiling. After Bridget left, if I had to accompany Edith, we hardly spoke to one another, and never to anyone else.

Then, around the time I started school and was making friends, one morning we locked up the house and went a long way in the motorcar, to a new house, because Father *had a transfer*. I didn't know what this meant but Edith said it was *an adventure* for the three of us. I was excited, we were in this together, discovering a place we'd none of us seen before.

But when the car drew up outside the small brick terrace on the dark street in the Northern town where Edith had grown up and would become home for the next ten years, there was a vase in the tiny front window, the unmistakeable green glass one that Bridget always placed on a doily on the piano, and here it was, with fresh daffodils. I knew then that Father and Edith had already been here. It was not an uncharted journey for the three of us. She had tricked me again.

Edith accompanied me to and from school, not speaking as we hurried, as if she needed to be somewhere else, me running to catch up, until I was deemed old enough to walk by myself. The children didn't understand me, and laughed at my strange accent. I learned to impersonate, and life got better. Imitation comes easily to me now. I take on the accent of someone else almost within minutes.

Father seemed happier in this new life, and we would see Edith's family all the time, Auntie Janet and Uncle Walter and the babies. Auntie Janet seemed to be permanently pregnant, and Edith doted on each child as it arrived and grew, a different woman with her own blood. We'd go on holidays with them to Wales, where we stayed in green wooden huts amongst grassy sand dunes and whistling winds. The grownups drank and played cards and laughed a lot. I babysat while they went to a pub in the village, fearing they would not return when it grew dark, or if one of the little ones started crying. I never let them see this when they got back, laughing and joking, pouring more drinks. Father looked sad behind his eyes, even when he was laughing. Then something changed, and we stopped seeing Janet and Walter. My father's silences returned, interspersed with bouts of rage.

We returned to Glasgow when I was sixteen, just before exam time. Once again, I left behind friends who I suppose had each other. I was glad to come home though, to this familiar smelling house that had been locked up all those years, and I could once again sleep in the bedroom that had been Ailsa's room. Bridget's annexe is where I still go to draw. I became friends again with Margaret. We remembered each other from being little, and we have been friends ever since. It was her house that I was visiting on Saturday evening, where we had been talking with her parents, as we often do, about the war and the world. In that house Margaret and I matter. On those occasions I never want to come home. So, when I got home from Margaret's and he wrongly accused me again, all I could think was that Margaret's father would never speak to her like that, whatever the circumstances.

Since we moved back, mealtimes are more tense, and my father talks little, except to instruct me to finish what I'm hiding under a crumpled napkin on my plate, or to complain to Edith about someone's incompetence at work that day and how he saved the situation. Mostly we eat in silence. The minute he arrives home from the work he resents, in the tax office he returned to, his evening meal must be on the table. My task is to watch for him coming along Knowe Terrace from where he will have alighted the tram, his familiar limping gait and cane swinging jauntily back and forth for the benefit of the outside world, then run down to tell Edith so she can take off her apron, open the front door to greet him and take his hat and coat before we put out the meal.

Following this tense repast, I go upstairs to the bathroom, turn on the taps and push my fingers down my throat. It is easier here, where sound doesn't travel as it did in the other house. Then I go back down and clear. My father washes and I dry, the two of us in silence. He joins her in the drawing room, which Edith now calls the *lounge* but I refuse to, falls asleep in front of the fire as she knits, needles click clacking, clock tick tocking, until he wakes and repairs in broody silence to the back room downstairs which we call the study for some reason. He locks himself in that joyless room where there is a bed and the locked bureau. He has been known to sleep all night in that room when he is in one of his black moods. At eight thirty he goes out to The Star Bar and the loquacious version returns two hours later.

This pattern has changed little, other than the new obsession with my compromised marital prospects. He talks about selfishness a lot, and one's duty, and of the war, when his leg and right hand were damaged, the reason he has difficulty climbing stairs if they are steep, or using implements. He had little choice after the war but to take a desk job, training as a tax inspector, commensurate with his lack of mobility and dexterity, and in my opinion suited to his suspicious mind and forensic eye for detail. His boast is invariably one of catching tax evaders, usually local businessmen, and if he can have them prosecuted and the case appears in the Glasgow Herald he is especially proud. The highlight is when his intervention means a spell in prison for a crook who will one day thank my father for changing his life. He likes to play God and I have been conditioned to regard him as occupying that role. I may cry, rage, rebel, but I believe the Deity of Father to hold the truth. I am all the things he calls me.

I don't remember when I started, but I draw all the time, on any paper I can find. It started with faces, and plans of houses I imagine living in. I think it was after I saw the sketch my mother had done at the back of the notebook. I drew for him, in the hope that he would be proud, but he only found errors, correcting me in one way or another. *The mouth is too near the nose, there is no point in drawing a house plan without scale.*

Back at Craigholme, Miss Peake suggested I should think about applying to Glasgow School of Art, where she herself had studied, and I ought to discuss this with my parents. He dismissed it out of hand. A woman should not enter higher education. There is no need for it, it causes problems in relationships and mental issues for the woman.

Women should aspire to marry, have children and not work. Edith followed this up with her suggestion that I could leave school now and find work in an office where I would have the best chance of meeting my future husband, as she had.

They lulled me briefly into thinking they cared about me in this regard, and for a few weeks I foolishly agreed, thinking if I made them happy we would at last be a proper family, only with a new husband. Then three things happened. One, I stayed on at school at the insistence of Miss Peake, who was horrified that my parents would even think of suggesting I leave school to work in an office. Two, the war broke out. Three, I met Joe Hendry at Govanhill baths during the boredom of this interminable summer.

Joe had been there all week, his wet muscular legs with their black hairs plastered down, real men's legs, swinging off the poolside as I swam my habitual ten lengths for my weight, knowing each time I swam past he would make me laugh. He looked like a more hirsute Cary Grant. I was lonely, Margaret was away all summer, he was home on leave from the Royal Navy, and he seemed to like me. We went for a cup of tea in a cafe nearby on Allison Street where he told me about his war experience thus far.

It wasn't important to me not to do it, if he used precautions, which he seemed to have a supply of. And there is a war on, he said. I don't understand what all the fuss is about. I thought, it's only my body, who cares about that, and I wanted to experience this mystery for myself. I know Miss Peake has done it, because she talked to me about her fiancé and how they had *sealed their bond to each other* before he left for his army post, and smiled secretly, so I knew she meant sex. Edith says

I have puppy fat, but I'm just bigger than her, that's all. Nearly everyone is bigger than her. I hate that it is so physically obvious we can't be related, even though I am glad. I heard her saying to a neighbour in Shrewsbury 'Yes, Gertrude's mine.' I thought, *I am not yours. I look nothing like you. Plus, you haven't earned the right. You are not my mother, even though I must call you that.* I never call her that in my head, or when speaking to Margaret.

As I wrote to Margaret, I'm glad I agreed to go back to that ground floor single-end on Daisy Street, clutching my wet rolled up towel and swimming costume, to contribute to the war effort. Joe was kind and funny and he had fresh smelling sheets. *Your first time*, he said. *Could be my last.* I looked for him at the baths a few times after that, but he was never there. It occurred to me later that perhaps he had been married, with a wife out at work, but at the time I thought he was just a shipshape sailor.

Margaret's reply was opened by my father without me knowing, eventually throwing the letter at me after several days of indirect interrogation about my social and aquatic routine, as if I were a tax fraudster and he had information on me that he was only going to reveal in staged interviews. He has no shame about his part in this: it is his right to intercept my post. He now follows me everywhere. I can't breathe. He makes accusations and forces me to stand humiliated in front of him for inspection before I leave the house, telling me to wipe off any trace of lipstick. When I announced that I had been offered a scholarship to study at Gray's in Aberdeen, he was incensed. He is furious because he will lose control.

As I sit here again taking in this bare, strangely modern scene, I start to imagine she may have escaped up here, while my father seethed below, unable to negotiate the steeper stairs. That would explain the lack of a *proper wife* and the sarcastic *precious mother*. If she did, if indeed she was neither proper nor precious, what did Bridget think of this situation? She said once, almost to herself when she was tucking me into bed, and it is imprinted on my brain - *your mammy was a lovely person hen, but these two, they only care about themselves*. My mother was a *lovely person*. Not only that, but she took a lover, a design engineer by the look of things, in the attic, perhaps a spy during the war, when my father was on active service.

Were those starstruck lovers assisted by Bridget, unlocking the back door when he tapped out a secret code on her window like a first world war version of the *French Resistance* we are hearing about today? Did he use the back stairs, hiding in the attic to draw up secret plans of arsenal for the government before making love to my mother, the two of them unable to resist their passion despite her being another man's wife?

Silver Fox Fur

Ailsa

Glasgow, September 1909

Flora and Ailsa are still alone.

The change in her mother is remarkable, thinks Ailsa, reminded of this almost daily. No more headaches, no more afternoon teas with those dreadful women, no more compliance over her daughter attending cookery and homemaking classes. She first noticed this after Flora had mourned her husband for the requisite period, staring into space, motionless, as if thinking over her place in the world, then one morning appeared at breakfast as if her body and mind had become inhabited overnight by another woman entirely.

Ailsa realised eventually that this might be the woman who had lived before the dead babies, before she married Charles even, when she was a girl in Applecross. Here is Mama today for example, relaxed, chatting with Bridget and Ailsa in the kitchen, laughing out loud - a new sound to Ailsa's ears - inviting other widows and spinsters, blue stockings she has met through her charity work, to evening soirées at Knowe Terrace. There they can be seen smoking cigarettes in holders, sharing stories or reading extracts from books out loud and discussing them over hot chocolate. One memorable evening recently Ailsa heard an uproar coming from the drawing room and rushed in to realise it was uninhibited laughter.

'Mama, is everything alright?'

'Yes dear of course. We have all agreed to stop wearing corsets to our evenings here. We had a vote. They are banned forthwith!'

Flora has learned to drive a motor car and now owns one. Her clothes are indeed looser and more colourful, her body softer, her hair shorter. She is now a woman of means. Charles's heavy engineering business on the Clydeside, the one he never reached on that fateful morning, has been bought over by his partner, providing Flora with enough money to keep her and Ailsa comfortable for life, assuming they are prudent.

We seem more like sisters these days, thinks Ailsa. Why is her mother so different now? 12 Knowe Terrace is a different house. Still outwardly the same, with its heavy furniture and dark wood panelling, but it seems lighter somehow, airier. The three women seem to talk louder and laugh more easily. Even Bridget, who had moved around silently before, carting her step ladders, endlessly dusting picture rails and flicking at ornate cornicing, beating rugs outside in the backcourt, now initiates conversation with Flora and Ailsa as she works: some local news picked up at Mr. Cranston's, or small pieces of information about her own life. Ailsa previously had no idea that Bridget's family were in Motherwell, for example, or that her own father had also been killed, in an accident at a local iron works.

Last month Flora invited Bridget's mother, who is a midwife, and her sister, for afternoon tea, then drove all five of them around Pollokshields in her motor car, showing them the villas and wide streets, explaining how it is a *garden city suburb* conceived by Sir John Stirling Maxwell of nearby Pollok Estate. Her running commentary from behind the wheel, not given in a showy way, was more from genuine interest in the project as conceived and undertaken, and the beauty she clearly finds in it. Having grown up in a tiny village in the Highlands, the daughter of a schoolmaster, only moving to Glasgow when she married Charles a year after they'd met when he was hillwalking as a young man in Applecross, Flora still retains the accent and much of the Gaelic language, lapsing into it occasionally, but never tires of the wonders of the big city that she first encountered as a young bride.

Ailsa was especially proud of her mother that day in the motor car, and is now so struck by the openness in the house and her mother's support for her, that she believes this is what true happiness means. Ailsa is taking informal drawing classes locally with a woman who has turned her front parlour into a studio, and is learning *Still Life*. She wishes it could stay like this forever, perhaps with a child of her own to add into the mix, to be raised by the two of them. A daughter ideally, who would not have need of a male role model. Either way, she has a plan. She will find a way to do that, and live at Knowe Terrace for the rest of her life, frugally, looking after Mama when the time comes, raising her own child, and working in some capacity, as a draughtswoman if she can find a firm prepared to take the risk.

Apart from her new circle of friends, Flora seems happiest now to live vicariously through her daughter, encouraging her to take up whatever activity she might wish to pursue. A tour of Europe? Join the women's suffrage movement? Formal drawing and painting classes at the newly extended School of Art? A visit to London perhaps to meet up with Truus Schräder, the younger sister of Ailsa's pen friend An, who has come from Holland and is staying with a family there.

In fact, when Ailsa reads An's letter more closely, she understands that the host family sounds somewhat bohemian and well connected in the art world, helping the girl to learn English and pursue her interest in studying architecture, which An thinks might suit Ailsa also given her expressed interest in past correspondence.

Reading between the lines, Ailsa gathers that Truus sounds quite strong willed and discusses this with her mother.

'She was clearly pushed into training as a pharmacist after being at a convent boarding school, but it has come to nothing.'

'Yes, they are a well-to-do Catholic family' replies Flora. 'The time you were going to stay I recall the younger sister was away in Amersfoort, in a school run by nuns.'

'Well it says here she has now been allowed to *follow her passion,* which is for the Arts. She wonders if I might like to visit London before the winter sets in. What do you think Mama?'

'Where would you stay?'

'An says the family has plenty of room and is encouraging in this regard. The couple would be pleased to have me stay.'

An's letter describes further how a companion for Truus close to her own age, to accompany her on visits to galleries and buildings of note, would be ideal, as the family regrettably has limited time available to do so.

Ailsa resolves to take up this suggestion immediately. 'I will write to An to thank her and to Truus directly, at this London address.'

Within days she has received a favourable and quite effusive reply from Truus and is preparing to leave Glasgow. Her mother and Bridget are excited for her and, as Bridget presses and folds fine woollens and broderie anglaise blouses, long skirts and silk undergarments into Ailsa's new suitcase, which has been inscribed with her initials, Flora makes a list of purchases.

'We must go into the Trongate for a new hat and silver fox fur and muff to set off your winter coat, and Scottish gifts for the London people' says Flora.

*

The fine October day scheduled for travel arrives and, waving to her mother from the train as it slowly rumbles out of Central Station over the impressive new Caledonian Railway Bridge crossing the Clyde, Ailsa feels like an adult for the first time in her life. She presses her head against the window, seeing the Glasgow she knows recede, passing the numerous church spires of Pollokshields as they too fade into the smoky haze and her breath begins to cloud the glass. She draws a shape with her finger on the condensation, the outline of a house, and makes herself a promise. Whatever happens in London, when she returns she intends to put her plan into action.

Cream Vellum

Gertrude

Stonehaven, September 1940

Before boarding the train at Queen Street early this morning I resolved not to return to that house so long as he remains alive. It has turned out to be a tumultuous few weeks. Shortly after the episode leading to the discovery of the attic room, with its unexplained contents, I ran downstairs on the morning of my eighteenth birthday when I heard the letterbox, to look for greetings cards, of which there were none, but among the pile of post behind the storm doors was a large thick envelope addressed to me.

Before my father could rise from the breakfast table, to break the customary silent half hour he spends behind his morning newspaper, and limp the length of the hall, I slipped it inside my housecoat, dropping the bills back onto the mat. I walked casually back upstairs, arms crossed, just as he emerged from the dining room. It is well understood that my father is the only one who picks up the morning post from the doormat.

He refused to say goodbye this morning, remaining locked in the study, so I was left with the feeblest of embraces from Edith and insincere platitudes about coming home at Christmas. My cases have been sent on ahead and so, as I pulled the lion's head knocker to close the storm door firmly behind me, I paused on the front steps before getting into my cab. Taking in for the last time The Knowe opposite, now a hostel for unmarried mothers, nestled within its raised landscaped grounds above a stone wall, its lime trees beginning to turn to gold, I felt in that moment a kind of freedom. Standing there I made myself a promise. One day I will come back and restore the attic, which, despite my single plea, he refused to discuss further or be drawn on, and I expect once sober regretted giving me the key. Some instinct has stopped me from quizzing Edith on the subject.

I have not let the pewter key out of my sight. Several times when I was home alone I went back up to try to make sense of it. I found, in a shallow drawer under the table top, folded plans of the top floor showing inner walls removed, dated 1921, and alterations to Bridget's annexe, sketched freehand on blue waxed paper with a Dutch watermark. Whoever had drawn up these plans for my mother did so shortly before I was born. Did I live up there too? My mind has been racing along these lines for days now, but there's no-one to ask and I have no idea where Bridget could be even supposing she is still alive. There are no neighbours left from then, I am too unfamiliar to ask in shops or at the church, and in the ten years we were away so much has changed. Throughout my life my father and Edith fostered an atmosphere where even the rare visitors, ones that possibly knew my mother, I now think, must have also known that the subject of her was forbidden. I don't imagine that those visitors, or shopkeepers, churchgoers and neighbours, would think for a minute that I know *nothing*.

Before the attic, I only ever pictured Ailsa playing the piano, or reading in the drawing room: an Edwardian lady in furs like in the photograph, while my father, damaged by the war but *head over heels in love*, adored her while longing in vain for her be a *proper wife*. I had thought that meant she was delicate and withheld certain favours from him. She could not suffer his nightly demands as Edith would later agree to.

When the connecting train to Aberdeen finally pulled out of the grand main line Highland junction of Perth General, four soldiers who had burst noisily into my carriage, heading home on leave, with their unusual twang, local Doric words unfamiliar to me, were jovial and carefree and as I listened to their banter my mood began to lighten. I look at my reflection, my tearstained face pressed against the carriage window, then lift my head back to watch rolling fields sweep by. As we approach Stonehaven, I catch the North Sea for the first time, grey and calm in the gathering dusk. Allowing myself to smile weakly at my reflection, I make myself another promise: I will be an artist one day, like Miss Peake, and don't need a family, or a 'decent man.' I will live life on my own, or be someone's lover.

I trace an outline of a house with my finger in the condensation on the carriage window. In the thick envelope, along with title deeds on cream vellum paper, solicitors McFarlane and Murricane informed me that I own a three-storey property at number twelve Knowe Terrace, Pollokshields, Glasgow, built for my grandfather Charles Bray in 1875 and left to me in her will by my grandmother Flora Bray, to be kept in trust until my eighteenth birthday by the solicitors. I met with McFarlane and Murricane, but it seems the only partner who would have known the background, a Mr. Robin Asher, died some years ago and the current partners are sorry, but they cannot help me further as to the circumstances surrounding the legacy. Discovering that I own the house barely registers with me. It is my father's home, and to have questioned my entitlement, to have acknowledged it even, would only have elicited rage and prompted a lecture on selfishness. What does register is that for the first time I know the names of my grandparents, and that my grandmother, Flora (book mystery solved), was someone to whom I mattered enough to leave me her house. So where was Ailsa in all of this? Disinherited through scandal?

Light Oak

Ailsa

London, October 1909

Meeting Truus for Ailsa has meant finding the friend she has long wished for. The two young women fit together like lost pieces from the same jigsaw puzzle, despite Truus being Ailsa's junior by six years and unlike anyone she has met before. At only twenty the shy but forthright *Hollandse* is poised, serious and self-assured. There is an honesty and a simplicity about the way she presents herself, a frugal quality, with her straight hair pulled back into a plain knot, her clothing cleanly tailored, with no elaborate accessories. What she does possess is a keen mind and is not afraid to speak it when roused. Often, Ailsa has noticed, she refers to An as her source in relation to views on politics, but there is an identity and humour about her that is all her own and immediately infectious.

She brings out a side of Ailsa that has been waiting to flourish, and to have a friend with whom she can talk, about life and ideas, is such a novelty that Ailsa feels that exuberance rubbing off onto her straight away. Truus is also kind, inclusive, helping Ailsa feel at ease with the family whose home she will be sharing for the next month. Mealtimes are joyous occasions, full of stimulating, lively conversation and ideas befitting these liberating times. Within a couple of days Ailsa is assimilated into family life and has formed a natural bond with Truus.

The girls share a bedroom and whisper well into the night about their individual hopes for the future, but also the losses of their past. Both had brothers and sisters who died before they were born. Prompted by Truus, Ailsa gradually opens up about Papa, whom she loved well enough but was dominated by, as was her mother. He could give Ailsa a withering look merely for showing her ankles; a strict disciplinarian, not in an aggressive way, more that his way was the only way, and everyone had to fall in line. He held absolute power over the household, quietly but firmly. He had not wanted for Ailsa and her mother to visit the Schräders that time a few years ago; it was only through her mother's quiet persuasion and her father's business links with Mr. Schräder, a significant contract supplying machinery for the Dutch textile factory, that he finally relented. Yet in the end he got his way. Now he is no longer alive, Ailsa feels guilt at how free she is by comparison, enabled only through his financial legacy.

Truus feels no such guilt. She talks of patriarchy and, as for money, men have had the advantage for centuries; how can we be blamed for trying to catch up? It's not as if we want to fritter it away on fineries. It seems her mother died when Truus was only four, and the strict stepmother she feels at odds with has not been able to fill that role. Truus has enough memories of her mother to know they had been a happy family, and that for her this is no replacement. She admits she rebelled, and her difficult behaviour meant she was sent to boarding school, a convent, which has clearly influenced her views. She speaks fondly of her father, and how he gave her a love of nature and of buildings, through their many long walks together. She says she cannot bear to upset him and loves him dearly, which causes her much confusion in trying to become her own person. This stay in London is liberating however, and Truus is now determined to find her own way in the world.

Ailsa has not met a Catholic before, and is quite shocked at how cynical Truus is about her religion and the hypocrisy she feels is endemic within the rules and doctrines. Of course Truus does not say this openly in front of her hosts, who are themselves Catholic and well acquainted with her father, yet seem quite enlightened about any subject discussed as far as Ailsa can see. Still, Truus seems not to want her unconventional views on religion to offend them.

Ailsa has never really thought about religion in this way, nor about how the Church of Scotland, only a few doors away from her house and so integral to the community, which she attended each week growing up, could somehow be a cause of indoctrination. It has always just felt part of her surroundings, like the library, or her school, part of the fabric of her life. In fact she can see now how powerful some of the men are within it, how they have influenced local thinking on many matters, and how this filters through and is not questioned. She has only ever thought of the Catholic church as something remote, an institution that families in the poor parts of Glasgow belong to, the men who worked for her father for example, most of Irish descent.

She thinks it odd that she has never known anyone personally from another religion until now. Truus is from a higher class to her own, indeed the only comparison she can make to the Schräder family would be the local families who live in the largest and most individual of the villas up in the Avenues, people like the Dunsmuirs, the McCorkindales and the Hamiltons, and Ailsa is sure none of these are Catholics. Yet

Truus, and the host family in London, are a long way from the class of her father's workers, and it now troubles her that she has heard and accepted that the Catholic religion is responsible for ignorance and violence, practices that belong in the dark ages, when she can now see with her own eyes how these new acquaintances want to make life better for working people and are enlightened and educated. She realises she has been living with a delusion and resolves not to judge anyone or anything in the future without first being sure of the facts.

'It is similar in Holland', says Truus, when Ailsa admits her ignorance of Catholicism, and how she can now see the discrimination that is rife in Glasgow. 'In addition to us, we have the Dutch Reformed Church and the Calvinists. Although some conservative Protestants object to the liberal Dutch Reformed Church, everyone is part of one, and only one - we call it a *zuil* - a pillar, based on religion, like Protestant, Catholic, or secular. Each pillar has its own organisations, such as political parties, schools, universities, unions, sport clubs, youth clubs, and newspapers. The members of different *zuilen* live side by side in our cities and villages, we do business with one another, but we seldom interact and rarely intermarry.'

Truus has already been in London for a month when Ailsa arrives, and will be staying for another five. Because her father can afford for his younger daughter to travel and study, he can indulge her with all the expenses entailed. Truus is a little more circumspect, saying wryly that her father does not know what to do with her. The relationship with her stepmother sounds to be strained, and Truus does not speak well of her. Too many rules; too much Catholic doctrine.

By contrast her older sister means everything, and some of the views expressed by Truus seem at first quite shocking to Ailsa. She hints at how women should not be constrained by the institution of marriage and that love should be given freely to more than one partner exclusively, man or woman. She has read the work of a number of philosophers and quite risqué novelists. Ailsa feels so naive, having spent much of her adult life thus far concentrating on reading about buildings and how to draw them.

The more Truus talks, the more Ailsa can see a connection between art, literature and politics, architecture even. In particular Truus has firm views about a simpler life, free from the trappings of wealth tied to materialistic show. She advocates a frugal existence, allowing women freedom to flourish. Truus seems not to care what anyone else thinks. She has her mind made up about how her own life will be. This chimes with Ailsa's own view about the societal structures in place for running a home, and how free life has been at Knowe Terrace for the past three years; how, before then, she felt constrained by her father's restriction of her ambition to be something other than a wife. For the first time she is able to put this into a wider context than just her own small world, and even wonders if perhaps her mother has been trying to say this to her without criticising her father directly.

By the time Ailsa arrives, Truus has already visited most of the city's landmarks in all their Baroque, Gothic or Georgian splendour, and has spent many hours at the Tate gallery studying the works of Rossetti and Turner. Ailsa has been to London once before, with her parents when she was fourteen, and has seen its sights, so makes a tentative suggestion. She has been reading up on the works of John Ruskin and

William Morris and would love to visit the new extension to the Victorian and Albert Museum to learn more about Arts and Crafts. She has read it is a *political ideal*, with its notion of apprenticeship and simplicity of design, and thinks Truus may find it interesting. Truus is delighted with this suggestion, as she deplores ostentation.

After the Victoria and Albert visit Truus is sceptical about some aspects of the movement, as she thinks mechanisation, which Mr. Morris was so against, potentially frees workers and enables economy of scale in production. Having seen first hand the benefits of industrialisation to her father's factory, she wants to better understand this contradiction. She despises the ornamentation prevalent in Dutch design, preferring the ideas of the emerging architect Berlage. She speaks passionately, with an increasingly excellent command of English, and has a way of making the things she feels strongly about resonate with deep and profound meaning, accentuated by her persuasive tone. The girls' interest is mutually ignited, and they agree that for the rest of Ailsa's stay they will concentrate on this architectural style alone, and consider its wider political meaning.

Over the coming weeks, when weather permits, Ailsa and Truus visit the houses that they have been told about through various introductions at dinner engagements and parties, at the homes of their hosts' friends, in districts like Bloomsbury and Chelsea. London society is contagious. Once you meet someone, they know someone who knows someone and before you know it, thinks Ailsa, you are being whisked here and there to be introduced to the residents of the latest and most beautiful homes.

They travel by rail and stay in guest houses to discover Arts and Crafts England, which is simple in detail and emphasises natural light falling through openings into interior spaces and onto light, modern furnishings and high light oak wall panelling. They are invited to view Leighton House in Holland Park, and on another occasion they have a wonderful evening with the Muffs, a socially progressive family, at Red House in Bexleyheath, designed by William Morris and where he himself first lived. From Kelmscott House in the Cotswolds and to what is left to see of the artisan workshops at Chipping Campden they travel up to the Lake District to visit Broad Leys at Windermere.

Thereafter they take in the much-lauded garden suburbs of Hampstead and Bedford Park, where Ailsa cannot help but think that these fall short of Pollokshields, which she would like to argue is in fact the first and best garden suburb in Britain, but she keeps that thought to herself in the interests of harmony. They have afternoon tea at Standen in West Sussex with the Beales, and everywhere someone is there to meet the Dutch socialite and her quaint Scottish companion with the *Pre-Raphaelite features*, as one effusive and slightly inebriated poet told her at a dinner party in Russell Square.

It is a heady time and an education like no other for Ailsa. People ask her about the noted 'Glasgow Style' and she realises that she knows more than she thought. She is able to tell them about the Glasgow Four and of Mackintosh's interiors, the homes he has designed but also the new Art School building, and the Tea Rooms, because she has visited these or read about them. With politics she is less sure of herself. Asked about movements such as the Socialist Labour Party which is seemingly flourishing mainly due to its Glasgow membership, she is embarrassed to know nothing, and resolves to rectify this on her return.

By the end of her stay, Ailsa is aware that she has been transformed by a short but intensive period of education, though perhaps not the one intended for her. She knows she has undergone some kind of epiphany that will never be undone and, although she is more than happy to return home for Christmas, and excited to tell her mother about everything she has seen and experienced, she knows she has grown a new outer layer. She likens this to a polished and resilient skin, with added confidence and positivity, much of it derived from being around Truus and her radical ideas.

Ailsa's only fear is that, once they part, she will lose the effect of this disarming Dutch woman who is such a life force and catalyst for change in those fortunate enough to come into contact with her. She seems to have an innate ability to find the best part of anyone she meets and to nurture it until it is allowed to flourish. The best part of Ailsa is her desire to be her own woman, to carve out a life for herself, something she always knew was her goal, unsure though on how to proceed. Now she is leaving London with absolutely clarity on the way forward and, as she embraces Truus for the last time, she tells her friend how she feels.

'No, no' replies Truus. 'On the contrary. You have shown me a new lifestyle. Arts and Crafts, simple rustic design, plain living. I'd never have found all that without you Ailsa. And we must both study architecture. I will begin in Hanover. My father is arranging for me to go there next. You must follow your dream too. Write to me soon.'

As the train heads north out of Euston, Ailsa thinks over all of their conversations and shared ideas about architecture and the design of a home, ideas she was not able to articulate before, and is determined not to waver from the course she has set for herself. She will rekindle her original desire, to become an architect, not simply a draughtswoman. An architect, like Fay Kellogg. Like her new friend Truus Schräder.

Polished Granite

Gertrude

Aberdeen, April 1945

Sunlight suffuses what might be a Japanese shoji screen as it glides soundlessly aside to disclose the interior of a square white room, a simple cube forming part of what I think is a house, where one corner, diagonally opposite to where I'm standing, appears to be open to the sky, as if windows, walls even, are missing. The voices come then, laughing, playful, a group of children welcoming me into their game. Little birds flutter and chirp outside the open corner that is brushed by the higher branches of trees. A smell of good coffee pervades and I'm asking to taste it. Two women, one red haired, one light brown, talking and drinking from blue and white mugs at a table beside the corner window, beckon me with smiles, hands outstretched. The room brims with light and love.

I reluctantly leave behind that familiar tranquility, that glimpse of something, a symbol perhaps. All my life, this dream, not often, but when it comes it lingers, bringing relief from the nightmares that conjure others from the past, freeing them to taunt the present, until I wake with exhaustion.

Fully alert now I assess the contrasting gloom over a washed out quilted counterpane that was once gold: the lacquered walnut veneered wardrobe and chest of drawers with their musty odours that linger on my work clothes; a mismatched dressing table below low eaves at the dormer recess with its three unforgiving mirrors a nod to art deco, a jagged glass sunburst positioned in front of the window to block any sun. The blackout blinds, despite bombing being a rare intrusion nowadays, and greyed-out nets, bear out the redundancy of that window. Peeling patterned wallpaper above a chipped wash hand basin and brown oilcloth flooring complete this dismal tableau along with the bedside rug, its faded beige and orange art deco fan shapes another throwback to fleeting inter-war optimism.

The redeeming aspect to this Aberdeen attic is its size compared to the rooms below, large enough to include space for a desk and hardback chair and a faded brocade armchair beside my Bakelite wireless on the tallboy. Apart from the wireless, my contributions, secondhand, are an easel and a floor mounted anglepoise lamp. Both stand defiantly in the centre of the long narrow room.

I check the alarm clock and rise grudgingly to light the gas fire in the meagre surround, keeping it low to eke out the meter money, and peer out onto the top landing hoping as always that the chilly bathroom below will be free. Four years I have lodged in this house in the knowledge that, if there were to be a fire, for example a lit cigarette dropped by one of the men when drunk, I wouldn't make it down the two flights of unprotected timber stairs to the front door.

Despite any misgivings with regard to my room, it is a sanctuary compared to the shared bathroom, its cast iron bath hosting a permanent legacy of ingrained grime and chipped enamel, never a place to linger and anyway inevitably someone else will soon be rattling the doorknob. The fact that it is shared with four young men working in reserved occupations at the local iron foundry means I am not in there except out of necessity. Sometimes, huddled in that scummy bath with the night wind howling outside the cracked windowpane and my soap ration clutched tightly, feeling abject misery at my self-inflicted situation, pondering the price of freedom, I allow myself to muse on the elegant porcelain bath left behind in Glasgow. Steam would rise all the way to the frosted glass rooflight as its polished brass taps gushed hot water from copper pipes ascending from the black and white tiled floor, its wide rim wrapping over all four sides, long enough and deep enough to lie completely flat underwater for as long as my breath would hold as a child. I used to wonder if my mother had done the same at my age. In the same reverie I free myself to drift across the landing to a drawing room where shafts of orange light are entering three tall windows, illuminating sandstone on window reveals before cutting across to emblazon the opposite wall on summer evenings.

I could have tried for admission to that more prestigious local School of Art, but chose to escape North. Four years on, I have come to appreciate this city's austere, brittle beauty, its *greyness,* so many polished granite buildings speckled in the moonlight, a gleaming beacon for German bombers during blackout. Siren City they call us. I have come to love cold, sharp edged Aberdeen, if not the board and lodgings on offer. I venture down a flight as the bathroom door is unbolted.

'Morning Robbie.' This muscled young man hunches over his cloth wash bag as he edges past me on the landing.

'Aye, Gerda.' His pet name for me, short for Gertrude, which I think belongs to someone exotic, like the artist Gerda Wegener for example, known for her erotica.

'Wee bit chilly' he continues, but he does not want to stop and chat, embarrassed in his vest and braces. I fantasise about Robbie sometimes. All of the men who lodge here actually. Their lack of vanity, their frankness and humour, drinking and rough language, a blatant desire for pleasure in an otherwise unpredictable wartime existence, arouses something in me. Perhaps because they are friendly towards me, like on the unexpected Friday evening after bumping into Robbie on Union Street, spent in Ma Cameron's, a shadowy public house with a notable absence of women and a number of male stares in my direction, which thrilled me. I flouted the unwritten rules of social norm and drank beer, felt popular, took off my glasses, laughed and flirted with Robbie and the others and had a sense of what life must be like for a man. My landlady Mrs Grier was less impressed when told by the neighbourhood gossip about my social *faux pas*, and had I not been a respectable student teacher who pays reliable rent plus extra for clothes' laundering and meals, I should probably have been asked to leave.

Back in front of the gas flame, I dress quickly in yesterday's short sleeved paisley patterned shirtdress and a green cardigan and sort out notes for class. Brushing out the tangled knots in dark curls and clipping on a hair slide, I check my face and neck reflected in the harsh light of the mirror. I look young for my age, baby faced, with soft rounded features prone to chubbiness if I'm not careful. I am not what you'd call a *looker*. I have a small scar at my hairline and, if I were to allow myself to put on weight, a slight double chin. My legs and nose are my best features. Recently my cheekbones have become more pronounced, my clavicle more prominent, and I look better. Eating less is made easier by rationing of course, but it is one thing, one actual thing in life, within my control. I put on my spectacles, apply a touch of lipstick then rub it off again.

Today will be a good day. A morning field trip to the Art Galleries on Schoolhill, next door to Gray's where I completed my Diploma last year (average grades for a student who can draw but cannot paint). Today, sixth form grammar school boys keen to please the Art mistress, each requiring a reference for entry to study art or perhaps architecture at one of our few Scottish establishments. A small group therefore, if a little full of themselves, from privileged families mostly, humbled temporarily by the possibility of being called for active service that would threaten to interrupt their passage into higher education.

This war has been more beneficial to women, young ones anyway. My own peripatetic teaching post across several Aberdeen schools is made possible because Art masters are serving with HM Forces. If and when the men return they will resume their posts and we will have little choice but to vacate them. In that event I plan to move to London and look for a design position, or further afield, to Europe. So many talented, creative people have left Europe for America and taken their talent with them. Perhaps I can fill some gap with less than average ability disguised by hard work and an eye for a trend.

I fell unplanned into the new *Industrial Design* specialism once I passed the general first year. The critical eye of Drawing and Painting tutors was all too apparent. Although I can draw a little, they could spot I lack the ability to *abstract*, so much in vogue now in painting. One tutor ridiculed me in front of the year group when he saw my oil based daubings, mocking me, *how did **you** get into art school.* As though it were a club I should not belong to. The three girls in my year were local, and already had their extended groups. It was too hard to join in, too exhausting for me, already worn down from too many fresh starts.

I know myself I view things literally, and represent them that way, without interpretation, and I don't need some pompous lecturer telling me. I realised early on that I lacked original ideas until I had seen a successful example by another and could interpret the essence of it, or if the outline of an idea had been sketched for me by a trusted college tutor, Miss Burnett for example. I learned quickly there is a wealth of design from this century out there, from before the war, which I studied late into the night, passing myself off next day as having the quality of creativity, reassured by knowing I was on prepared ground. Technical drawings are more prescriptive, I could not go wrong there, and enjoyed the mechanical process. I was prone to working long hours at night drawing up a presentation. The sheer relief at being beyond the crippling *ideas* stage. No, my *forté* is recognising good ideas, despite having few of my own: this is ideal for teaching, so with luck and experience I may secure a post at an art school one day, like Miss Burnett, whom I observed closely. I do not enjoy teaching children. Art at this level is too abstruse for me, and I have few approaches to draw on. Being a tutor to adults studying design is my preferred destination. They will generate ideas, and I will put Miss Burnett's teaching style to use.

It is hard to assume authority over these boys, being only four years older. Do I behave differently with the girls? Yes is the answer. I want boys to like me where I imagine girls don't anyway, so why bother? Girls can see through me, can too easily mock me if I drop my guard. I can't take the risk. They sense that I have no entitlement, no safety net of the kind they take for granted.

A choice that could have been avoided. One that another daughter might have avoided. *All you ever think about is yourself.*

Another girl might have laughed along, not sulked when called *ridiculous*, been less vain when told she was *putting on the beef,* agreed about a lack of common sense, shown more gratitude, been less *selfish.* And not ruined her chances of marriage. *No decent man will want to marry you now.*

The lesson starts well. Dadaism is a movement in which I actually have an interest. The visiting Max Ernst exhibition is a coup for Aberdeen, given the war, not to mention the artist's own volatile romantic and political life at this present time, so I have no difficulty imparting some real information. I don't know why, but that avant garde era in Europe has always held my interest. It is a different type of abstract. Hard edged, a potpourri of ideas, often through the medium of a collage, iconoclastic, random visual statements, design based. I would go as far as to say that, sometimes when I need a lift out of the dark thoughts when they come, I imagine myself as a left wing anti-establishment artist posing as undercover spy or resistance fighter in somewhere like Amsterdam. In these scenarios I am a different woman, one whose life is valid, notable. When the war is over, I am determined to see Europe.

I escape for the school holidays each summer to the same damp cottage on a working farm near Ellon to join a small band of Land

Army volunteers. That way I can appear to be going home to Glasgow. Not that anyone here really asks. The advantage of working across a number of schools is that staffroom chat is not required. Christmas is more difficult. I tell Mrs Grier that my family spends Christmas abroad and I prefer to stay here. I think she believes me. Generally though, the last day of any term depresses me. Everyone else whooping with joy as they go off to rejoin families. I close the attic door behind me and wonder how I will fill the time, and with whom.

As I inform the smattering of assembled boys about the origins of Dadaism, emphasising that it is from a time actually only shortly before they were born, one chap leaning on the atrium balcony catches my eye. I have not noticed him before, but now, in this light and in the surreal and degenerate art world of nineteen twenties Cologne we have momentarily transported ourselves to, I see he is watching me from under dark hair that flops over one eye, taller than his two friends, still seventeen I imagine, school blazer slung over his shoulder. I am flustered, and possibly sounding shrill, obsessive. I hope not.

Afterwards I make it my business to stay close to him, as if coincidentally, as they meander around the exhibition. I stand near as if intent on one painting. He has an attractive habit of flicking his hair back, and makes his friends laugh, but not, I find, at my expense. He has manners, because he includes me in a joke. One of his friends asks about the artist Dada, which this boy pretends to play along with, calling the artist by a first name of Jimmy, and draws me in.

'Your friends are teasing you I'm afraid' I say to the red faced friend. 'There is no artist called Dada. It is a common mistake though' I reassure him. 'It is the name of the movement, of the group.'

I am able to explain in good humour that the name was derived purely from a child's nonsense word. I choose not to elaborate, for instance that it also means *Father*.

Did the dark haired boy, who I notice has sparkling deep blue eyes, include me so I would know they were not laughing at me, at my possibly obsessive interest in this art movement? So I could play into my role as expert? What I do know, because he is telling me now in the tearoom where I happen to sit across from him and am asking the boys about their ambitions, is that Daniel Ogilvie, the grandson of a Rubislaw quarryman and son of a stonemason turned successful granite merchant, intends to honour the family tradition. There is a quiet confidence about him, yet he is quite without vanity. He will study architecture and one day design durable modern buildings of granite, not of *transient concrete and glass* like the ones I showed them on slides last week, and I have no doubt he will succeed. As we walk back down Schoolhill for the afternoon drawing class, he holds eye contact with me for just a second too long. I'm sure of it.

*

Aberdeen Grammar, one of my better schools, has an enlightened headmaster who is happy for the Art Department to hire models for figure drawing. These models are nonetheless required to be fully clothed so, in my opinion, do not enable the sixth form boys to study anatomy in enough detail.

I formed this opinion five years ago whilst at school myself, in Glasgow, in support of my own Art mistress Miss Peake, who was equally unsuccessful in a similar request, despite Craigholme being an all girls' school. My preference, which I have requested several times, in the way Miss Peake did, is for life models to enrich the contents of students' portfolios and their understanding of anatomy. This is thought to be unsuitable for impressionable adolescent boys and would not go down well with their parents.

I find favour with the boys by letting them know of my fruitless endeavours, playing the role of teacher both progressive and flirtatious, who commiserates with them as we scoff at a headmaster clearly unable to imagine any unclothed model other than a nubile female. Such ignorance is common and misplaced, we agree, among those unenlightened, less *creative*.

As I set up our current model, the seventy-five-year-old somewhat scrawny Agnes, who supplements her breadline income where she can, in her chair beside the coal fire in the Art studio, each boy arranges himself behind an easel with his board and charcoal pencils. By this method, I am able to lean in over each shoulder from behind and suggest a line here, a shadow there, how to measure by eye and pencil a better proportion of head to body or body to chair. I am on safe ground here in terms of appropriate teaching style, having experienced it myself at Gray's.

Daniel Ogilvie is last in the semicircle, and I anticipate my imminent proximity to him with a disturbingly quickening heartbeat. I hear my footsteps on the bare floorboards in the otherwise silent classroom. As I lean in I can smell his hair oil, his fresh male sweat from below his shirt sleeve, not unpleasant, as he lifts his right arm and closes one eye to extend the charcoal to measure the delicate proportions of Agnes.

As I remove the pencil gently from his grip, our fingers touch and the effect is electric. I make my suggestion, hardly required as this boy can produce a fine drawing with a few carefully placed lines. As the bell rings for the end of class, he is last to clear up and leave the art room.

'Daniel, can you hold on a moment please.' I can't help myself. He waits, his school tie knot loose now below his open white collar, revealing a clearly visible Adam's apple as I look up at him. 'You have a lot of talent for drawing. I'm sure you know this. I'd like to help you prepare your final portfolio for submission if you'd allow me.' I remove my spectacles, hoping they have not left an indent on the bridge of my nose.

He does not answer, so I go on, my words coming too fast now. 'Sometimes it is what you leave out, to have fewer pieces but keep in your best ones. It is quality not quantity that impresses a selection panel. They have many portfolios to look through, and a single line drawing can make all the difference.' This is true, I know from experience. Miss Peake took such an interest in my own submission, and it helped.

'I can bring it in to show you tomorrow' he says, and looks genuinely pleased, blushing at this interest shown in him.

'Good. Stay behind after class. It is last period, so we will have time to go through it together then.'

'Thank you. Miss O'Neill.' He emphasises my title slowly, but not sarcastically, as he smiles and maintains eye contact with me again. I think I look away first. He does not appear to mock me.

Daniel has a month in which to submit his portfolio to Robert Gordon's in support of his application to the architecture course. He also has examinations to sit, so I resolve to limit any suggestions I will make.

At the initial appraisal, I advise him to leave out a few of the less impressive watercolours, add in more looseleaf sketchbooks, and to window mount his best drawings. The sensitivity of his work is profound and he possesses raw, real talent that comes from within. He has a light touch, and knows instinctively when to leave a drawing alone, which is rare in one so young. His charcoal drawings in particular are truly sensual, as is his limited knowledge of anatomy. He has drawn his own face and hand beautifully, from numerous angles, and quick studies of members of his family also feature in his moleskin sketchbooks. I note there are none portraying a girlfriend or suchlike. By contrast, the finished and mounted portrait of his grandfather, entitled **The Quarryman** and showing a craggy face sitting with a pint of ale and in his working boots, depicts a lifetime of hard graft combined with such dignity in the old man's eyes that I am momentarily breathless. All Daniel lacks is a life model, and he could equal Michelangelo.

His architectural drawings by contrast are lightly shaded, textured pen and ink studies of Aberdeen's finer classical buildings. His love of granite is evident, and his elevations possess a traditional three-dimensional quality that transforms them into works of art. He needs no help from me for his portfolio. He will walk into the course.

'Daniel, these are truly remarkable' I tell him honestly. 'Do you find it easy enough to get people to sit for you?'

He laughs. 'No. My grandfather is the only one who sits still long enough. I'd like to get more of a range. Younger people, different poses. I'm tired doing self portraits, and I've got too many of Agnes.'

'You can draw me if you like' I suggest as if spontaneously. I have been reading up on the Pre-Raphaelite Brotherhood's thrillingly unconventional liaisons. 'I have time if it helps. Not for tuition money of course. I'd just like to help.' My mind is suddenly on fire.

It's only my body. Who cares about that.

Wrought Iron

Ailsa

12 Knowe Terrace

Pollokshields

Glasgow

4 March 1910

Dear Truus

The winter months seemed to go on forever. I expect you will be leaving London for Hanover soon to begin your architectural studies. Perhaps you are already there and this letter will have been forwarded to you.

I have some news on that front too. In January I enrolled at the Glasgow School of Art, to study decorative design and illustration but with a mind to transfer to the architecture course if they will agree to accepting a woman. It is a slow process and, if I succeed, I will be the first woman to enrol for architecture. Meanwhile we are busy learning about colour and pattern. I enjoy illustration especially; this term we are designing a book cover incorporating typography, but I still work away on my architectural sketches when I get chance.

I have an amusing story to tell you. I recently had a strange encounter with an interesting character, a young man who introduced himself somewhat flamboyantly in the park, proffering a flower and saying he had noticed me on several occasions beside the wrought iron railings above the railway cutting, or sheltering under the iron canopy of the station building, appearing to be sketching details of 'his' new tenements, which indeed I had been! He reminds me of the more eccentric characters you and I met in Bloomsbury, bohemian in appearance and possessing quite a wit.

He is actually supervising the final touches to these new homes, the ones I mentioned to you, in the 'Glasgow Style', reminiscent of the Arts and Craft examples we visited, but in tenemental form. It turns out Mr. O'Neill is a draughtsman employed by the architect Robert Crawford and has invited me to visit their offices, as I expressed my interest in architecture. I decided to accept and Mama agrees I should go as it is exactly where my interest lies.

Dear Truus, I often think fondly of our time together, and do miss it, and you of course, but the daffodils are finally out in abundance and Spring is in the air, so I must not dwell on the past. We shall meet again!

Write to me from Hanover and tell me of your studies.

Your dearest friend,

Ailsa.

Cream Silk

Gertrude

Aberdeen, May 1945

Daniel comes to Mrs. Grier's on the nights she is at the Belmont, in other words Saturdays and Wednesdays. I am not too concerned about justifying this arrangement, as I already supplement my income with private tuition. It is not unusual for a young person, younger than Daniel admittedly, from one of my schools, to come to my room after tea, where I will have set up a still life. This usually consists of a bowl of fruit, and when fruit is unavailable, bread rolls in a basket complemented by a colourful scarf or striped tea towel, and perhaps a vase of pansies, or a bare branch, depending on the season.

Mrs Grier has sanctioned this general arrangement, given her reluctant approval providing no paint gets on the rug. I have assured her we only use a medium that can be cleaned easily, such as pencil or watercolours. Never oils, which I am not good with myself. I have not mentioned this departure into figure drawing to Mrs Grier, as I really do not see the necessity; it is all just drawing, and anyway I will sit, clothed, on the hard-backed chair while Daniel (who is in fact my only figure drawing pupil, although that is no business of Mrs. Grier's) will be at my easel.

He seems more relaxed after a few of these sessions and is fully immersed in the activity each time. He has great powers of concentration which I do not break, though I might wish to, apart from instructing him to stop at the appropriate time. He comes for an hour and a half, long enough for us to discuss and agree a pose and a medium, keep the pose for two half hour sittings separated by a tea break, leaving sufficient time allotted to review the work and make any adjustments.

The first few times we do not converse, both awkward, aware that we are treading a fine line in terms of the professional relationship of young Art mistress and male sixth form pupil. I am beginning to anticipate these sessions with romantic notions of artist and muse, spending hours thinking up my next pose, not least what I shall wear and how I might sit. I select fabric to best show my *anatomy*, silk usually, a robe or a dress, newly purchased in Falconers from my savings and modest enough to cover me adequately yet clinging enough to show contours and bone structure.

I choose flattering positions. As the weeks go on, I may adjust my robe to fall open slightly in order to reveal the muscles of a calf, a knee or an ankle bone, and on one occasion slip the straps off the shoulder of a cocktail dress to better accentuate bone structure, of the clavicle for example.

He is surely as aware as I am that the balance of power is not normal, that we are guilty of pushing boundaries, but it suits us. A model is not normally the one to determine the pose; rather the artist will demand whatever position he or she wishes to suit a desired composition. In this situation, however, I am the teacher, therefore in control, engaged in the education of a pupil, and as such can take up any (rehearsed) pose I choose, once I have suggested a medium. My body weight has further reduced, driven by my wish to show the bone structure of an elbow, the breastbone and so on.

In our breaks I put on a robe and we chat a little about other matters as we sip hot tea, but I find that, despite being the one in charge, I become nervous and find it hard to talk about myself. Perhaps because I am the teacher, but also because I want to give over this time to Daniel, to make him relax, and of course to like me. He is shy too, which is endearing, but not too shy to talk about himself when prompted. He is seventeen, he has a girlfriend called Jane who he knew growing up as their parents are friends, he thinks the war will soon be over, he has two younger brothers and a dog called Nell.

I already know he has a dog because I have watched him, from a safe distance, walking it across Victoria Park near his home. I have come to know the times he walks his dog and have on one occasion walked right past his welcoming family home, well uphill from my lodgings, shortly before lights out, where I saw his parents appearing to dance a slow waltz in soft lamplight through a bay window.

I had checked the school records for his address and date of birth. I am writing him a reference for art school, so am permitted to access his details and read his back school reports, all of which are favourable. Daniel Ogilvie is an outstanding student, and will one day have an assured career in his chosen profession. He will become a decent man. What he doesn't need is a scandal.

No decent man will want you now.

Willow Wood

Ailsa

12 Knowe Terrace,
Pollokshields,
Glasgow.

3 July 1911

My Dear Truus

Do you approve of my new lettering? I use this to annotate drawings.

So, you are to be married! Mr. Schröder (such a similar name to your own will confuse me! Will you be Mrs. Schröder-Schräder?) and you are clearly very much in love, given your account of the whirlwind romance. I am happy for you.

Your new life in Utrecht will bring much opportunity as you say, and It is good that your future husband is himself involved with the Arts, and supports your wish to continue with the architectural studies you began in Hanover. As he is a lawyer you will have complementing professions and I'm sure a stimulating life together.

Your letters continue to inspire me. The themes around society and the design of the home are of great interest, and much in line with my own thoughts. I am learning to prepare scale drawings, and I have been given an old drawing table from Michael's office, and other equipment. Mama is not sure where it should live. It has pride of place in the drawing room for now, which I say is surely a suitable room for drawing! (in our eccentric English language the term 'drawing room' derives from 'withdrawing', as in what ladies do after dinner, so perhaps not! This I learned in those dreadful homemaking lectures that I spoke of).

I am teaching myself the <u>laws of perspective.</u> My transfer to the Architectural Studies course is now agreed, helped in no small way by the opportunity I've had to volunteer in the office over the past year, where I have learned a great deal. I draw up surveys, and am allowed to annotate drawings with this lettering style, having studied calligraphy as part of the illustration course. I begin formal classes as a day student of Architecture next term. Hoorah!!!!

Mama sends her congratulations on your betrothal and her regards to your family and I send my dearest wishes to you and An, and of course to your handsome beau Frits.

With deepest affection,

Ailsa

Ailsa cannot help but feel something of a hypocrite, offering her compliments to Truus on her forthcoming marriage without question, after everything they discussed in London: their mutual plan to become architects, and how marriage or courtship meantime would be bound to stifle such ambition. This development not only contradicts that resolve, but has come about so quickly following Truus' stay in Hanover and her attendance at classes at the Institute of Technology there, which she wrote to say she had enjoyed so much. Now suddenly she is to marry, in just over a month.

Ailsa thinks this might be Truus' father's doing. Perhaps it is the Dutch upper class equivalent of an arranged marriage, for whatever reason Ailsa cannot imagine. If Truus is in love, as she undoubtedly seems to be, with this dashing lawyer eleven years her senior, then all well and good. If it is only to escape from her old life, to be independent, or to please her father, then it will very much depend on the character of Frits Schröder, who is apparently the son of an associate of her father and similarly from a prosperous Catholic family. He is taking on such a free spirit, such a strong woman with radical ideas, who may well come to find marriage confining.

Ailsa knows her friend well enough to know she would not compromise herself easily, and Truus did say in her letter that Frits does not want children either and is supportive of her ambition to be an architect. Perhaps he is a radical lawyer and their union will be extraordinary, and between them they will change others' lives for the better.

A fleeting thought then crosses Ailsa's mind. During her time in London, she took on board all the ideals and theories quite literally, such as those about women's rights, and how society could be, or will be, according to the bohemian set they mixed with. Could it be that some of the talk was really that, just talk, and not everyone intends to live according to such strongly held views when it comes down to it, that in fact they have no real intention of doing so? Ailsa certainly intends to, but then she knows she has the luxury of not being beholden to, or financially dependent on, a man, and has her mother's unstinting support. Could that be the key difference? She sighs, and again feels the pull of guilt that her own ambition may only be realised because of her father's death.

She reminds herself of her resolve not to be so quick to judge others and decides she will visit the Netherlands next summer, the experience once denied, and to see how married life is suiting Truus. This year though she is too busy. She was lucky enough last summer, with Michael O'Neill's help, to have gained an offer of experience in the offices of Robert Crawford, which she combines with her Art and Design classes. Nothing too onerous, and for no remuneration, she was at first only permitted to accompany Michael on site visits and to observe the other draughtsmen converting measurements, which she helped to note down, onto scale drawings. She learned how to make blueprints from originals, and how the planning approval process works. Within the space of a few months however she is possessed of her own cubicle, drawing up and annotating surveys and design proposals.

She often smiles to herself thinking of her father's remark about a lack of female lavatories in architects' offices. Mr. Crawford's offices in Bath Street, as indeed with most offices in town, do not provide ladies restroom facilities, it is true. In fact, until recently the very idea of a lady needing to use a lavatory anywhere but in a home or a private establishment was unheard of, certainly uncatered for. With her characteristic determination, Ailsa assured Robert Crawford from the outset that it was absolutely no problem for her to slip out of the office when required to visit the Ladies' Restroom at Miss Cranston's Willow Tearoom on nearby Sauchiehall Street. She combines this with a welcome pot of tea in the 'Room de Luxe', the exclusive ladies' room overlooking Sauchiehall Street on the first floor, with its vaulted ceiling and full-width, curved bay window.

On the best days, like today, she is able to observe the eccentric Kate Cranston, who sweeps in and out in her trademark grey corduroy costume and little bowler hat perched jauntily on her head, busily pointing out something or other to the waitresses or manager, or simply casting her eye satisfactorily over this, one of her empire of four tearooms. They are so fashionable now, not least because of the free rein she has given the eccentric 'Toshie', as the newspapers affectionately call him, and his wife Margaret MacDonald, to design exquisite interiors and, as in this case, the exterior façade.

Described as 'a fantasy for afternoon tea', the Room de Luxe features a colour scheme of grey, purple and white, a soft grey carpet, a silk upholstered dado, chairs and settees a rich rose-purple, and silver painted tables with high-backed chairs. The walls are white, with a frieze of coloured, mirrored and leaded glass panels. One side wall contains a fireplace and, opposite, the wall features Margaret MacDonald's gesso panel inspired by Rossetti's sonnet *O Ye, all ye that walk in Willow Wood*. 'Sauchiehall' comes from the Scots *sauch* meaning willow tree, as her mother has confirmed. This is complemented by crisp, white tablecloths and blue willow-pattern crockery, and very much contrasts with the masculine interior of the men's smoking and billiards rooms on the second floor, the dark wood panelling designed for men to drop in from their offices for a leisure break without the temptation of alcohol.

Out of all Miss Cranston's establishments, this one is Ailsa's favourite. It is ironic to think that not long ago she regularly endured afternoon tea here with her mother's previous set, where the overriding interest was the style of dress. The interior was hardly given a passing comment. It served merely as a glamorous backdrop for gossiping and preening. Even today, as she glances around the room, she assesses that she and Miss Cranston are the only business women here.

*

On the days that Ailsa is due in the office, Michael frequently shows up unexpectedly at Knowe Terrace at the precise moment Ailsa steps over the threshold, saying he had an early site visit in Pollokshields and, what luck, on such a glorious morning he can escort her to work. At other times he is to be found in the waiting room at Pollokshields West station, saying it is no problem for him to alight the Cathcart Circle train at Ailsa's stop, as he travels this route anyway, and they can resume the last leg of the journey, one final stop, together.

These chivalrous encounters are not prearranged, and their frequency is starting to annoy Ailsa, who likes to be solitary on her morning journey into town, to mentally prepare for whatever task is ahead. One time, when she decided to take the tram (Ailsa avoids trams generally since her father's accident and this occasion was to be a test of her resolve), Michael arrived late for work, furious, having waited for some time at Pollokshields West for her to arrive.

Lately he has started to appear at the Willow Tearoom simultaneously, by coincidence, whereupon they must use the Tea Gallery much to Ailsa's annoyance as she prefers the oasis of the ladies' Room de Luxe.

Ailsa finds Michael kind and solicitous, a rather eager young man, witty and gregarious, and good company. Naturally she is grateful that he has facilitated this opportunity for her to experience the world of work, something which has undoubtedly influenced her gaining admittance to the Architecture School, and quite unprecedented for a woman. He did go out of his way to make the introduction to Robert Crawford, something Michael likes to joke that she would never have had the courage to do on her own. Yet the proprietor was so taken with her sketchbook and serious attitude during their private interview that she could indeed have walked in off the street.

The fact that she had scribbled the name of the architect down in her notebook when the modern tenements on Fotheringay Road were first described in the newspaper, then had begun to scrutinise their build, meant she may well have done exactly that given a little more time, but she will only think of this years later.

Michael is younger than Ailsa by three years, but has been proprietorial over her work experience, almost as if she works for him. He does not seem to grasp that soon Ailsa will have the benefit of the best tutors in Scotland, when the days of Michael explaining how to use a measuring stick or a scale ruler will be behind them. He changes the subject if she talks about her thrill at the prospect of undertaking the Diploma.

She wants to continue to be his friend, as he is good company, and her only Glasgow friend in fact. She has enjoyed the picnic lunches in Maxwell Park, supplied by Bridget for the days when they are on site, and he does fuss over her and make her laugh. Some instinct stops Ailsa from saying much about her London experience, or of Truus, as Michael can be scathing about unconventional ideas or people. His bold cravat, and the proffering of a flower as first introduction, symbols which she had interpreted as creative idiosyncrasy, were no such thing. Michael is conventional to the core and rarely seen without his three piece pin striped suit and starched high collars, which Ailsa has noticed are slightly frayed. She has not seen the bold cravat again.

Her mother has been welcoming, as she enjoys Michael's company, and on two separate Sundays he has been found in Knowe Terrace on Ailsa's return from her walk, already chatting with Flora from Papa's armchair in the drawing room as Bridget is serving tea with an uncharacteristically dour expression. *Michael was just passing and called in to see you after your walk*, her mother says on both occasions, as though Michael knows Ailsa is out walking and her return is imminent. Why would Michael be in Pollokshields on a Sunday afternoon, *just passing*, when he lives with his invalid mother in Cathcart? He takes his supervisory role of the new tenements too seriously, clearly.

*

'What do you think I should do on the subject of Michael?' ventures Ailsa over breakfast one Saturday in September. Ailsa will soon be registering on her new course and leaving the work experience behind her, and is wondering how to continue her friendship.

'The subject?' queries Flora absent mindedly, her head in a new pamphlet.

'He seems perhaps a little too attached to his role as mentor, don't you think?'

'I fear it is you he is attached to my dear, not his role. Men cannot simply be friends with women, or indeed mentors. You must be firm with him if you have no romantic inclinations towards him.'
Ailsa laughs at this ridiculous idea.

'I have never led Michael to expect romance and I'm sure he would agree. We are friends, simply.'

'Ah, but where you will have seen, say, a provided picnic as a practical requirement for shared sustenance in the middle of the day when you are nowhere near a tearoom, Michael may have seen such a picnic, or rather several such picnics, as an invitation for courtship. Similarly your agreement for him to help you with your drawing. It is not your fault, dear, it is just the way men are', Flora says resignedly.

'I do wish you had mentioned this before, Mama.'
It is true that Michael seems more distracted lately, and less interested than he first was as Ailsa expounds her latest theory on the design of a home, the possibilities of domestic work-saving layouts and furnishings than, say, Truus would be in the same situation. When they have been relaxing on the plaid travelling rug beside the duck pond for example, or over a cup of Earl Grey tea at Miss Cranston's, Michael seems to

have lost his earlier enthusiasm for their discussions on modern architecture. Yesterday in the tea gallery he reached forward and absentmindedly lifted a lock of hair that had fallen over her eye as she was mid-sentence, which disarmed her momentarily, but she managed to carry on. On another occasion he continued to gaze at her over his eyeglasses when she had asked a question of him, requesting his view of a simple cabinet she had sketched, seeming not to have heard.

Ailsa puts his teasing at what he calls her *radical ideas* down to playful affection, as an older brother might, one she might have had, and certainly not as a suitor, for which she has no time or inclination. When it comes to the world of men, Ailsa has yet to experience desire. One day, when she is almost drowning in desire, she will look back on this time and understand it differently, and feel shocked at her lack of awareness. She will see how naive she was. For now, she is simply irritated.

'I will speak with him.'

'Don't be too hard. He is a rather sweet young man, if a little pushy.'

Michael has from time to time offered to help Flora with motor car problems or practical matters at Knowe Terrace, such as a leaking tap or a draughty window, despite her having access to the services of both a perfectly good local handyman and mechanic. Michael was a member of the Boys' Brigade in his youth and is currently actively involved in the new 'Boy Scout' scheme, so to offer help is in his nature, he assures her.

In similar vein he likes nothing better than a brisk hillwalk over rugged terrain and up steep inclines, a pastime that he repeatedly suggests to Ailsa as a good idea for her and seemingly increasingly common among ladies. She relented only once, whereupon she twisted her ankle badly on the Cathkin Braes and was laid up for several days, which she did not enjoy. She prefers to walk in the local avenues and park, something Michael tends to scoff at.

Michael is starting to scoff a great deal, Ailsa now thinks. He scoffs openly at her attending the School of Art, saying it is a waste of time and money, and she now realises he must have thought her interest in technical drawing to have been a mere summer dalliance for a bored and idle young woman, and her decorative design and illustration course as nothing more than a genteel hobby.

Ailsa knows she is *driven* when it comes to architecture, and that this may be tiresome for others, although her mother seems interested enough, even if she cannot read plans. By contrast Michael's talent lies in his ability to draw, usually to translate a design prepared by one of the architects into a scale drawing, and he does this well. He possesses a natural talent for drawing, but little imagination for design. When she has sketched simple ideas, perhaps at lunch on a napkin, casually discarded, imagining her version of an entry for the erstwhile House for an Art Lover competition, or a possibly more logical layout for the Shawlands apartments that Mr. Crawford has been commissioned to design, Michael has on several occasions, without her knowledge, squirrelled these away and perhaps a week later presented her at Knowe Terrace with a set of final plans and elevations, fully rendered, as if of a real proposal.

Ailsa was at first flattered by this industry on her behalf, wondering aloud where on earth Michael found time to produce such fine drawings, which he assured her was his own. On closer inspection she could see that Michael usually interpreted the proportions she had in mind wrongly or, when unable to grasp some design aspect of her scribbles, he had inserted his own, rather dull, badly proportioned version. She would never dream of telling him this of course, as he has a tendency to sulk if challenged, or react quite oddly. One time he screwed a rather fine set of elevations for the design of a cottage, sketched by Ailsa some days before and tossed aside, into a ball which he flung onto the drawing-room fire. Ailsa had merely suggested the first idea had needed more thought.

If anything, Michael could be described as *over enthusiastic* but someone who clearly loves trying to help. The thought that he would try to change, or thwart, Ailsa's ambitions, has not yet entered her head.

*

In fact Ailsa does not speak with Michael after all. She thinks it would embarrass both and may well be unfounded, and tells her mother as such.

On the Friday that she will be in the office for the last time, she is surprised to learn that Michael is not there. Something about his mother, who is ill. Ailsa is therefore unable to arrange a future social arrangement as an alternative to their accustomed daily encounter, but expects that he will come calling at home on a Sunday in the near future, and hopes that he will, for she is fond of Michael.

She thanks Robert Crawford profusely for the opportunity extended, but he only kisses her hand affectionately and says that he was the winner and if she is ever looking for a position once she qualifies she must promise to come to him first.

Before catching the tramcar home that day, Ailsa decides, on a whim, to stroll in the late afternoon sun along to the nearby School of Art and climb the short, steep incline to Renfrew Street. She turns to look up at the new building's powerful presence, thrilled to know she will be walking in there on Monday to begin the Diploma in Architecture, one woman sharing a studio with a group of young men starting out, but is sure enough in her own knowledge and small amount of experience to be able to hold her own from the start.

She will learn from the best. She has heard that guest lectures from Europe's leading figures in the world of design and architecture are commonplace under the leadership of Director Fra Newbery, the Englishman who has given Glasgow an international design reputation and created the culture that has become embedded. William Morris himself, and Voysey, both visited at the invitation of the Director and each gave a memorable lecture. The fact that Mr. Newbery chose to commission a former graduate of the School to design the new extension, with its fine library and interior detailing, its exquisite light, is the highest inspiration any new student could be given. Mr. Mackintosh's genius yet again is in play there, in a building that Ailsa will inhabit daily.

She was previously taught by both men and women on her design and illustration course, including Fra Newbery's wife Jessie, and has joined the Art Club which the Director has set up, a wonderfully stimulating place where both sexes mix socially and much lively debate occurs.

As Ailsa springs happily onto the tramcar a while later, back down on Sauchiehall Street, carrying the tools of her trade in her bag like any time-served apprentice, all around her she notices scores of high spirited workers spilling out of offices. On this glorious Friday evening, they will be rushing to wherever they stay in this bustling city, hot and therefore keen to remove work suits and neckties. Ailsa feels as she felt when she left London, that another layer has been added to her armour. So euphoric is she, so distracted by optimism for her future and this modern world she will inhabit, that she fails to see the familiar figure shadowed in the doorway of a tobacconists across the street.

Grey Satin

Gertrude

Aberdeen, May 1945

As the weeks pass I feel sure Daniel and I have become closer and, as he relaxes, I discover he has a kind of nervous energy that transforms into humour, which he likes to put to playful use by making me laugh, usually at myself. Perhaps as a foil to my role as teacher, he turns the tables when we take our breaks, teasing me about small things: my accent, my lax style of discipline with the younger boys, that type of thing. Thankfully never about how I look. In my experience there is a fine line between teasing and mocking, and he does not cross it.

I encourage this teasing, happy for the attention, to allow us to behave as peers. Sometimes, the best times, are when he is serious and reveals something of himself. He does this rarely and generally avoids giving straight answers to questions. He does not like questions, so I am careful. There is chemistry I'm sure in this compound made up of his jittery humour and my jangled bursts of laughter in response.

'I was thinking we have enough' I say on a Wednesday when he has finished a topical study we have been working on for several sessions: anxious woman standing by tallboy as if thoughtfully tuning the wireless, dressed in grey satin camisole and wide legged pyjamas, head inclined as if listening intently for news from the Front Line. I have rehearsed this next statement, knowing it had to happen tonight, and that I would say it lightly, casually.

'You have a good number of pieces to choose from and you'll be submitting your portfolio next week. We can stop these sessions now, as you have your examinations coming up.'

He looks briefly crestfallen, which is encouraging.

'But I enjoy them' he says with a meaningful smile, his blue eyes dancing, and for a moment could be a man of twenty-five or more. I am grateful that he does not ever call me Miss now. He does not call me anything.

'I was hoping we might work up to a pose with more, er, anatomy' he says.

He is finally making his move. I look at him then for a long time, until I can think of what to say.

'Well, we should really wait, if we are to continue, until you leave school in May.'

I am ecstatic. We both know the implications of this.

'Do you ever discuss our private tuition with the other boys Daniel?'

'Never. And I wouldn't. Nor with my family. They think I'm at a night class.'

I decide to trust him. Once again, I can't help myself. Neither of us says another word on the matter. We arrange for him to return on Saturday. I will eat nothing until then.

Now that sex has reared its ugly head.

Black Ice

The Christmas Vacation is almost here before Ailsa's realises it. Her first term has been a nonstop whirlwind of meeting new people, navigating the curriculum, purchasing equipment and materials, attending lectures and classes, and visiting buildings of note. Her fellow classmates are like-minded, wide eyed enthusiasts, not standoffish in the least, young men embarking on the same course through various modes of study. Some are full time, like herself, others attached to architectural firms and released to study day classes part time while attending evening classes as a supplement. Some hope to complete their Diploma within four years, others in seven or eight, but all appear humbled to be here. Such a hotchpotch of characters: fun, but serious too. Not one is complacent; there is something about the School that makes one feel privileged, in awe of its rich culture. They have discussed this over lunches in the refectory.

The curriculum is broad: in this foundation year students attend classes at both the School of Art, in Life Drawing and Arts subjects, and the Glasgow and West of Scotland Technical College for Descriptive Geometry, Mechanics Lectures, Stereotomy, Builders' Quantities, Mechanics of Structures, Chemistry, Geology and Physics, as well as various classes in Architecture.

Ailsa loves it all in equal measure. She works long and exhausting hours. Bridget's brothers have very kindly moved Crawfords' heavy drawing table up to the top floor of Knowe Terrace, to the room that was once her nursery, which has now become a studio for her to spread out without Bridget fussing about mess. A typical weekday sees Ailsa catch the tramcar home after class and join Flora for supper, where she exchanges the highlights of her day with her mother's own, before repairing to her studio to work. Flora has become a willing and ardent listener, fascinated by the characteristics and antics of the young men in Ailsa's year group, almost as if they are close personal friends, despite never having met them.

Tonight Ailsa is telling Flora about the forthcoming Christmas Ball, an annual all night revelry for which fancy dress is worn and much collective effort on the part of students and staff goes into the design and decoration of the Assembly Hall.

'It is a tradition Mama, apparently a quite notorious one, and it has been known, in past years, for dishevelled Vikings or masked creatures from Atlantis to be found wandering the streets of Garnethill for days after. Anyway, the point is, each student may bring a guest.'

'Why don't you ask Michael?' suggests Flora, causing Bridget to momentarily pause in mid air as she is dishing up the winter version of her legendary cranachan pudding, the raspberries having been preserved in syrup from the summer crop. Flora continues. 'We haven't heard from him in months. Why is that, do you think?"

'I've been wondering that too' says Ailsa. 'I feel guilty about Michael. I've not enquired about his mother's health. We haven't seen him since

I left Crawfords. I thought he would have called on us before now.'
She ponders this awhile.

'I have an idea! I will take the circle line and call on him at home this weekend to invite him. The Ball will be such fun.'

Ailsa remembers that Michael shares a two room and kitchen in a tenement in Cathcart with his widowed mother and younger sister, although Ailsa has not met either woman, and Michael was never forthcoming. She does know his mother is housebound and suffers badly with her nerves, and his sister Grace works at the local paper mill beside the Cart. She knows where they live from Michael having reluctantly pointed out the tenement from a tramcar as they were passing it one day en route from a site visit in the area, with Ailsa insisting he show her.

The following Saturday afternoon Ailsa takes the train the few stops to Cathcart and follows her instincts until she spies the familiar row of tenements on Holmlea Road. Enquiring of a woman and child at the close mouth, she learns that the O'Neill family stays in 3/2.

The stair is presentable and well swept, and Ailsa enjoys the climb to the top landing, such is her love of tenemental properties. This close may have a rather plain glazed tiled dado compared with the more decorative full height art nouveau tiling of Pollokshields or Shawlands, and is lacking proportions and intricate stained glass on its half landings, but is attractive enough with its terrazzo stone treads and glazed doorways.

She smiles in anticipation as she presses the right-hand side doorbell on the top landing. The storm doors are ajar, indicating the family to be at home, and Ailsa stands ready with her box of festively wrapped

Christmas shortbread and card in hand. She is therefore much taken aback at the sight which greets her when the figure behind the obscured glass eventually opens the door.

Michael looks gaunt and has dark purple circles under his eyes, as though he has not slept. He is dressed in a grubby collarless shirt and braces, and has not shaven. He takes a moment or two to realise who the caller is, fumbling as he puts on his eyeglasses, at which point a shadow crosses his face as if he wishes he had not opened the door at all. In fact he attempts to close it momentarily before he stops himself. Ailsa is flustered then, shocked by this unexpected reaction.

'Michael, I came to see how you are.....and to ask after your mother. We haven't seen you in quite some time.' She instinctively presses the glass panel in the door with her gloved hand to keep him talking.

'Wait here' whispers Michael, glancing back into the hall as if to gather his thoughts or perhaps out of concern for another, closing the door fully as he retreats. The weather is bitterly cold, and Ailsa has on her fur muff and velvet hat. After some time Michael steps out and pulls the door behind him, roughly buttoning a tweed overcoat and forcing his bowler hat so low that it hides his face. He runs briskly down the three flights of stairs, almost as if Ailsa were not there, his boots clattering on the cold stone. She has to run to catch up. Once out in the street he lights up a cigarette, and she notices his hand is shaking. She has never seen Michael smoke before. He cannot seem to look at her.

'Michael, whatever is the matter?'

'You should not have come here.' He looks everywhere but at her.

'Why not? Michael, of course I should. Why have you not called at Knowe Terrace as you used to? It's been three months.'

'I'm surprised you even remember me.' He looks at her now, and she sees hurt in his eyes, not the dismissal his attitude indicates. He is shivering, and Ailsa can smell stale drink on his breath. He makes no attempt to move from the spot. She decides she must take charge of this strained situation.

'Come' she says, ushering Michael along the road to a small bakery and tearoom which she passed earlier on a corner. It is stuffy inside, a combination of wet clothing, yeast and smoke. Cheap tinsel hangs from shelving and across wall light fittings. Ailsa manages to find seats beside the steamed-up window. She goes to the counter and orders tea for two, and soup with bread for Michael. She was not mistaken. He is ravenous, or perhaps eats hungrily to avoid talking. They sit in awkward silence until he has finished. He lights a cigarette then and sits back, less shaky now, staring at her intently, cigarette dangling from his lips. There is a coldness in his gaze, in his defiant stance. Ailsa thinks it would be inappropriate to mention the Christmas Ball at this point.

'How is work?' she asks, hoping this past mutual activity will spark conversation.

'Managing to survive without you.' There is no disguising the familiar sarcasm in his voice. She refuses to be taunted by this, as she knows Michael resorts to hurtful remarks when he is upset.

'Michael, have I done something to displease you? I wish you would speak plainly and tell me what is wrong.'

'My sister is with child and is to marry the scoundrel responsible, and my mother has suffered another breakdown as a consequence. Is that plain enough for you?'

'I'm so sorry to hear that. But…. I don't see what I have to do with this. Why are you angry with me?'

He snaps back without hesitation. 'You women never understand how men take advantage of you given the opportunity. I have seen you, shamelessly cavorting with at least two men, in broad daylight, on Renfrew Street.'

'You have seen me? Why didn't you greet me? I would have been moving between lectures with some fellow students. Michael, what is this? I am in a mixed class group. It is natural to socialise. We walk in small groups between buildings.'

Ailsa is becoming angry. She should not need to justify herself to Michael, and cannot believe he has seen her and not approached her, especially as Renfrew Street is not a busy or wide street, being set back and uphill from the main thoroughfare of Sauchiehall Street, very much the sole domain of academics, art students and school pupils. Nor can she imagine why Michael would be there, when his office is several blocks away on Bath Street, and to her knowledge Robert Crawford has no commissions in that district. Shamelessly cavorting? Possibly mildly amused by a shared joke, but certainly in a professional capacity. She has been careful not to become too friendly with the other students, given her mother's warning about misinterpreted friendship with men.

She tells him this now. How for the past year she thought of him as her best friend, her only close friend, other than Truus, but that she knows that men may wish to take advantage of friendship, so she has been careful not to encourage him in this regard. In fact, she believes she has never encouraged any man in this regard.

'And I have never taken advantage' he responds. 'I was looking after you. There is a difference.' After a long pause he continues. ' You must know how I feel about you Ailsa.'

'No, Michael, I don't. Because you never told me. If you had, I would have gently informed you that I am not interested in courtship, or romance, with anyone at this time. I value our friendship and thought you did too. I see now that was a mistake. I came here to invite you as my guest to the Christmas Ball. Another mistake, I expect.' She wants to add, *and I don't need looking after*, but stops herself as it will seem ungrateful and can only inflame an already delicate situation.

Michael looks incredulous. 'A Christmas Ball? Why on earth do you suppose I would want to mix with a bunch of fantasists and fornicators? Sodomites some of them. You must see how these supposedly *creative* men will use you, Ailsa. I did not agree with you wasting your time on this Diploma when we were undertaking perfectly good tuition for you at Crawfords, but oh no, you were determined. It is unnatural for a woman to go into higher education and it is a waste of money. It is legally impossible for you to register with the professional body, so you can never be qualified to practise. What is the point?'

She starts to interrupt but he talks over her. 'The Institute is an all male organisation and I don't see that changing in our lifetime. I'd hoped we could start a little business at Knowe Terrace one day, where you could design home interiors if you wanted to, and I could complete the Diploma if the business demanded. You wouldn't need to go out to work.' He takes her hand, gripping it tightly, lost now in his declaration. 'I am head over heels in love with you, Ailsa, you must know that.'

In that moment Ailsa sees it clearly for the first time; all of it. Michael had pictured a life for them both, had been formulating it even, and she had no idea. He had simply assumed it, and never thought to discuss it with her. He would be the one to qualify, meet clients, be in charge, and she would be at home, coming up with ideas which he would present as his own, and eventually it would be his name, his firm, his family, his house, his decisions. He would sulk if she disagreed, or worse, become angry, throw things onto the fire. He would lead his Boy Scout troop and want marriage. If Ailsa had sons, he would mould them to be like himself, and as for daughters, they would have no life at all.

She has to wrench her hand free, then stands abruptly and throws coins onto the table from her purse before giving her final word.

'If you had thought, even for a moment, to discuss this with me, to seek my opinion, or tell me how you feel, I would have told you that such a life is the last thing I wish for. And I do not love you Michael, not in that way. I'm sorry. I was your friend, and you sought to abuse it. Maybe I will not be allowed to register or practise as a chartered architect, but I will learn, and it will not stop me designing. I will earn my own living, and I will be useful.'

As she starts towards the door, Michael grabs her arm roughly, twisting it violently. 'And you were happy enough to use me while it suited you.' Here is the other Michael, not the one bowing and proffering a flower, introducing himself humbly and feigning interest, but the one that lies just below the surface.

'It is you who are the fantasist, Michael.'

With that she stumbles, shaking, out of that drab little bakery and hurries towards the railway station, oblivious of her boots slipping alarmingly on the slush and black ice. Ailsa is not prone to anger, but her eyes are stinging now with fury, not only at him, but at herself for blindly letting this happen. What a sorry mess.

She tries to calm herself as the circle line trundles the five short stops to Pollokshields West. By the time she steps off the train a new layer of armour has covered her, this time one of self protection. She must write to Truus immediately, to share with her the mendacious flattery and manipulation that a man is capable of, the arrogant assumptions cynically made on behalf of a woman when really he has a quite different agenda. One does not always see it coming.

Sugar Paper

Gertrude

Aberdeen, May 1945

I let Daniel in and he hangs up his battered corduroy jacket behind the door. As he removes a selection of pencils from the top pocket, as he normally does, I move across what feels like infinity from the door to the bed, slip out of my housecoat and stretch into the prepared pose: right side, head propped up with right hand, left hand placed down side of left leg, facing full on. We don't speak. I am someone else, somewhere else, Paris perhaps. My hip bone feels sharp beneath my elbow. I know my skin is pale. I look the best that I can, because I have indeed prepared this *languorous* pose, this fantasy, practised it over and over since Wednesday, reflected in a side mirror turned toward the bed. I am pleased with how this other woman looks, at this precise moment in time, unabashed, boldly facing forward, hair left to dry in tangled, untamed curls, a wilder look. I only wish my hair were red. The pre-Raphaelite waif, the muse, plucked from obscurity by a tall, dark, handsome Left Bank artist. I remain still, as if a statue.

He does not take his eyes away from mine, even as he lifts the equipment closer to the bed, smiling briefly. He begins a drawing just like every other, silently, eyes and hands moving steadily as he works with his pencil, faster now, rubbing lines with his thumb as he goes. What part of me is he touching? Shading the underside of a breast, perhaps smudging a dark triangle of pubic hair, a shadow in the curve of a thigh? I follow his eyes as they roam.

After ten minutes I change position, unannounced, emboldened now, turning to face the bedhead, so that he must start another drawing. Now he can see an arched spine, rounded buttocks, legs tucked under at the knee, one hand on the bedhead rail, the other pressed into the bedspread; shape and form necessary to any artist's development. I change again without warning after another ten minutes, so he needs to begin again, quickly, fluidly, as I pull up my knees and sit upright, facing forwards, head turned in profile.

We have a rhythm now, of ten minute poses, which he understands as he silently whips off each sheet of rough cream sugar paper and begin the next. We do not stop, but continue to work in this way until he has six or seven studies. By this method I know that it would be difficult to identify me from these *esquisses*, some because my face is turned away, others because there is no time to fill out the facial features behind the wild hair. None are lewd; they are all derived from classical works by other artists that I have studied and rehearsed at night. Titian, Rossetti, Picasso.

When I decide it is time, I tell him to stop. He does, then lights a cigarette. He rolls the drawings carefully and puts them into the leatherbound tube he always arrives with, slung over his shoulder. These are not for show, even to me. We understand that it is not my place to comment as I have on previous occasions, nor to suggest changes. I stretch out of the last pose, unhurried, knowing he is still looking. As I put on my cotton housecoat and tie the belt slowly, I am embarrassed now, shocked by my boldness, eyes cast down, no longer that other woman.

He washes graphite from his hands, tidies up his pencils, puts on his jacket as I cross to the door and wait for him to join me. He must be seen to leave at the usual time. When he does, he touches me for the first time. Placing a hand against my hip over the thin fabric of my housecoat, he traces a contour lightly all the way up to my neck, then lifts my chin. He presses a finger against my lips before bending down to kiss me just once, lightly, on the forehead, intimately but proprietorially, like a father might do to a daughter he loves and is reluctantly saying goodbye to. As he opens the door he turns.

'Thank you' he says, simply.

I lean against the closed door for a long time afterwards. I have fallen in love with a schoolboy.

All you ever think about is yourself.

Walnut with Black

Ailsa

Utrecht, July 1912

The late afternoon train from Amsterdam is smoky and hot, workers mostly, tired and expressionless, but for Ailsa the journey holds only anticipation, surely betrayed by her face, for she receives one or two inquisitive glances. She is a woman travelling alone, flushed and somewhat ruffled, a look she cannot seem to avoid wherever she goes. She is dressed plainly in a brown calico smock and a now creased linen coat with matching ribbon to her boater, carrying both suitcase and portfolio. An oddity therefore.

Ailsa is on her way to meet Truus at the Utrecht home she shares with her new husband, a man Ailsa is yet to meet, and she can hardly contain her thrill at finally having set foot on foreign soil.

Yesterday morning the feel of that ground underfoot as she stepped off the boat sent a shockwave through her, as if treading onto the surface of another planet. The landscape as she travelled inland was flat and wet, channels of water stretching for miles, dotted with the windmills she has only read about, and long straight tracks with people working allotments or cycling alongside fields of yellow crops in bright sunshine.

And her first sight of Amsterdam!

Such industry, such a rich world contained in canal houses with their slim façades and beams extended out from the carved attic profiles for hoisting goods up from the waterways. Her overnight stay after the long journey allowed her to spend time walking, to marvel at the brickwork everywhere, the bustling industry similar to London, except here there are the working barges, horses, noise, narrow cobbled streets, bicycles. She found the newness of it all exhilarating: the smells of cheese and beer and something she could not identify; watching Jewish diamond merchants, women setting up colourful flower stalls, couples crossing little bridges over canals. As she boarded her carriage for Utrecht inside the vast Gothic railway station, she knew in her heart she would be back here one day. It had been love at first sight.

Arriving now at Station Centraal in Utrecht she easily locates the electric tramcar for Biltstraat as directed by Truus, alighting soon afterwards on the island platform of Biltstraat station. The brick and timber building, with its overhanging iron shelter, is not unlike the train and tram station ticket offices at home, except for the location: tram lines and the building itself prominently positioned in the centre of what appears to be a two way main thoroughfare. Everywhere is flat. She is used to Glasgow, where any route seems to lead uphill from the river.

Biltstraat is located in what seems to be a wealthy new commercial district, boasting large mansion style buildings along both sides of the wide street. Ailsa locates number 135, an imposing cream stuccoed villa on three levels, the lowest a row of arched windows set slightly below the pavement line, providing a semi basement. This results in an elevated ground floor, with six tall symmetrical windows across the frontage, scrolled detailing above every lintel. A central arched entrance is arrived at by stepping down from the street.

The colonnaded façade is topped off at its centre by an elaborate scrolled arch at roof level with rather pretentious porthole, urns and weather vane, in Italianate neoclassical style. Behind this will be the typical Dutch mansard roof, Ailsa thinks: a clever design concept that allows usable attic height due to a flat central roof area often incorporating a skylight.

Across the street Ailsa notices the predominant use of brick, as in London, except in the Netherlands it seems more celebrated. Here on the Biltstraat, mansions seem to be competing, each one trying to trump its neighbour with yet more elaborate brickwork. Details are picked out in a contrasting colour in a most pleasing style on the exterior, biscuit coloured bricks against red indicating horizontal floor levels or accentuating arches over openings. So delicate, so different to the fortress-like stone of Pollokshields villas. In another respect, the competition for individuality is exactly the same.

Turning her attention back to number 135 she notices a busy lawyer's' office on the lower ground behind the arched windows and directly onto the bustling street as Truus had described. It must be convenient for Frits to live and work in one building, yet possibly allows little escape for Truus.

Once admitted by the housemaid, Ailsa puts down her luggage and marvels at the scale of the elaborate central hallway that indeed boasts the grand lightwell she suspected it would from the street. A palatial connecting staircase and open landing on each level has rooms off to the sides; the proportions are impressive, and with so much light, it makes Knowe Terrace, with its own modest light well above the deep narrow hall, seem tiny by comparison. This is more akin to one of those stately homes that one visits, where royal families or aristocracy live, and takes Ailsa aback momentarily.

She has always known her friend to be from a higher class to her own, yet somehow she had not imagined quite such opulence. It is disconcerting, given how Truus is so passionate about simplicity and her preference for the style of Berlage or English Arts and Crafts, not to mention her social convictions with regard to housing. This dwelling could not be more of a contrast and positively exudes wealth and societal position.

Her musing is broken by Truus exclaiming delight as she rushes downstairs to throw her arms around her friend. It is an emotional reunion: so much has happened in the three years since they parted, and Ailsa is relieved to see that Truus has at least lost none of her *joie de vivre* and sparkle. She is positively glowing. Right away she can see that Truus is with child, and cannot hide her shock.

'I know. It just happened!' laughs Truus, looking down and patting her bulge. 'But now that it has, we are delighted.'

Ailsa isn't sure what to think, but is now even more intrigued to meet the man who agreed before marriage that he did not want children any more than Truus did. They go upstairs for Ailsa to freshen up and then for the tour, passing through a maze of rooms with high ornate ceilings, each one opening not only off the landing but also through to the next adjoining room, again in the style of aristocratic residences.

Ailsa still cannot take it in that Truus actually lives here, clearly a colossal house to manage, but no doubt there are servants and staff to do that. The back windows on each of the three floors overlook well tended gardens, and the whole effect, if one ignores the blatant opulence, is architecturally striking. The guest bedroom, larger than the drawing room at home, and where Ailsa will sleep comfortably for the next three weeks, has a most agreeable aspect overlooking the rear gardens.

Truus seems to sense Ailsa's perplexity. The irony of a woman who expounds the theory of frugal, uncomplicated design for living having such a home for herself cannot go unremarked.

'I love it and I hate it' says Truus with some seriousness. She speaks quickly, as if trying to justify her choice, if it was indeed her choice. 'I love the light that floods down through the central hall, and these little balconies at all the windows overlooking the garden. It is good to live upstairs, where it is lighter. I would hate to live on a ground floor. Perhaps it is the Dutch fear of flooding, but it seems unnatural to me to be at street level or below, like some choose to live. So dark.

'No, what I hate is the flamboyance, all this ornate detailing, fussy plasterwork everywhere, and Frits' preference for traditional, over-elaborate furniture. Also, each individual room is too high and narrow in comparison to its width. They are badly proportioned, don't you think? And of course, it is far too big!!!' She stops and shrugs apologetically. 'What can I do about it? It comes with my husband's business. It is expected of a successful lawyer to have a home that reassures clients he knows what he is doing. As you know, it is not my taste at all.'

Ailsa sees that Truus has lost none of her passion and that still she sees the positive in every situation and in people. Her love for her husband means she puts him first, even though it compromises her own beliefs and opposing taste. No doubt the pregnancy is also down to that selfless nature. Ailsa's thoughts turn to Michael briefly, but she stops herself from thinking that all men are going to be manipulative. She has yet to meet Frits, so will not prejudge.

It is true that, once one steps off the magnificent hall into any of the rooms, whether it be the drawing room, the bedrooms or the dining room, they are tall and narrow, certainly not designed using the principle of the *Golden Section*, which Ailsa has been learning about, a principle about ratio and proportion which goes back all the way to the ancient Greeks. The Parthenon is a good example. There exists a simple formula for the ideal ratio of length to width, whether it be applied to a simple sheet of paper, a table, a building, or a painting, and this calculable mathematical proportion is said to be aesthetically pleasing to the human eye because it appears in nature, in the human body and in plants. There has certainly been no Golden Section applied to the design of these rooms.

*

The stay turns out to be exactly the tonic Ailsa needs to shake off her distressing situation with Michael, which has left her deeply upset, and has disproportionately distorted her view of the world. Neither did it end with the altercation in the bakery: Michael has since written a number of long, rambling letters, repeating the same declaration of love, despite her responses to dissuade him, and in the end she stopped replying. One evening in late February, dark by five o'clock, he stepped out of nowhere it seemed, as Ailsa was walking down Hope Street from the School to Central Station on her way home, apologising desperately, as he had done in the correspondence, asking her to reconsider their situation. She had to endure him until she left the train at Pollokshields West.

Another time, in the Spring, Michael surprised her by emerging from a wooded area, dressed in full scoutmaster dress, accompanied by several youths in similar attire. She had been walking through woodland on Pollok Estate, part of her new route of a Sunday since last year when the Maxwell family granted public access to their parkland, whereupon he appeared to step out right in front of her on purpose. He claimed to have been showing the boys how to light a fire by rubbing sticks together when he had happened to spot her through the trees. In the presence of the youths she was forced to exchange pleasantries and move on.

Whatever Michael tried to say, she could not shake from her memory the expression on his face in the bakery cafe, or him hurting her arm, and has lost all trust in him, even though he apologised repeatedly for that rough behaviour. She played down his obsession when Flora questioned her, but the reality was he would not seem to take no for an answer and had it in his head that they belonged together and he only wished she would let him prove that to her.

So now, Ailsa has been forced to face just how naive she is, how artless and unsophisticated when it comes to relationships. She tells Truus the whole story, how since Christmas she has thrown herself into her studies with added vigour, avoiding any distraction, wary of giving signals to her fellow students or to her tutors that could compromise her and cause possible recriminations down the line, such as those she received from Michael.

She has gained a reputation for being distant and reserved in class, which she resents, as it is not her natural disposition. She knows Flora has become worried for her, ever since she stopped regaling amusing anecdotes about whatever Arthur or James or Bertie said today, or about her tutor's comments on her latest design project, or indeed on the activities of the Art Club. In fact Ailsa has stopped going to the Art Club altogether.

Here in a new environment, with no possibility of Michael making contact or appearing out of nowhere, by talking it over with Truus, and once again being around her friend's infectious personality and independent thought, Ailsa gains a fresh perspective and realises that, by having allowed Michael's behaviour to affect her own, she has let him win. She had done nothing wrong. Truus is certain no-one could accuse Ailsa of being a flirt. It is simply not in her nature, nor to be coquettish. She feels a weight lift. Truus convinces her that it was not her fault. In future, they agree, she will resume her natural behaviour around men, who are everywhere in the world, especially in the world she inhabits. She may have no designs on men for now, but will relax freely in male company. The matter is decided.

Frits turns out to be a good example: welcoming, well educated, happy to debate with his wife and her Scottish friend in good humour, but displays no anger or arrogance if they gang up on him playfully, and laughs much of the time. The three discuss ideas over dinner each evening, including women's rights. To Ailsa's surprise, Truus uses Michael as an example of how a woman can unwittingly become the victim of social repression. She is unable to freely express herself, simply wishing to live differently but within a code of morals, without being castigated.

Frits is older, an enlightened man who seems experienced in matters of the heart and relationships, and alas takes a view similar to Flora's: that it is just human nature. *Vive la différence,* he laughs, a phrase Ailsa has not heard before. He has the way of a lawyer, happy to listen to all sides of an argument, then to cleverly steer the discussion into calmer waters as required. He clearly adores his young wife, and is a good foil for her more extreme theories. Ailsa hopes the couple will always engage in healthy and good humoured debate, although she is not convinced that Truus will win so easily.

Over the coming week Truus and Ailsa do all the things she has longed to do. They visit the medieval old town, with its canals, Christian monuments and the university. Ailsa at last visits the iconic Domtoren, a fourteenth century bell tower, and the Gothic Cathedral of St. Martin on central Domplein Square. She finally meets An, whom she feels she knows already from their adolescent days, when they wrote often as pen friends.

An is just as Ailsa knew she would be: possessed of an energy that she is channelling into writing nowadays, vociferous in her views on politics and religion. The sisters are extremely close, and Truus still looks up to An as much as she did when she spoke of her in London. Ailsa notices that, in An's presence, Frits is less accommodating in debate, less good humoured. Perhaps he sees An as a threat, an unsettling influence possibly on his wife, but it may be that Ailsa imagines this.

It doesn't take long for Ailsa to realise she has neglected her wardrobe and appearance since becoming a student. Never one to be overly interested in fashion, she has nevertheless slipped too far into the constant wearing of artists' smocks over simple calico or lawn dresses, grey usually, with ink stains she can do nothing about. Her hair is positively unkempt, its tangled red curls half way down her back, spiralling out from her hairline and making her look quite tousled but, as Truus laughs, in an attractive, bohemian way.

Truus also has simple taste in clothing, but is able to afford fine fabrics and well cut dresses and costumes. They spend lazy mornings in Truus' bedroom, after Frits has gone down to his office, laughing and idling on the bed in their night shifts, going through her wardrobe. This room is different to the others. Still grand in scale, with its high ceiling and elaborate cornicing, but imbued with Truus' taste rather than that of Frits; more austere, spare, with simple, elegant furnishings. Perhaps Truus does get her own way sometimes, thinks Ailsa, when she has something with which to bargain. The marital bedroom is one example.

Truus takes pleasure in making clothing suggestions for Ailsa to try on, even to keep one or two outfits that she herself no longer wears, especially in her present condition, and to take them back home with her when she leaves. They are beautiful and expensive items that Ailsa would never dream of allowing herself to spend money on, given that she needs so much for equipment and materials.

She understands for the first time the value of good tailoring and quality of fabric. It is not so different to architecture: there is an art to a good cut on the bias, the way a fabric drapes over the body, the careful application of a detail. It is the same with hair. Truus, who wears her own straight hair tied back in a simple knot, takes Ailsa to a salon where her hair is tamed, conditioned and cut a little, enough to allow her natural curls, without the need of Marcel tongs, to curl gently around her face and the remainder to be piled high around her head in a soft fashionable pompadour style.

Ailsa knows she will never be able to sustain or replicate this look when she is back in Glasgow, pouring over her drawing table or rushing from class to class, but for now she is simply enjoying a pampered summer holiday indulging in new experiences and the pleasure of close female friendship.

Truus and Frits spend time looking through Ailsa's portfolio, which they had asked her to bring, and Frits suggests they attend an evening event at his Art club, where a number of local artists and craftsmen are staging an exhibition of their work. The pieces are considered quite radical according to his sources, and he has acquired three tickets for the Friday opening, which he thinks the ladies will enjoy. It will be an opportunity for Ailsa to meet some of his associates, most of whom Truus already knows, including one or two architects who have heard about this exotic foreign creature in town: a *female* studying *architecture*! In fact one impudent fellow has asked when is he going to meet the *Schotse Architectress,* as she has become known at the club, or is Frits Schröder keeping her all to himself?

*

As they browse the exhibition on a glorious Friday evening, small clusters of businessmen and their wives can be seen socialising or studying paintings and pieces of furniture at close quarters, discussing them animatedly. Ailsa is introduced to this one and that, and made welcome by all. Frits is obviously relishing this business opportunity over culture, so the women, who have spent hours getting ready and have chosen to wear complementary outfits of empire waisted unboned tea gowns of beaded satin, drift away on their own.

Truus points out a dark haired young man with a pencil thin moustache and beard, a cigarette hanging from his lips, dressed in artisan clothing, who is animatedly explaining a basic looking chair to someone, lifting it into the air and turning it round to show the joints. He is strikingly handsome.

From behind her hand Truus says 'I've met him before. A few times.' Ailsa notices that Truus is smiling, as if thinking of an amusement.

'Who is he?'

'When I was engaged to Frits we were busy fitting out the new office. This young man here had helped his father to deliver a desk they had made to order. I hated it immediately and I think the son agreed with me, going by the smile on his face that day.'

It turns out the father, Rietveld, a local furniture maker well known for quality copies of traditional pieces, had made the inlaid black ebony and rich reddish walnut desk, an extremely intricate and elaborate design, which Frits was delighted with of course. Truus, being her usual outspoken self, derided the design and teased Frits, much to Rietveld senior's annoyance. His son had said nothing on that occasion, just smiled, but had returned with his father now and again to carry out repairs to other pieces, and finally Truus had got him to speak his mind.

'One time' she confided, 'a few months ago, I happened to be alone with him, and he volunteered how much he had agreed with my opinion on that first day. We had such a long discussion, the two of us. He is a very interesting man.'

'Not to mention very handsome' teases Ailsa. 'In what way is he interesting?'

'His thoughts on modern design, simpler style and construction, without ornament, were in harmony with how you and I feel. I found him very stimulating to talk to.'

'We should look at what he is exhibiting' says Ailsa, intrigued.

Truus is still talking about the day they first met.

'Then of course we were interrupted by his disgruntled father. Unfortunately I never discovered his first name.'

'Then that is our mission tonight' says Ailsa.

In high spirits and full of mischief, the friends decide to make this their objective for the evening: to find out the Christian name of Rietveld Junior. In fact this is easier than they think, as his work is on display: simple, modern chairs and gifted technical drawings to explain and accompany the designs.

'So, he is not all talk', whispers Truus. 'He actually creates modern pieces.'

They go over for a closer inspection while Frits is still busy talking shop with a client, and discover, when the young man offers them his hand drawn business card, that his first name is Gerrit. He recognizes

Truus right away, and they reminisce about the earlier incident, when they felt like two naughty children under the wary eye of his father. Ailsa notices he wears a wedding band. He seems young for marriage. She is introduced to him, and Truus, as always, proudly boasts of her friend's chosen occupation and course of study.

'Ah, yes, I have heard about you' Rietveld says to Ailsa. His dark eyes seem to perpetually sparkle and he has a spontaneity about him that is quite infectious.

'Should I be worried?' Ailsa teases.

'No, no! All good things. This town is very small, that's all. You must meet architect Piet Klaarhamer, my own tutor. He is here someplace. Now, may I show you ladies this beautiful chair' he says with a flourish.

Ailsa is always impressed with how well everyone can speak English here, even if it is a little broken as in Gerrit Rietveld's case.

By coincidence, when the women go back across the room to join Frits, the architect Klaarhamer is in conversation with him, alongside another man who has turned away to view a painting. They are introduced, and a discussion follows around the benefits women can bring to architecture, of which there are none yet in the Netherlands according to the architect, who is most impressed by Ailsa's ambition and tenacity.

He seems worldly, around forty years of age, and has studied under the influential Hendrik Berlage of Amsterdam, who in turn has recently visited America, returning much inspired by the work of one Frank Lloyd Wright, now a great influence on Berlage's own work. So much so that he now gives excellent lectures on the pioneering American's buildings.

At this point the Schröders get caught up in a separate conversation with a passing and needy client, so Ailsa continues speaking with Klaarhamer by herself. 'I am familiar with the work of Frank Lloyd Wright, and would indeed love to see Berlage's work while I am here.' She senses someone close by.

'Well then,' continues Klaarhamer, turning to his right. 'Johan here is working for Berlage over the summer, in the Amsterdam office. Johan is one of my students. One of the better ones.'

For the first time Ailsa looks properly at the man who has been hovering to the side slightly, and he joins them now.

'Johan Peeters, meet Ailsa Bray, from Glasgow.'

She is first aware of his height, which must be six feet at least. He is stocky with curly light brown hair and a full, now unfashionable style of beard, and looks reassuringly rumpled but fresh, with a mustard waistcoat and striped shirt, mismatched to a pair of chequered breeks. She smells a not unpleasant aroma of pipe tobacco and thinks he looks as if he has thrown on whatever clothes first came to hand, resulting in an overall appearance of eccentricity, but certainly no dandy. This lack of vanity in another appeals to Ailsa, being one who is herself often so immersed in thought about whatever creative activity she is currently working on that she cannot remember if she has just washed her face or was just about to wash it. At such times she has to feel the cake of soap, to see if it is wet or not, to get her answer. Johan Peeters seems to carry no guile or self importance and his manner seems gentle. A gentle giant, thinks Ailsa.

Peeters shakes her hand as one professional to another and bows slightly. 'I am delighted to meet the Schotse Architectress at last' he says, with a smile that reaches all the way to his eyes. Green eyes, she notices, and also that his accent is slightly different to the others.

'Schröder has been singing your praises' he continues. 'I would very much like to see your own work if you have time. We admire the Glasgow Style, especially since the German house competition and the Viennese collaboration with your Mr. Mackintosh.'

He is referring to the House for an Art Lover competition of a few years ago, in which Mackintosh received a prize for his stunning design despite being disqualified due to late entry.

'And if you are up in Amsterdam during your stay I'd be pleased to introduce you to Berlage's work, in particular the new Beurs, the Stock Exchange.'

'An excellent idea, Johan' says Klaarhamer. 'Ailsa, my dear, you must give my regards to Eugene when you return to Glasgow. I knew him well in Paris.'

This reference is to Eugene Bourdon, Director of Architecture at the Glasgow School. Ailsa knows him well enough from the inspiring talks he gives, in his attractive broken English with its French flourish, and of course from his reputation. Monsieur Bourdon is a highly thought of *Beaux-Arts* architect, and is a great influence on the entire culture of the Glasgow School. In particular, and much to Ailsa's delight, he has insisted that the students produce quick, conceptual sketches, highly finished perspective presentation drawings, and large scale details. He emphasises design as of equal importance to the knowledge of building methods in any architect's training. Ailsa has the utmost respect for him, but can hardly just address him *en passant* in the 'hen run' to relay his former Dutch associate's regards, but she doesn't say this.

Truus comes over and, in her naturally gregarious style when surrounded by the familiar, suggests the two men join them for dinner on Biltstraat the following evening, where they can view Ailsa's work and spend a pleasant evening cooling in the garden, given this overbearing heat. They will eat a late supper, plus Klaarhamer can continue the legal discussion he was having with Frits earlier over some matter to do with copyright. This is settled, and details are agreed.

As they go to leave, Ailsa notices Truus turn to smile and nod directly to the young furniture maker Rietveld, who is looking back at her from across the room, despite an entourage of young men around him. She sees him respond likewise, with an almost imperceptible smile as they hold each other's gaze momentarily. It would be inappropriate to mention it, but Ailsa has noticed a spark between these two, despite an obvious disparity in their class. She follows Truus out of the hall with an odd sensation, as if she has just witnessed some kind of foreshadowing moment.

However, at this precise moment in time, gathered together on a fine summer's evening in the medieval surroundings of Utrecht, indulging in the simple pleasure of a progressive cultural event, no-one in that room can possibly imagine what horror will befall most of Europe and shift the balance of the wider world long before Truus will meet this young man again.

Sweet Sherry

Gertrude

Aberdeen, June 1945

The war is over. Despite the festivities all around, for me there is only a sense of anticlimax. Of course it is a great relief, but I know that my time here will now end.

I resolve, recklessly, to write to Daniel. If I tell him that I have no intention of compromising him, perhaps he will visit me again. I tell him the future for me is uncertain, I may be leaving soon, given the changing status of my teaching post, and would like to discuss this with him in private. I offer a time and date for when his exams will be over and he will have officially left school, and slip the sealed envelope unobserved into his battered satchel on the bench in the Art Room. The boys are preoccupied now, chatting with palpable relief about finishing school and avoiding the war service that hopefully will no longer be immediate or even compulsory.

Daniel has not made eye contact with me since our last session, and I cannot help thinking that, unless he is genuinely embarrassed by what happened, he must find me desperate. I cannot bear to think he only wanted the thrill of drawing a naked woman, any naked woman, but especially his teacher, offered exclusively and willingly, and found her wanting. The short period when I was in control of this relationship, this *arrangement,* has passed, and the one in control (how quickly men, boys even, do this) is Daniel.

As agreed I am keeping my distance to allow him to sit his exams, but I have been anguished that he has not looked at me once, even in the days since I slipped him the note. When I have been invigilating exams for example, slowly pacing the aisles, inevitably brushing past his desk among the tight rows of boys, so many heads bowed, I am willing him to look up but he does not.

I even write out a copy of the reference I have submitted for him, suitably impersonal but glowing nevertheless, composed without bias, and pass it to him openly, brightly calling out his name, explaining its context loudly as he is leaving the exam hall one time. I do it in such a way that he can be reassured I am not betraying any intimacy, if that is indeed the correct term for what we had, nor am I attempting to write to him a second time. He takes it and thanks me, gruffly, but keeps his hair flopped over his eyes, continuing to discuss the exam paper with another boy as they bundle out of the door. I cling to the thought that this is his bungled way of being discreet.

When the appointed Saturday evening arrives I am prepared for disappointment but still hopeful that he will come. I have heard via staffroom talk that he, along with one other boy, have been offered conditional places on the Architecture course in Aberdeen. He must surely be more relaxed now and fairly confident of his results. He has officially left school as of yesterday and must surely see that as a rite of passage. There is nothing to stop us now from seeing one another as consenting adults.

I wait, breathe, breathe again, stomach churning as I pace the depressing, claustrophobic room that once felt like an exotic boudoir, an artist's garret, whenever he was here. Since then I have never been so low yet, when it was happening, so elated. I am wearing a frock that says I am neither teacher nor temptress, possibly girlfriend. My hair has been cut a little and tamed. I have set a bottle of rather sweet sherry, the only type I could find locally, on the table with two glasses and an ashtray, for I have seen Daniel smoking lately when walking his dog. He may not be used to alcohol, but this is an occasion for celebration. I try not to be sick as I pour myself a small glass.

Earlier than expected, by half an hour, there is a rap at my door. I knew he would come. Trying to look nonchalant I cross to open it with a bright smile.

'Are you the schoolteacher? O'Neill?'

The tall elegant woman before me is unmistakably the same woman I watched being lovingly waltzed by her tall silver haired husband through the lit bay window of a room with colourful abstract oils on canvasses around the walls, tastefully chosen to match the plain soft cushions and buttoned leather Chesterfield sofas; whereupon a young boy, younger than Daniel, entered to show them something, a drawing perhaps or a comic, and they all laughed as they drew him effortlessly into the dance. Even if I had not seen her before, she has such a look of Daniel that it can only be his mother. She is beautiful and expensive.

'Cordelia Ogilvie. May I come in, or would you prefer to discuss this out on the landing?'

Head spinning, I step aside and indicate for this self assured woman to enter. She gazes disdainfully around the room, taking in my easel, the bed, the sherry.

'Mrs. Ogilvie' I acknowledge politely, swallowing hard. 'Would you like to sit down?'

'I won't be staying. I am here to tell you to stay away from my son.' Standing just inside the door, she snaps open the metal clasp on her hard snakeskin handbag and takes out a familiar envelope. 'I found this in Dan's bag and read it, thinking it to be official school correspondence.'

I start to protest but she talks over me. 'And…. I found... explicit drawings, below his bed, which speak for themselves. Please don't insult me by denying what has been going on here.'

I feel my father's presence in the room, that familiar tone. I am transported back to other recriminations. How quickly I accept guilt, inadequacy. Indecency.

'I don't need to spell out what it would mean for you if I report this to the school governors, of which I know several personally.'

She hasn't reported it.

'We've done nothing wrong, Mrs. Ogilvie. I was helping Daniel's portfolio content, that is all. Have you spoken to him?'

'No, and I don't intend to, providing you stay away from him and leave Aberdeen. Dan has his whole life ahead of him. The war may have allowed unnatural situations to arise, such as women like you being in positions of authority, but that is no longer the case. He is a young man who will meet someone his own age when he is good and ready, as it should be. He doesn't need to have his head turned by an older woman who is clearly seeking to take advantage of him. He has been spared the war, thank God, and now you need to leave him alone.'

'I'm hardly an older woman, Mrs. Ogilvie. I'm not yet twenty three. Daniel has been coming here for tuition, that's all. He is extremely talented and I've tried only to help him. I would never do anything to harm his future.' My face is burning. I wish now I hadn't sampled the sherry. 'And for the record I'd like to know what you mean by 'women like me'.' I briefly try to take the moral high ground, a familiar if futile position.

'You are from Glasgow, need I say more, and you have been seducing my son. It stops now. It is very possibly illegal, and certainly immoral. You may behave like that where you come from but we don't here. You are leaving anyway I understand, and the sooner the better.'

'I have...we all have...been advised to look for permanent posts, yes. I doubt there will be many going in Aberdeen once the men return. But I would like to stay if I can.'

'You won't be staying. Take it from me.'

So, a word in an ear, nothing to incriminate her son or cast doubt on his good name, but enough to plant suspicion about my character. Poison dropped from the lips of the wife of an influential businessman and one of a respected family in the community.

'Does Daniel even know I wrote to him?' I can hear my voice breaking. Was the letter undiscovered when she found it?

'He does not, and you will not contact him, nor will you tell him of this conversation, otherwise I *will* go to the school, who may well contact the police.'

I become defensive now. Surely I have not committed a criminal act (except in my own imagination). As one *in loco parentis* I know the rules. This was art. The kiss on the forehead was one of friendship. (How quickly I delete his hand tracing an outline from my hip to my mouth, yet that act has sustained me and I relive it constantly. It surely signified desire?) Though this explains why he has not acknowledged me. He never saw my note.

'I see you waited until I had submitted his reference and he'd left school before coming to threaten me.' I say this as I move to open the door, wanting this to be the last word. It is then I notice Mrs.Grier on the landing, who has heard everything. She wears a mocking triumphant expression, reminiscent of Edith's when knitting during a tirade.

'Go home to your own family, and stay away from mine' says Cordelia Ogilvie before sweeping out of the door.

I have no family. I wanted yours.

Rising Tide

Ailsa

Utrecht, April 1914

Johan is there to meet her off the boat at Ostende. She sees him in the crowd as she disembarks, towering above the others waiting at the port. My gentle giant, she thinks, here for me.

This morning they will travel by rail to Brussels then to his parents' home in Leuven, stay for a few days so Ailsa can meet his family, then on to Utrecht for her to begin a term of study under Piet Klaarhamer. She will be alongside five other students, in a private arrangement that has been agreed between the Director in Glasgow and Klaarhamer himself. The two men have exchanged correspondence over the past few months, at Ailsa's request initially, and agreed a personalised course of study for her. In addition the two men seemed to enjoy rekindling their earlier acquaintance in Paris. Ailsa has not seen the content of the letters that have passed between them, but has seen the testimonial written for her by Bourdon, and was genuinely surprised by his praise for her and complimentary remarks about her ability and character.

She had no idea she was thought of in this way by her tutors, but it seems they regard her as equal to the men on the course, in fact possessing advanced skills when it comes to design and detailing. In addition, they confirm she is no stranger to hard work, nor indeed to negotiating building sites and even scaffolding.

Now approaching the end of her third year, she is finding a niche that suits her and which can only be enhanced by this opportunity of a term under Klaarhamer. Of course being able to be with Johan, and to see Truus again, is part of the appeal, but Ailsa has been upfront about that too. She cannot hide her love for Johan Peeters from the world, nor does she wish to. In fact she wants to shout it from the rooftops.

Johan wraps her in his habitual bear hug, and she once again takes in the scent of her Belgian lover: pipe smoke mixed with warm wool, a sweet foreign smell she always thinks, unlike anything at home, and one she does not forget in the months they spend apart. He laughed when she asked to take one of his old fishermens' guernseys back with her after their last summer together, to hold close and keep his aroma with her, to sleep with at Knowe Terrace until the next time she would hold him. As he stoops down now to meet her lips, she feels his rough beard brushing her face before he holds her head tightly against his chest. She can hear his heart beating. They laugh at the sheer pleasure of touching after so long.

'I've missed you, Architectress' he says, using the nickname she is affectionately called at the studio in Utrecht. She has noticed that the men refer to each other by surname habitually, so she thinks they do this to avoid calling her Bray, or alternatively patronising her by using her Christian name.

'The waiting gets longer each time. But now we can make up for it.' His eyes take in every part of her face, cupping it, stroking back her hair with his big hands. 'Three whole months. No, in fact it will be more, including the summer.'

She decides to leave until later her concerns over that, the financial necessity that cannot be ignored, plus her growing worry about the troubles in Europe, especially the Balkans. The newspapers are filled with foreboding, but that is too serious a subject for this moment of reunion.

Once they are settled on the train with her suitcase and portfolio stored, she ventures to explain her concerns for the months ahead. The significance of Ailsa's situation will not be lost on Johan. At thirty, most women would be married with children and leaving financial matters to their husband. Yet Ailsa is not most women, and they have discussed this. He knows that she plans to live and work in Glasgow where she can be close to her mother, and has no intention of marrying. He also knows she wants a child because she told him early on that this was her plan, and to remain independent. The conversation they have not had is the one concerning any future together, or Ailsa asking him to father a child. She wants this passionately, but does not yet know if she has the right to ask.

'Johan, I need to find work if I am to stay on this time' she says, her hand resting on his arm.

She is aware how openly they touch each other in public, how intimacy always reveals itself. 'My expenses are beginning to bite. Mama has talked of selling our home and moving locally to a flat, but I have assured her that will not happen. I've taken over running the household finances now, and Mama is well covered. We will be fine as long as I work alongside studying, as you do. This opportunity is wonderful, and to be with you, and near to Truus, but finding work will be essential in the summer. My scholarship will cover Klaarhamer's fees and my expenses for this term, but by the end of June I must find paid work, here or at home.'

She decides that the wider discussion can wait. Perhaps here in Belgium they will be able to tell her more real facts than those she reads in the pessimistic press at home.

Since she met Johan two years ago, Ailsa has matured into a responsible and tenacious woman, and is more than ready for professional work. Their growing feelings for each other, since the night they first met at an art exhibition, and their first kiss in the gardens of Truus' home on Biltstraat after a week when Johan had shown her the Amsterdam she had not seen when passing through the first time: the Beurs, or Stock Exchange, with its vast red brick interior, three open multi-storey trading floors in an atrium under an iron and glass roof, its entrance below a high clock tower, which Johan said is over one hundred feet high. It was like nothing Ailsa had seen before, except perhaps St. Pancras Station. They visited the site of the Scheepvaarthuis at the harbour, still a work in progress, with charming and exotic decorative detailing of ironwork, brick and hardwood. It is being designed by two architects of the Amsterdam School, organic in design, reflecting Dutch colonial power throughout the interior and exterior design of the Shipping House. A truly beautiful building.

At dinner on the Biltstraat that first time, Johan had been genuinely impressed by her portfolio, as had Klaarhamer, and she realised then that the course in Glasgow was a match for anywhere, as was her own work, even then. She had looked around the dinner table that night, at these engaging people who were now part of the substance of her life: Truus, her dearest friend, and Frits, a man she had come to like enormously in the few weeks she had known him, and now these two new acquaintances, professionals who treated her likewise and spoke eloquently of influences from America and Paris. How lucky she felt, and then remembered that all of this came about because of Papa's business links with Truus' father.

Quietly in that moment she thanked Papa, made her peace with him. If he had lived perhaps she would have arrived at this point eventually, through her own determination, and he would have come to realise that she needed something beyond the confines of home. He was a kind man at heart, just of a different generation to hers.

The influence of Bourdon, under the leadership of Fra Newbery, meant her work stood up well next to the innovative work of Klaarhamer, even back then. When she returned home after that first summer, already falling in love, something she had not been looking for but had found her when she least expected it, had caught her unawares, she hated parting from Johan even more than leaving Truus. But she also returned to Glasgow possessed of a confidence and with new ideas that she could share with her fellow students.

She became her old self again, open and receptive, able to participate fully in social and educational discussions and to drop the reserve she had falsely acquired. Her colleagues possibly thought she had emerged from a period of bereavement or mental illness, but no one spoke of it, to her at least. She did not see Michael at all during her second year, but she was always looking over her shoulder.

Ailsa came back to Utrecht the following summer to stay with Truus, who by then had not one, but two small children, Binnert and Marjan, taking up much of the family's time, and so she was able to get to know Johan better, although they had written to each other many times over the intervening months. They became inseparable, and spent many lazy hours making love in his tiny apartment on Annastraat or sitting in the dark cafes and tiny bars alongside the canal or off the square, telling each other everything about their lives up to that point. Ailsa even told him about Michael, and the misunderstanding that had occurred.

Back home for her third year of study, she put in a request to specialise in domestic architecture. This was expected of a woman in any case, given that the profession needs a female perspective on matters such as the intricate details of running a home and labour saving design. She has been allowed to undertake a project that will underpin her final thesis, looking at modern developments in housing in both Scotland and the Netherlands, given her now established links to that country.

Ailsa is therefore thrilled to have been awarded this travel scholarship to spend a full term in Utrecht, studying alongside Johan and four other men. She was awarded the Alexander Thomson Travelling Studentship, which had been set up by the Glasgow Institute of Architects following the death of the famed architect. Charles Rennie Mackintosh was a previous recipient of this studentship, in 1890. She does not worry about working with Johan, as he leaves her space to work and to think, and has never once tried to influence what she chooses to research or her approach. She loves this about him. He has his own style, influenced by his work experience with Berlage, and now, under Klaarhamer, his furniture and interiors are very much in the style of a group that is gaining a reputation of some importance in Utrecht.

Johan's parents are academics, not wealthy like Truus' family, but must have enough to help fund his tuition in the Netherlands with such a prominent tutor, who had first spotted Johan's talent on a teaching visit to Leuven. Providing he supplements his studies with paid work, as he did two years before with Berlage, and last summer working for Klaarhamer, Johan can afford to rent an apartment in Utrecht with enough left over for food, a few Amstel beers and his pungent pipe tobacco. Ailsa loves this too. She can be overwhelmed by Truus' wealth, although her friend does not force it on her, or onto anyone, and she would hate for Truus to know of this effect. It is simply the way things are.

'We could work together' he says. 'It's up to you, but over the next two months we could look for a commission to undertake over the summer.'

She doesn't hesitate to warm to this idea. Johan and Ailsa are equal partners, so different to the balance that would have existed between herself and Michael, he acting as mentor and benefactor yet without the element of creativity, Ailsa being the one with ideas. They were never going to be compatible professionally, nor had she ever even considered it.

She pushes Michael from her mind. He is always there, sitting on her shoulder, critical, cynical, sucking the joy out of any situation. He would not approve of Johan; she can hear him now, a voice in her head, calling Johan idealistic, unkempt. But to her, Johan is a man who has inner strength and a love of beauty in all its forms. In those dark cafes that first summer, eating simple stews in rough bowls with hunks of bread and drinking beers together, he talked about his early difficulty in being able to read, to understand and communicate, and how his parents had found him a special tutor to help, but he was a dreamer, and found his outlet through his imagination, and through drawing.

She fell in love with this quiet, humble giant of a man, his laughing green eyes and light curling hair, his long beard, ideas about how people might live, a man who himself lives in the moment and finds pleasure in nature and the pursuit of a simple life. Clearly intelligent, and two years older than Ailsa, he has found his niche under the careful eye of Klaarhamer.

Johan is a colleague of Rietveld, the young man she met at the exhibition two years ago, and last summer she twice joined the two of them for a meal. On those occasions Ailsa observed how similar these two young men were, in their openness to new ideas and love of design, as she listened to them talking passionately about concepts of light and space and form. Rietveld also studies under Klaarhamer, when he is not working for his father, and he too has his own unique style.

Johan wants to visit Glasgow, and this is something they intend to do at the end of her stay, so that Ailsa can introduce him to Flora, who is naturally excited to meet him after everything her daughter has told her. All in all, they have a busy time ahead.

*

Ailsa settles in well with Klaarhamer's group, and loves her morning bicycle ride from the Biltstraat to the studio on Korte Jansstraat. She is set a project designing in the style now associated with Piet Klaarhamer, who has developed houses constructed from reinforced concrete, and in his instruction to Ailsa he demonstrates a passionate commitment to ensuring the interiors receive a maximum of natural light. This has a profound influence on her thinking about design and her thesis will focus on light and the use of modern materials in addition to labour saving solutions and space.

In terms of his furniture design Piet Klaarhamer reminds Ailsa of Mackintosh, advancing a take on Art Nouveau by using simple construction methods to produce objects with an elegant charm and which despite their solid nature present a light and honest character.

In addition to producing furniture for numerous interior design, shopfitting and architecture projects, Klaarhamer's reduced, functional furniture is sold directly through the Utrecht department store Vroom & Dreesmann, thus making him one of the best known Dutch furniture designers of the moment. His studio is consequently very busy, and new ways of thinking about materials, furniture, architecture and space are constant, with large sheets of paper covering the walls and much lively interaction within the small group. Ailsa feels part of something that she senses is special.

She notices that Rietveld also constructs pieces of furniture for Klaarhamer in his father's workshop. It is a different teaching approach to Glasgow, very much hands on, live commissions, and Ailsa imagines it like the Dutch Masters of old who learned to paint by first copying the works of older Masters; the students here learn to understand the nature of modern furniture through constructing Piet Klaarhamer's designs before moving on to their own.

In the evenings she dines with Truus and Frits or, if they are otherwise engaged in a business or social commitment, with Johan at his apartment. Occasionally Johan joins them at Biltstraat for supper before returning to his apartment. Ailsa has lost none of her independent nature, and their lovemaking is confined to afternoons or evenings, never over a whole night spent together.

She mentions to Truus one morning at breakfast, after Frits has gone down to work, that she sees Rietveld around regularly, but realises this has been a mistake. Her friend looks into the distance, as though imagining some other life she might be living, as she holds her baby girl Marjan on one arm and encourages little Binnert to eat his fruit. The plans for Truus to continue with the architectural studies she began in Hanover are very much on hold for now, even though the two women discuss ideas at length about modern home design. If she is not with her children, or entertaining the members of Frits' family who live in Utrecht, Truus is at some function or other, fulfilling her duties as the wife of an increasingly prominent lawyer. There simply is not time for anything else, and mostly she seems happy enough. She is a loving and attentive mother, not strict at all, and has strong views about the children's education.

Tonight over dinner, Truus is busy telling them all about Maria Montessori, an Italian who is experimenting with a new method of learning, focused on discovery, freedom and choice. Young children develop as individuals and learn by creative activity, uninterrupted and not delivered by direct instruction. It is gaining great respect and momentum in Europe and Truus is quite convinced by its methods. Out of nowhere Frits makes it absolutely clear the children will attend Catholic schools, without question, already endorsed by Truus' father it seems, and there follows quite an altercation between the couple in front of their friends.

These debates are becoming more heated, Ailsa has noticed, not theoretical anymore, and starting to impinge on the daily lives of the Schröders. An, who is due to marry next year, visits less frequently, as relations between her and Frits are increasingly strained. An is involved in the arts and in women's rights, and is gaining quite a reputation in political circles. Her fiancé is highly regarded in his work under a new specialism focused entirely on children's health, called paediatrics, and does innovative work. Truus enjoys spending time with An's circle of friends, who sound to Ailsa to be far too radical for Frits.

She wonders how this situation will evolve, but for now a pleasant evening has been marred by another confrontation. These arguments are usually about how the children are to be brought up, or religion. Truus is becoming more sceptical than ever about Catholicism and is rejecting her faith, which is agonising both for herself and her husband. They do love each other, anyone can see that, but religion is such a big part of people's lives here, impinging on business and society generally, much more so than at home, therefore Ailsa tries to listen but not to judge.

*

The question of paid work is resolved towards the end of June, when Johan and Ailsa take on a commission, led by Klaarhamer, for a bungalow in Huis ter Heide. This will pay enough for her to be able to keep herself financially. She has taken a small apartment on the Oudkerkhof, closer to the studio and to Johan's apartment, and to leave the Schröders to work things out without the distraction of a house guest.

She worries for Truus more and more. This morning the two friends are sitting inside a cafe on the Oudegracht drinking coffee. It is cooler inside. Truus is showing Ailsa the contents of a letter that Frits wrote to her during a particularly difficult time recently when Truus had left him to stay with An for a few days. She reads his words aloud: *'I take life as it comes, have a practical approach, and try to adapt it to my way of thinking. Your sense of right and wrong is determined by your reading, by your intrinsic self, and your life is shaped by these theories. You give precedence to that which most suits yourself, your nature and feelings. Herein lies, I believe, the essential difference between us; this is what makes you more theoretical and me more practical; you are more concerned with the spiritual, I with the material. You do not perceive society as it really is; you see society in its essence, how it ought to be. The differences manifest themselves in all our interests.'*

They are discussing the truth of this wisdom when Johan appears in the doorway, his bulk blocking out the bright sunlight momentarily. He is clutching a copy of the *Telegraaf* and, looking unusually serious, sits down at the table and speaks urgently, his eyes on Ailsa the whole time.

'Archduke Franz Ferdinand of Austria has been assassinated in Sarajevo along with his wife. There is talk of Germany and Austria going to war with Serbia. They are saying here in the newspaper that Holland will flood the Waterline defence to demonstrate neutrality.'

'What will that mean?' asks Truus.

'We will be in a state of siege. Architectress, I think perhaps your stay here may be a little longer than expected.'

Common Brick

Gertrude

London, August 1946

In those first few miserable months I came to realise that my digs in Aberdeen were palatial compared to those of Acton or Finchley, both of which I have now had the bug-ridden displeasure of experiencing. In the beginning I preferred to get outside to pound the unfamiliar London streets, doing the rounds of the top names, lugging my portfolio, overdressed, too hot in my wool costume that had suited the Aberdeen climate. Being unused to the heat, I was glad to enter the cool, dark offices of genteel architects, kindly pipe-smoking middle-aged men with time and patience. A few were able to offer words of advice but no job to a young Scottish woman who can write a suitably sycophantic letter asking, not for a job necessarily, although that was the underlying aim, but for advice on her portfolio, while skating over the details of her year in teaching practice and subsequent hasty departure.

One year on, I spend an inordinate amount of time wondering how I can let Daniel know where I am without his mother finding out, just in the hope that he may want to get in touch. Perhaps I can persuade him to visit, where I can show him the Greater London Plan for building new homes and estates following the destruction of so much. I'm sure he would find this interesting. I collect information on it all the time and visit the bombsites. I even attend lectures by London City

Council in preparation. I have so much to tell him. I know redevelopment will be planned in Aberdeen and other cities, but London has been so badly bomb damaged and homes destroyed on such a massive scale.

We could start again, this time as professional equals, and I could assist his development as he works towards qualifying. I could find him work experience here. I know he intends to remain in Aberdeen, but a summer job in London can do no harm. Just to see him, talk to him, and to care again about how I look, to want to get up in the morning, even to walk with a gait that does not feel like I'm literally dragging my feet. I won't care if he marries and has a family one day. I'd be happy to be his secret, like before. Anything, just to know he cares and thinks about me.

After Cordelia Ogilvie's dramatic exit, Mrs Grier told me to pack my bags and be gone by the end of the week. I subsequently found myself, the following morning, in a different bed with a blinding headache. As I came to, I recalled vaguely that I had drunk a whole bottle of sherry then gone looking for a shoulder to cry on. I had little recollection of the hours in between that and waking up in a single bed on the floor below. Robbie wasn't even there. He must have had double time for a Sunday and gone while I was sleeping. As I tried to creep back up to my own room unseen, Mrs Grier came out of nowhere and stood in silence on the landing, her arms smugly folded, eyes following my walk of shame in last night's frock and carrying my shoes.

I managed to fit my wireless into the suitcase along with my hastily stuffed clothes, but had to leave the lamp and easel behind. Slinging my portfolio over my shoulder once she was out at church, I lifted the case and put my keys through her door. It being a Sunday I was unable to use my bank book, so checked into the Station Hotel on Guild Street, from where I would make my getaway. If Daniel's mother did not spread gossip immediately, Mrs Grier certainly would. It was only a matter of time before the story would be all around the various schools, grossly exaggerated no doubt. I didn't know Robbie well enough either, to know whether or not he would brag to his friends, plus I had no doubt poured out the whole sorry mess to him the night before. It was only a matter of time before Daniel would find out about Robbie too.

Nauseous, perched on the edge of a hotel bed, I wrote to the Education Department explaining my having to leave unexpectedly due to a family bereavement and that I would not be returning. The men were being demobbed sporadically, so we had been promised an extension to our contracts on a term by term basis. I had been paid up to date so did not need to give a forwarding address, only to apologise for the short notice. After sealing the envelope, I had an unrushed soak in my hotel bathroom and then tried to sleep, head throbbing and in turmoil.

In the morning I slipped out to the bank and withdrew all my savings, posted the letter, paid the hotel and bought a rail ticket. I caught the first train for Perth, with onward connections to Edinburgh and London, face once again pressed against a railway carriage window, gazing out at the grey North Sea, running away, bridges burned, shamed, alone, only this time in the opposite direction. Was this to be the pattern of my life?

*

My arrival in London coincided with the post war frenzy to establish Britain's competitiveness in the world of design. This resulted in the creation of the Council Of Industrial Design to oversee the Herculean task, and where I am now employed through the advice and contacts of one of those kindly gentlemen. My limited savings from teaching dwindling fast, I took this temporary post as general dogsbody to help set up the forthcoming **Britain Can Make It** exhibition at the V & A, which promises to be a commentary on the best of post-war British design.

As a result I am now rubbing shoulders on a daily basis with bright young things and well known names of the design world who, between them, are the emerging establishment and hierarchy of the newly formed Council alongside their own private practices. For anyone else, this would present an ideal opportunity to make a good impression and land a proper design job, but I can already see I do not belong in their world. There are any number of girls from the top private schools calling themselves designers, no doubt less qualified than me, but with whom I cannot hope to compete. They have the accent and ease that comes with a privileged and entitled upbringing in the home counties, no doubt sponsored by loving families and nepotic business connections. These girls know how to look and act to catch the eye of some architect only too willing to buy them dinner and discuss their future. I feel provincial and old fashioned, the girl with the unruly hair, round glasses, weight increasing by the week, no family connections or pedigree, and to make matters worse, a Scottish accent. No-one notices me as I take notes at meetings or order materials for an exhibition stand, but at least, by my invisibility, I am able to observe for future reference the actions of the real trailblazers as they pioneer this design revolution, observations which may come in useful one day.

Britain Can Make It is scheduled to open at the end of September, so we have only a few weeks left to put the finishing touches to the **Furnished Rooms** section of the exhibition, which is my section. Other sections cover all manner of the best post-war British made industrial products collated by the Council's Selection Committee, ranging from textiles and flooring to cutlery, glass, household commodities, packaging, Utility furniture approved by the Board of Trade, lighting, garden tools and so on, but the room settings are the climax and by far the most interesting part, where these products come alive, in **Things In Their Home Setting**.

My curator, Nigel Penhaligon, is friendly and, when he found out that I am qualified in art and design, asked me to help with the titles of the different room settings and to make up family profiles for each, based on their class, occupation, location and so on. I relished this task, as it meant I could conjure up fictitious families and scenarios, rather like looking into a brightly lit living room window from outside, and create each family member from my imagination. We have had cartoons drawn up for the DESIGN '46 catalogue, where each family is depicted either in their existing home or freshly transported onto some new common brick housing estate currently at the planning stage.

These profiles were approved by Committee, with a few revisions, mainly to ensure the imaginary wives are 'house proud', homemakers who complement whatever hobbies their imaginary husbands have, and for imaginary daughters to simply 'love excitement' or similar, whereas the imaginary sons must be off to university or pursuing some serious interest. I managed to retain the role of the wife in a token imaginary Scottish family as one who writes novels. I expect the Committee allowed this on the basis that she was some form of alien species that I'd know more about than they do. The architect who is designing this stand, Mervyn Noad, had a laugh with me about it the other day. I like him a lot, he is Scottish and very modern, and has travelled all over Europe and Scandinavia. It helps to meet Scottish people down here. We share the same humour, as if we belong to a secret club that no one else understands. I wish I were back in Aberdeen. I'm desperately miserable here.

Once approved, the profiles were put out as a brief to the various architects and design experts who had been selected and will be credited with their work in the exhibition and catalogue. The specification of materials and furnishings they propose, all the best of British of course, are required to be selected from a list of suppliers or approved in advance by the Selection Committee and will form part of the catalogue of articles and photographs. No doubt the accredited professionals taking part will get further business on the back of this prestigious opportunity.

My subsequent role has been to order for each room setting, based on the specifications, and work with suppliers on quantities. This is safe territory, as I don't have to come up with ideas myself, but can simply adhere to the experts' drawings, using my design knowledge to interpret them. As the sets are built, I oversee the work and use my initiative to dress each one personally with accessories. I like to get it just right for when each architect or designer comes to inspect his or her stand.

I particularly like Dorothy Braddell, a designer whose stand focuses on ways to make domestic management easier for women. She pays special attention to the kitchen and the ways that good planning combined with well-designed appliances and workflows can reduce domestic labour. I've never really thought about this before. She has written various publications on the topic, and coined the phrase 'Where There's Dirt There's Danger.' She goes by the pseudonym Darcy Braddell, which is her husband's name, so that people take her seriously, because of course he is an architect. However, on this occasion she has allowed for the title Mrs. to preface the name, which she says she does not always do. I also like Marjorie Holford, who has designed a quite lovely bedroom setting. These professional women are so open, so generous, not like Edith at all, and I wish I knew them personally. I had to go to the ladies' for a cry when I got an unexpected hug from Dorothy. I'd forgotten how good physical contact with an older woman felt. It made me long for Bridget all over again.

The most eccentric professionals here are Maxwell Fry and Jane Drew, real life celebrities, modernists who dress in a kind of colonial bohemian style, and apparently know Le Corbusier personally, among other notaries, such as the radical evolutionary biologist Julian Huxley. They have both been divorced from other people and are now married to each other, and I could spend hours just listening to them and watching them from afar. I love people like that. Totally oblivious to what anyone else thinks. I think one has to grow up in a certain kind of unconventional environment to be that cavalier. I do envy them.

I confess to feeling a thrill when one particular architect compliments me on my interpretation, where I have placed the furniture and so on, based on his original drawings. His name is Austin Lord, he is in his late forties probably, and originally from Manchester. I like his Room Setting the best, and had already noted before I met him that he'd specified materials from factories and suppliers in the North or from Scotland. Unlike the other men, apart from Mervyn and Nigel, he takes time to talk to me, and even asks me things about myself. I make sure I am there whenever he is due on site.

All talk now is of the opening night, so I am going to have my hair done in a permanent wave and spend endless nights sewing a wasp-waisted dress in the style of Balmain, very much in vogue at present, to wear for the event. To fit into the tight waist I must starve myself and lose some of this weight over the next few weeks, which should not be difficult as we are rushed off our feet. I've decided that on the opening night I will position myself at Austin Lord's stand, to see if he brings a family.

Clear Blue Water

Ailsa

Utrecht, August 1914

135 Biltstraat,

Utrecht.

10 August 1914

12 Knowe Terrace,

Glasgow.

Dearest Mama,

The authorities have advised that I should remain here for the time being. I am safe and well and you must not worry.

I hope this reaches you, and that you are not unduly anxious about this war in Europe, which we hear will be sorted out within months. Let us hope so.

The Netherlands is neutral and has good defences: the New Holland Waterline - the rivers and lowlands - have been inundated, resulting in us being cut off by a ring of water, and the military are mobilised to anticipate any breach of this, which no-one expects. Everyone says this neutral position has been agreed and makes us safe.

Johan is worried for his parents, as Germany is using Belgium as a means to reach other borders, but stories are rife from Belgians who have come here, saying that this is causing trouble and there is some resistance. I know the British government is unhappy about this too and is going to help sort it out. Johan will bring his parents back here.

I am staying with Truus and Frits until we know what is happening. Johan has left for Leuven to find out more, but will return shortly.

That is all for now dearest Mama. I send my love to you and Bridget, and hope that Glasgow is not feeling the impact of this war, which must seem so far away to you.

I will write again once I have news of my return, which should be soon. I have written to M. Bourdon to explain my predicament and will work and study here meantime, as we continue to be busy.

Please write to me care of the Biltstraat address.

Much love,

Ailsa.

Sapphire Ring

Gertrude

London, March 1949

At first I think it is one of the false sightings that I experience routinely. A hand gesture, dark hair brushed back casually from a forehead, a certain height in the distance, a fleeting posture, a corduroy jacket. In the same way people see a loved one, presumed dead or missing in action, coming towards them only to discover it has been wishful thinking or an overactive imagination. The stranger in question nears and passes by, oblivious to their scant physical resemblance to another. This has happened often in my four years in London and, even though statistically it would be almost impossible, it is a kind of comfort nonetheless. *Almost impossible* is not *impossible*.

Therefore the sight of Daniel, the real Daniel, across the vast expanse of the exhibition hall at Olympia, one of a group of young adults heading my way, visiting students perhaps from Robert Gordon's, is less of a shock than it might be. As though I had been expecting to see him today, just like on any other.

Despite the many imaginary encounters, I had not thought out my next move. This is unlike me, as one who likes to rehearse any impending situation in order to maximise success. I panic. Do I leave my post on the stand and hide in the staff area until I formulate a plan and check my appearance? I could lose him and that is unthinkable. Do I wait here, hoping that the group visits the Austin Lord Associates stand to view the **'living room looking through into a dining room'** setting, and wait for his eyes to alight on me? This could backfire as he may become embarrassed in front of the group, if indeed the scandal became common knowledge in Aberdeen circles. Do I approach him enthusiastically, as a former teacher who has spotted one of her ex pupils, and brazen it out? This would also prove risky, as others in the group may have been pupils of mine and wonder why I have singled him out.

I decide to do what I always do: I follow, surreptitiously, until I can position myself in his sightline, where he cannot fail but notice me, and hope he makes the first move. If he does not, then I will know he chose to avoid me, and will have saved us both the embarrassment.

'I think I'll take my break now' I say to Paul, yawning nonchalantly, as if bored.

'No problem Gerd' he replies, his eye on a potential customer who is stroking the teak shelving unit in the living room space and examining the glassware, as her husband seats himself in the man's armchair, the open dining room behind his head displaying a table setting of the finest cutlery Sheffield can offer. Paul will be able to cover my areas of product knowledge if asked, as I know his inside out whenever he goes for his frequent cigarette and coffee breaks.

In the busy throng it is easy to manoeuvre my way in and out of the various stands and temporary house façades. I know the layout of the Ideal Home Exhibition intimately, having spent the last month here on a daily basis, even before it opened, so know the shortcuts to keep one step ahead of Daniel's group. The exhibition is a warren of room settings and garden landscapes, with displays of labour saving devices designed to allow women to cut down on what is an average of seventy hours of domestic work in the home per week. This year there is the introduction of something called a microwave oven.

No doubt a London trip from Aberdeen has been organised to coincide with this annual event, which this year is especially well attended due to unwanted publicity following the two Communist Party members who showered leaflets from the balcony down onto the passing entourage escorting Princess Elizabeth and the Duke of Edinburgh around the opening. "*'Houses for all, not for the few,' 'Houses for working people and not for the rich.*', their propaganda stated. No wonder; there is still a severe housing shortage despite all the grand plans after the war. Needless to say the Princess and the Duke ignored the incident and carried on their way, smiling and chatting to the organisers in that oblique way that royal families do.

To check my appearance, I stop off at a mirrored dressing table inside one of the **homes with steel windows**. My affair with Austin has kept my weight down, so I must be roughly the size I was last time Daniel saw me. I'm not dressed as I'd have preferred, had I known, frumpy in my tweed skirt and red sweater. Not exactly New Look, but it will have to do. I pinch colour into my cheeks without drawing attention to myself. This is as good as I'm going to get.

Daniel's interest in a set of low stone fireplaces means he lingers there by himself after the group has gone ahead. He is not going to see me unless I do something obvious. He is alone, so I decide to take my chance and face him.

'Hello Daniel Ogilvie. Still interested in stone I see.' I am awkward, trying to keep my hands still.

He looks startled then confused, flicks his hair back and looks momentarily from side to side to check who else is around.

'Hello' he says, still unable to give me a name. 'This is a surprise.' He gathers himself. 'What are you doing here?'

He must be twenty-two now, his stance upright, confident. The floppy dark hair and chiselled features haven't changed but his chest has filled out. I want to take him home with me and sit him in a chair, make him tea, watch his hands as they draw, his eyes as they roam, follow his concentration, kiss him on the mouth.

'I'm working here. I work for an architectural firm and we have a stand. Over there. I do these every year.' I point vaguely at nothing in particular.

'How long have you been in London?'

'Almost four years now. How are your studies going?'

'Going well thanks. We are down here on a three day visit, for this and some other sites.'

The conversation is pleasant enough, but tense, stilted. I still have no idea if he was told the reason for my hasty departure. There is a pause, then just as he starts to say, 'Why did you…' we are interrupted by a girl, who takes Daniel's arm and, laughing, says *Dan, I lost you. We're all going for lunch now.* She is dark haired, round faced, younger than me. She looks like me.

'Oh, sorry' says Daniel. 'Er, this is Susan, my …...' He halts, then introduces me. 'This is my art teacher from school.' No name. Old habit.

'Gertrude' I say, shaking her hand, smiling. 'Are you on the architecture course too?' I feel like the grown up.

'Yes' she laughs. 'They admit women now.' She has an Aberdeen accent. A cultured one. She is relaxed, self assured, like she will have a family who loves her. She keeps her arm locked through the crook of Daniel's, fingers pressing into the brown corduroy. She is wearing a sapphire and diamond engagement ring.

'Well, I won't keep you both' I say brightly. He is looking at me oddly. 'Here's our firm's business card.'

I give one to each of them from my skirt pocket. 'Next time you're in London, come and see us. We do some interesting work, although mainly interiors: houses, ships and so on. I can show you round the office.'

She is pulling him away to join the others, impatient but smiling. 'Nice to meet you' she says. He looks back briefly as they walk away. I can't read his expression. I put my hand to my ear in desperation, imitating a telephone, just for a second, so she doesn't see.

'Bye then' she waves, turning briefly.

I watch them go. She is gazing up at him, chatting and laughing effortlessly. Cordelia Ogilvie will have given her seal of approval.

*

The telephone call a few days later is awkward. I am in the middle of a busy office; Daniel must be in an Aberdeen telephone box pushing coins into the slot. We exchange pleasantries briefly. I hate the telephone.

'So, why did you leave without saying goodbye?' he asks, lightheartedly, as if being melodramatic but not seriously. He can talk like this now. No longer a bashful schoolboy lost for words. He has grown up.

I resolve not to tell him. If I say that his mother came to see me and effectively ran me out of town, it will backfire. I already know that the fiancée will mention they met Daniel's art teacher from his schooldays; that is bad enough. I can hear her saying it casually, over dinner, one of the stories of their London field trip, and can imagine Cordelia's face.

'I went to your digs and asked' he shouts down the wire. 'A bloke said you had left in a hurry but he didn't know why.' Robbie must have kept quiet. I knew he was one of the good ones.

Eventually Daniel heard through the school that I had a bereavement. I mumble something about it being a difficult time and I had to leave as soon as I heard; I say sorry. I realise at this point that he doesn't know. The whole episode has been contained. Cordelia Ogilvie kept her word, and Mrs. Grier's network didn't reach as far as I'd imagined it would.

'I will actually be passing through London in June, going to Italy' he says. 'Maybe we could meet up?'

I give him my address in Islington and he writes it down. I'm hardly listening to the details, but Daniel is telling me that he has a travel scholarship and will be touring Italy to study classical stone in architectural form. He tells me that he is engaged to Susan, and that she is spending the summer in America. He will be staying in a youth hostel close to King's Cross but perhaps we could meet for a drink. He provides the exact time and date of his arrival and says he will call for me at my flat at seven in the evening. The pips go and I lose him.

Daniel wants to see me. He is coming to London. He did find me attractive, not desperate after all. Tears of joy spring into my eyes as I put down the receiver, and I have to go to the washroom to compose myself. Paul asks me if I'm alright. I can tell him most things, but not this. I don't want Austin to know.

My relationship with Austin is tired now, for both of us I think. He comes to my flat when he can, less often now, but it is far from ideal. At first it was exciting, an older man who was kind to me, gave me a job, took me out for dinner a few times, found me an unfurnished flat through his contacts, installed me in it then seduced me. It helped me to care about how I looked again and lose weight, and I felt less lonely. I'm grateful to Austin, he is a *decent man* who would never intentionally hurt me, but I never lost my feelings for Daniel.

Austin is married of course, with a family. I once took a train to Dunmow in Essex and sat on a pretty village green, watching the ducks and looking across at his rambling thatched cottage with its modern extension at the back, from the front like something off a chocolate box or a jigsaw. I waited until the lights were turned on and I could see the tasteful interior through tiny leaded panes of glass and the family moving around. His wife comes to the office with the teenage children occasionally, so she is thankfully not a mystery. I just wanted to see how he lives, and to contrast it with a down-at-heel rented flat in Islington. It is a different world. I expect homes have an inscape too. Unless you know what really goes on, they can appear like a chocolate box from the outside.

After all this time, I think he and I might both be happy for an excuse to stop this. I will have to find another job, but things are picking up and I have experience now. I'm sure he will give me a good reference. I have totally revamped the samples library, and am the office expert on sourcing any product or material. I don't draw often, but I put together a mean sample board for client presentations.

I have less than three months to prepare, to get the flat looking good, to find an outfit, to lose more weight, change my job. Nothing is more important than Daniel coming to see me for one evening.

Live Wire

Ailsa

Utrecht, November 1918

Ailsa dangles baby Hanneke on her knee, barely noticing the gurgling of this happy child who is smiling up at her, too young to understand what is happening. The war has ended, and this morning Ailsa placed the key to Johan's apartment under the Delft tile for the last time. Should he be alive and return to Annastraat, which now seems almost impossible, he will find the key where he always left it, and then the letter from Ailsa on the oak kitchen table. They have tried everything in their power, especially in Frits' power as a lawyer, to discover Johan's fate, but any word from Belgium that does still come indicates his whereabouts remain unknown. Ailsa refuses to believe he will not come back. *Almost impossible* is not *impossible*.

Truus is dealing with the housekeeper before she accompanies Ailsa to the port. Frits is already in the motor car on the driveway at the side of the mansion, looking impatient, and the bags and portfolio are packed onto the rear shelf. Binnert and Marjan will stay behind with the nanny, while baby Han will ride with her parents. She is fractious and needs to be with Truus, and the rhythm of the engine soothes her. The mood is sombre and they speak little this morning; Ailsa is tearful, trying to shield this from the others. She should be happy to be going home, to see her mother again after such a long absence, but she is torn. To leave Utrecht now means giving up on Johan's return.

The early days of the war were hopeful, when news from Belgium reached her several times: scribbled notes from him smuggled in with people who managed to find refuge in the Netherlands and were told to find *the Architectress, Utrecht* by going to the studio on Korte Jansstraat. It wasn't difficult. In the beginning, refugees found their way here. Ailsa was convinced that Johan would arrive back with his parents, the reason he had travelled in the first place. He wanted nothing to do with war, and knew that this country would be the safest place for all of them. He had convinced Ailsa to stay in the Netherlands, and she has done, for four years.

There have been opportunities for her to travel back to Scotland, especially when Mama was ill, but the dangers outweighed them. Her mother convinced her that all was well, her sister Catherine had come from Applecross to look after her along with Bridget, and she was improving daily. So Ailsa stayed.

The study under Klaarhamer has been a solace. The group has been incubated, no-one coming in or out of the country, and it is undeniable that talent has flourished as a result; as though these young men, and indeed Ailsa herself, felt a need to contribute somehow, and they have done that through designing for social change. Homes and furniture are functional, easily constructed, and the artists in a new group, started last year by Theo van Doesburg, which he calls The Style, or *De Stijl*, have intellectualised their craft, making it rebellious and anti-establishment, by abstracting forms in design, reducing them to the simple horizontal and vertical. Creative people who normally would have been in Paris were trapped here, and talent came to the fore in Amsterdam and Utrecht. In that way it has been an ideal environment for Ailsa. Except for the terrible war, and for the loss of Johan in the midst of all this, she would be returning home now full of inspiration and new ideas.

The stories in the press are almost incomprehensible: the numbers of young men who have lost their lives, and the horrors of what has happened next door in Belgium she can hardly bring herself to read. They were told that some of these stories were false propaganda, especially in the early years, designed to get sympathy and support from America. But to read about women having breasts chopped off, of babies being slaughtered and thousands killed, of German desecration of Belgian cities, universities and libraries, the torture of anyone who tried to rebel, in what was supposed to be a neutral country, had been terrifying. The Rape of Belgium the papers called it. To think that Johan, and his parents, disappeared without trace in that scenario, even if some of it is exaggerated, has, over time, destroyed Ailsa's spirit. When she heard that an electric fence had been erected around the border between Belgium and the Netherlands, she almost gave up hope completely. Hundreds of people were killed by that live wire, trying to cross unawares. Could that be what has happened? The not knowing is the worst. Ailsa asks herself these questions again as they drive to Rotterdam.

The port is bustling now that trade and free movement are made possible without fear of being blown out of the water, and Frits parks the motor car as close as he can to the busy embarkation area. They climb out. Frits removes the luggage. He kisses Ailsa on each cheek and grips her shoulders as if to empower her.

'Ailsa, you must, for your own sake, try to move on with your life. The reality is, if Johan had survived, we would have heard by now.'

'You could be right. But if I had been his wife, there would have been a telegram. As it stands, they will not know to contact me' she replies. In her heart, she knows Frits is right. Johan would not have let her suffer in this way if he were alive.

Frits promises Ailsa that he will continue to try to discover Johan's fate, and will write to her with any news. He goes in search of a porter.

Truus holds her friend close now, and they whisper endearments. The two women are so attuned nowadays, they hardly need speak. They only need look into each other's eyes, to embrace, to understand the other's emotion. Baby Han is sleeping now, rocked by the motion of the motor car, and Ailsa touches her little cheek for the last time, hoping that this new child in the family will bring Truus and Frits fresh hope for their troubled marriage. Perhaps with the war over, everyone will begin to look outward, and frustration will abate, even at a domestic level. Truus wants a life like An, full of new political and social ideas, surrounded by likeminded people. She has none of this stimulation with Frits' family in Utrecht, or with anyone they know, apart from Ailsa, who hopes that they find the compromise they both seek to sustain their marriage.

Later, as she waves from the top deck, the port disappearing into a cold morning fog, Ailsa is reminded of another time long ago, when she stood as a young girl on a similar deck. A lifetime ago. She is returning to Glasgow with a wealth of knowledge and a strong portfolio, more than enough to secure her Diploma once she sits her final examinations, but lacking the passion she once had for putting it to use. The homes she helped to design under Klaarhamer, using concrete and brick, with plain interiors, large windows, groundbreaking in their modernity, no longer excite her without Johan to share it all with. How strange, she thinks, that a few years ago she had no interest in romance or partnership. Once someone enters your heart, once you let them in, she now knows, there is no going back. Ailsa cannot ever get back to how she was before and nor does she wish to. Waiting for him now for almost four years, she is in limbo. She can neither go back nor move forward emotionally. She has sunk into a deep melancholy, which she tries to hide and will continue to hide when she is reunited with her mother. To know she has lost him, to think what torture Johan may have had to endure at the hands of the Germans, and to know she will never have the child she so desperately wanted with him, means she finds no joy in life at all. This grief, for a life she might have had, is overwhelming. If this boat were to sink now, she would find relief in it. She cannot imagine being happy ever again. She looks up at the cawing seagulls, and wonders how they find the energy or purpose to follow ships for sustenance that must rarely come in these lean times. They must be going through the motions, exactly as she is.

Purple Wisteria

Gertrude

Islington, June 1949

We walk up Richmond Avenue on a balmy evening to The Albion, where I have planned to take Daniel for a drink. I am glad it is not raining, as it has been sunny whenever I pictured this scene in my mind. The purple wisteria is still in bloom on the front of this historic coaching inn, nestled in a Barnsbury side street, my favourite Islington pub. I used to come here with Austin in the early days for half pints of bitter in dark corners. Now I sit very publicly in the shady pub garden under the overhanging wisteria while Daniel goes for drinks.

I have had weeks to put together my look. The soft yellow cotton skirt is full, accentuating my hips, and gathered in at the waist, topped by a white broderie anglaise sleeveless blouse and matching pumps. He returns and drinks deep from his pint glass. I sip my Dubonnet, having rehearsed that I will wait for Daniel to speak first. I have reached up to this point in my mind, but no further.

He avoids the obvious past connection we have, and we are on our second drink before we drop the generalities. He has proudly shown me the Kodak 35 camera that his parents bought him for the Italian trip, which was slung over his shoulder when he arrived at the flat. His hobby is architectural photography, and he develops his own reels of film in the college dark rooms. He asks about my job briefly, we discuss where other pupils are now, his study tour, my flat (which he entered briefly). He admired it and asked did I own it, to which I replied, as I always do, *no, it is rented on a long lease; I own a house in Glasgow left to me by my grandmother.* I love to say those words to anyone who asks. Not because I wish to impress by owning property, but because it would appear I have family. I sound normal, cared for, loved. Only Austin knows the truth.

'I thought about you after you disappeared' he says at last, emboldened now by the ale. 'For a long time I didn't go out with girls. It felt like we had unfinished business.' I realise that my enforced departure worked in my favour. It made me look cool, aloof, in Daniel's eyes, back then. The mature one. I must try to retain this image. My father's words come to me then, about men and anticipation being everything, but I bat this away. It is too cynical. I take another sip of my drink.

'What we did was inappropriate Daniel. We could have, no - *I* could have, been in a lot of trouble' I say, wise after the event. 'That doesn't mean I didn't want to see you again though. Leaving without saying goodbye was one of the hardest things I've ever had to do.' I don't want to play it too cool. 'You seem to have got past it now though.' By this I mean Susan. It needs to be said.

'She reminds me of you' he says. 'To look at, I mean.'

'You're engaged. You must love her' I venture. He smiles but gives nothing away. He hasn't lost his desire for privacy. He is not going to disrespect Susan by discussing his feelings, or their relationship, and I love him for that. He asks me about suitors, and I too am vague, saying there have been two or three, none of them serious. I don't mention Austin, and he doesn't push me further.

By this exchange we create the rules of engagement. Our real lives are our own. What we will have here is something else, a fantasy, as in Aberdeen. Looking around us, I think how far we have both come in a few years. This feels almost sophisticated, not a boudoir fantasy in a dingy attic, and requires less transformation. I don't need to pretend I am his Parisian muse. I can slip into being a London mistress without altering a thing.

Back at the flat, inhibitions lost by too much drink and no food (I have opened a bottle of wine), he kisses me on the mouth for the first time. As I attempt to lead him to the bedroom, he stops me and asks if I will do something first. He asks do I mind. I don't. He plays with the camera settings. This is just for him, he says; he has never forgotten that day. We laugh a little, nervous, knowing to what he is referring, but he is serious. I remove my skirt, slip out of my shoes, my blouse, my underwear; I lie on the bed. I realise what happened in Aberdeen has shaped his desire.

I am flattered. I trust him. I imagine him thinking of that day in his private moments, when he is with Susan even. A schoolboy fantasy carried into manhood. He will develop these photographs himself in the dark and hide them. I change positions, trying to remember the poses, until he has run off a spool. I tell myself this is Art. He is an artist, with a new specialism, photography, and I am his model. We laugh together at the memory, the release of it.

When we finally make love, it feels like we are already lovers who have been intimate for a long time. We don't think that this is the beginning, although it is; we think our bodies are familiar, because we

have both imagined this so often. Afterwards I ask, *do you feel sad Daniel.*
I say I have heard that men feel sad after sex.

No, he laughs, *I feel grateful.*

I want to tell him, but don't, that I am the one who is grateful. Like
a starving child.

Peated Malt

Ailsa

Glasgow, 1921

Ailsa reads Piet Klaarhamer's letter over again. He seems understandably upset. Enclosed with the letter are back copies of the magazine *De Stijl*. There are no articles about him nor any pictures of his furniture or interiors. His letter is bitter, particularly toward his one-time disciple and apprentice Rietveld, and it seems their friendship has been irrevocably damaged as a result. Klaarhamer clearly believes himself to be at the zenith of his creativity and influence, but the magazine has published pictures of furniture by Rietveld and none by Klaarhamer.

……..My use of concrete for house construction and my architectural contributions in and around Utrecht have been completely overlooked.

Rietveld's understanding of art, architecture and design has come entirely from myself, Bart van der Leck and Robert van 't Hoff. They all seem to be acknowledged by De Stijl where I am not.

Since the time you left, I have undertaken my most important and prestigious project so far; furniture for the bedroom of the sons of industrialist Cees Bruynzeel. The Bruynzeel boys' room furniture, according to van Doesburg, isn't as forward thinking as the work Rietveld is producing. He says Rietveld's designs fit the world that De Stijl is preparing the Netherlands for, while I apparently still have one foot in the past and am not brave enough to move on!!!

She flicks through the magazine editions and can see how radical Gerrit's work has become. He uses crossed over joints, like scaffolding, pared back surfaces and flat planes in his lacquered wooden furniture, and it is true that he has taken the earlier ideas of the De Stijl group, of which Ailsa was briefly an associate, to a whole new level.

It seems trivial to her now, how impassioned the group becomes over such matters, given what has happened to Johan. It is a travesty, she supposes, that the De Stijl group does not acknowledge Klaarhamer's undoubted influence on the younger men. She thinks though that it is hardly Gerrit's fault, it sounds more like the way van Doesburg operates. Perhaps it is because Klaarhamer is not possessed of the charisma that Gerrit has, indeed that in his own way Johan had. She wonders what work Johan would be producing now if he were there. Would he be included in this radical magazine as one of the chosen few? Would she? Johan and Ailsa were each beginning to formulate their style when war broke out.

When she returned to the School of Art here, despite her numbed state of mind and lack of enthusiasm for work, for life itself, her tutors and the other students were truly moved by the modernity of her portfolio content, and the projects she had undertaken under Klaarhamer. The Glasgow School had stayed still, understandably, with war raging and so many of its finest lost or away serving in battle. Saddest of all to hear was the death of Eugene Bourdon, killed at the Somme, something Ailsa had the displeasure of having to write to Klaarhamer about, to inform him of this tragic news. The two men had known each other well and had rekindled their correspondence in recent years, inspired by Ailsa's request to study in Utrecht. It was little comfort but she was able to say that Bourdon had been awarded the Croix de la Légion d'Honneur, the Croix de Guerre and the British Military Cross during his time in service in France.

She can't bear it at times. So many good men lost in that senseless war. Some had rushed to join, thinking it an adventure, or a duty, in Johan's case, on a temporary mission to a supposedly neutral country. By the time men realised the scale of the atrocities and their own fate, it was too late. How fortunate the Dutch were to have stayed out of it. Back in Glasgow, and seeing first hand how people's lives have changed, how women, her mother included, took on or bore so much that was previously unthinkable, it makes arguments about inclusion in a design magazine seem petty by contrast. Yet she can understand why her old mentor feels aggrieved.

Flora's war involved assisting bereaved wives and mothers, offering practical advice and counselling, and becoming involved in the suffrage movement. Ailsa realised once she was back in Knowe Terrace that her mother's illness had been nothing more than sheer exhaustion, and bringing Aunt Catherine to stay was simply a ruse to help with her war work. Even now Flora spends each day dealing with matters on behalf of her women.

Ailsa spent a lot of time talking to Bridget when she first came home, catching up on the missing years, hearing about the events she was absent throughout, and pouring out to Bridget about Johan and her life in Utrecht. One of Bridget's brothers was killed in France, and the other has shell shock and is quite changed. The war has touched everyone one way or another. It shows in the faces and ravaged bodies Ailsa sees in the streets and on trams.

Frits wrote not long after she returned to tell her the dreadful news that Johan's parents did not survive. They were victims of a purge of academics near the start of the war who were seen as dissenters and actively resistant to the German occupation, especially to the destruction of their academic library. They were killed in the most deliberate and terrible way, shot by German troops after being rounded up from their hiding place in the university chapel.

So, terrible though that news was when it came, did it mean that Johan was elsewhere? Could he be alive? How many years will she go on telling herself that lie? There is no way Johan would have left her waiting like this. She has to move on. Many are worse off than her. Women have lost their sons, their own blood, and wives have lost husbands, the fathers of their children, and are left to cope.

The one thing she has is her Diploma in Architecture, her only barrier still being admittance to the Royal Institute, which persists in not admitting women. She decides she must keep busy, that even if she continues to be refused entry, she can undertake small commissions in housing, which is her area of interest and expertise in any case. She will open her own practice, as an architectural designer, and find work with whomsoever she can. She will employ the Dutch model of master and apprentice that she is now so familiar with, and take on young women to train under her guidance and tutelage.

This idea grows, and she sets about kitting out the attic floor in Knowe Terrace for this purpose. There is enough room for four light wooden table mounted drawing boards and a plan chest, and the kitchen and bathroom facilities make it self contained. The back stairs can be used for coming and going, meaning that Flora and Bridget are not troubled by strangers tramping through the main house. Not that Flora would mind. The entire house has a free, distinctly bohemian air to it these days, and if not for Bridget, chaos would reign. A few more women will make no difference.

Ailsa takes out the roll of blue waxed paper she brought home with her. It is a good quality to draw on; her favourite. She has the original blueprints for the house with the title deeds from Papa's study. Overlaying the wax paper she traces the attic floor through the blue tinge, showing the inner non loadbearing brick partitions removed. By leaving the walls around the two rooflight voids and retaining the tiny kitchen and lavatory, along with the stairs to the roof, she can create an open plan office space for at least four women to work and communicate openly, plus an area for modelmaking and meeting clients. That is if they are lucky enough to acquire any.

She may have lost her lust for life, indeed in the future, but she can try to do some good by taking on women who have an aspiration to learn a craft or a profession. They will not need to feel beholden to some man to give them a start. Ailsa will give them that without demanding any return. She will create a workshop area in the back yard, where furniture can be built and stored without damp, and create a safe environment for women to learn and work. She will have the attic painted white, and let light flood from front to back. On good days they can climb the stairs to the roof and sit outside there for leisure breaks, hidden from the world, taking in the sunshine and the view. There will be some who have lost their husbands or fiancés in the war, some with children who need an income to support them. She will provide a creche in Papa's study, and these women, who did useful work during wartime and are now expected to go back into the home again, will flourish and make a living for themselves.

If only she had a child of her own, it would help make up for the loss of Johan, and give her someone to devote her life to. She aches for the child she never had; at thirty-six and on her own she has left it too late. She knows she is trying to recreate the woman's attic from Chipping Campden, but in a work context, not a home with a child. It will have to do, and she will nurture craftswomen instead.

Local bricklayers, joiners, and decorators, vacant eyed, damaged men, glad of the work, carry hods of demolished bricks down the back stairs, replaster remaining walls and fix new soft pine wainscoting around the walls. They whiteout all woodwork, even the repaired floorboards and rafters. The drawing boards, plus ancillary equipment, are bought from an auction: an entire collection left over from one of the numerous architectural firms who lost their men to the war and went out of business.

Pleased with the end result and, seeing how her mother and Bridget are enthused, Ailsa realises that this can give all three of them something new and positive to involve themselves in. She has seen the sadness in Bridget's eyes. Everyone has suffered loss. She feels selfish that she has become so melancholy, for too long, over her own loss. She will try, every day from now on, to build a new purpose for 12 Knowe Terrace.

She goes into town to register the business, and to place an advertisement in the post office directory and newspaper. She will make an appointment in the tax office first for advice on revenue and charges.

Initially she doesn't recognise the gaunt face looking at hers across the desk, the right hand shaking as he lifts his eyes from his blotter to take down her details. As he registers recognition, Ailsa sees the damage that war has caused in yet another.

'Michael?' is all she can manage to say, bringing a gloved hand to her mouth.

*

Like so many, he cannot talk about his war experience, except to say he was a prisoner of war for some time in a place called Langensalza, where the treatment was little better than the trenches. She can glean that a grenade damaged the nerves in Michael's right hand to the extent that he can no longer draw. She remembers this one indisputable thing about Michael: he could produce fine architectural drawings like no one else, even her fellow students. His right leg was also damaged in a blast at Aisne, and he was gassed, before being captured along with others from his regiment. It took him a long time in the camp to be able to walk again and learn to write with his left hand. Back in Glasgow he is retraining as a tax inspector. He has said she must not worry if he starts to shake at the sound of any sudden noise.

It seems to Ailsa a lifetime ago, that wintry day when they argued in the bakery in Cathcart. As they sit here, in a different cafe, on a sunny day in St. Vincent Street, all of that seems forgotten, and Michael appears changed. He is a shadow of his former self and less arrogant. Ailsa tells him about her time in Utrecht, and her studies, and of course her plans for the future, with her business, but not of Johan. Michael is living with his sister and her husband, and the child; his mother has died. He does not see eye to eye with his brother-in-law, who did not fight in the war due to myopia, and other than that Michael seems alone in the world. Even his Boy Scout work has gone. He is too crippled, he says, to be of use to boys. His days of being of use are over. At this Ailsa glimpses a little of the old self pity coming through, but overall Michael seems humbled and so she dismisses the thought. They agree to meet again, and she is conscious that he is treading carefully, trying to avoid giving her advice, or telling her how to set up her venture. He has learned something then, she thinks.

Flora is pleased to hear that Ailsa and Michael have met. She always liked him and could not see why they fell out all those years ago. She wants to invite him to tea. Ailsa feels sorry for him but she can even admit to herself it felt good to see him again, a reminder of an earlier time when life was simpler and full of promise. She believes in the goodness of people, and part of her wants to put those bitter exchanges behind her. Michael loved her, and she understands now what that feels like. She was cavalier in her treatment of him, and should have seen the signs. No doubt he did feel encouraged, but she knows now that, if they can communicate, and he does not mistake friendship for anything else, they may find solace in each other's company. She agrees to invite him.

*

Over the coming months Ailsa is busy with the apprenticeship of four young women who have a genuine interest and aptitude for technical drawing. She finds she is a natural teacher, and has managed to obtain work on new housing for families who have lived in slums where there were sometimes ten to one room, with as many as forty families sharing one outside lavatory. The sanitation alone has been deemed unsatisfactory, and the overcrowding as a cause of disease. The recent Addison Act means that the slogan 'Homes fit for Heroes' results in the first 'garden suburbs': low density housing for rent, built and owned by Glasgow Corporation, on acquired land in new settlements such as Riddrie, Sandyhills and Knightswood. Rather than tenements with a common entrance passage, 'four in a block' flats are proposed, with individual entrances. Around a thousand homes, a mixture of semi-detached and terraced cottages with gardens and three-storey tenement flats, with cavity walling and electrical servicing, are to be constructed.

Contractors Sunlight Building know the power of marketing, in Ailsa's case a 'woman's touch' for the design of the new kitchens, so are happy to give her work. With her gender, architectural training and experience on the Continent, Ailsa knows she is being promoted as something of a novelty, but she studiously ignores this and concentrates on having secured the work. Sunlight also promote new technologies and materials, including prefabrication and flat roofs, with traditional materials like stone, and the requisite skilled tradesmen, being scarce due to wartime losses and emigration. In line with the fashion for 'sun baths', and physical wellbeing, the marketing boldly claims that flat roofs admit more sunshine at ground level than traditional pitched-roofs, not to mention the opportunity for a *rooftop gymnasium and sun deck.*

Ailsa, over time, teaches the women how to produce drawings to an acceptable standard and to design simple furniture, using the approach she learned at Klaarhamer's studio. They practise first on improvements to Knowe Terrace for Bridget: heating in her annexe, plus her own private bathroom and kitchenette. Ailsa hopes to encourage the women to apply to study part time at the School of Art or at the Tech. One of them, Lisa, a young widow, has a natural flair for design and the good sense, intuition and personality to become a successful businesswoman and possible associate for Ailsa, who is starting to see that life will go on.

When Michael comes to the house, by invitation, she sees that for him too the shadow of war is lifting. He is careful not to push his opinions onto her or Flora, and even seems proud of Ailsa's efforts. He must surely now see before him a professional woman who has achieved far more on her own than when he was trying to mould her into something she could never be. She is so much more than that. After a while she relents and allows him to help with her accounts, as she pays a small stipend to her apprentices from the commissions she is bringing in, and will pay tax.

Ailsa exhausts herself with the work but feels she is at last doing good. She knows from Flora that the houses they help to design will not benefit the poorest families living in the worst squalor, despite promises by politicians, but for families who will move into one of these garden suburbs it will mean better health for their children and less domestic labour for the women, previously used to constant tidying, folding and washing with so many people living in one room. This is everything that she and Truus had talked about before the war.

Michael is deeply unhappy with his living arrangements and talks about little else when he comes for their fortnightly dinner engagements. After a time Flora suggests to Ailsa that they offer him the ground floor room that was Papa's study, and at one time the morning room, to rent. It is little used these days, as Ailsa is almost always in the attic, and Flora conducts her community work from the upstairs drawing room. The old artificial segregation of activities in the house is gone, and the relaxed atmosphere which began after Charles died has only increased with the passing years.

Ailsa is unsure: a man in the house, even one as contrite and humbled as Michael, would change the dynamics. They decide to ask him to stay for Christmas and New Year, for two weeks, to share in the festivities and to rest, but Ailsa insists they will lay down explicit house rules.

Michael is happy to have the respite from domestic tension; he will take meals with his hosts in the dining room, and otherwise use his own room for his leisure time. The drawing room is not for his use, nor the attic floor. Ailsa cannot imagine having this conversation with Michael ten years ago. He is grateful, and rewards his hosts by bringing Christmas boxes and extravagant sweetmeats, which they open on Christmas Eve when Michael is invited up to the drawing room after dinner, along with Bridget.

*

When the festivities are over and a warm glow has settled on the house, and Michael has been staying for a week, Flora invites him up to the drawing room in the evening for a drink and to enjoy the Christmas tree by the fire. As is customary now, Flora sits in Papa's armchair, which always pleases Ailsa, and she and Michael sit at either end of the soft velvet couch. They enjoy a conversation about the further work that Ailsa is taking on in the New Year, and Michael has yet another story of a nameless tax fraudster to tell them which is shocking but quite entertaining. Flora is tired, as so often these days, and retires early. Bridget brings up sandwiches and coffee, and Ailsa and Michael are left to enjoy the Skye peated malt sent by Aunt Catherine, while Michael smokes his new pipe, a present from Ailsa.

'Michael, I hope you don't mind me mentioning this, but I have heard you crying out in the night.' His room is below hers and the screams are at times terrible. At first she thought it was hungry winter foxes, who sound like crying children in deep distress, but this is far worse.

'Do you have nightmares?'

He stares long into the fire, to a place far away, eyes blazing. They are both uninhibited by the effects of the pure whisky content.

'Sometimes' he says eventually. 'I am back at the front.'

He cannot, will not, say more, but she sees tears for the first time in his eyes, glistening in the glow of the fire. He is crying.

She cannot help herself. She goes to him and holds his head to her chest as he pours out his grief. No words come, but he is releasing something held long inside. It begins slowly, then erupts into uncontrollable sobbing. This will help him, she thinks.

When Michael eventually recovers, he lifts his head and holds her face in his, tenderly, like Johan used to do, except more eagerly, more desperately.

'I'm so sorry for the way I treated you Ailsa. You must know that. It was wrong, and I spoiled everything between us. I loved you too much and was wrong to hound you afterwards. I only sought forgiveness.'

'Michael, there is no need to apologise. I did not appreciate your feelings enough. I was too young then to understand about men and women. I know about love now, and it is I that should be sorry.'

She tells him then about Johan, about the time they had together and his long absence, how he returned to Belgium to find his parents and was almost certainly killed along with them or she would know by now. She tells him of her dashed hopes for the future, how she wanted a child and a life with Johan, even across two countries. She never wanted marriage, but a life, a free life, with a lifelong bond of love with him. Michael listens, as he must, and now it is she who is crying.

They laugh after a time, at their own sorrowful circumstances, at themselves sitting here crying into their whisky. They pour another and toast their mutual forgiveness.

'I wish I could do something for you Ailsa' he says. 'I know you can never love me, but I only wish to make you happy.'

'There is something' she says tentatively.

Ailsa has thought about this. She has never lost her desire for a child. Certainly she is emboldened by the whisky, but possibly she has wanted to ask this of Michael for some time without admitting it even to herself.

She puts the proposition to him now, even though in her heart she knows it will never be enough for him. A day will come when Michael will want more; he will not be able to accept these terms that she is spelling out to him, even though he is slowly and carefully nodding his assent, willingly saying *whatever you want, whatever you want. I only want to make you happy.*

The pact is made then, and they go forward, even though she knows what will lie ahead. She will fight, if necessary. She will remind Michael that he agreed, on this night in front of a dying fire, not to pursue her for more, that she cares for him but can never love him; if she has a child, he can be involved in that child's upbringing, as its father, but he will make no claim on Ailsa, none whatsoever, and the child will be in her custody to raise and live as she wishes. She knows this from having seen Truus so compromised in the way she had wanted to bring up her children. Michael promises again.

Even as they perform the act, there on the soft velvet cushions and over the week to come when she slips down to his room, to Papa's old daybed in his study, when Michael cries out in the grip of some terrible nightmare and she holds him close until the terrors subside, tiptoeing back to her room when he is spent and breathing quietly again; even in the sober light of day when she repeats their agreement while out on a winter walk, that he will have no claim on her and she wants no financial support for a child, even then she knows in her heart that a day will come when she can see herself saying to him, as he tries to alter boundaries, 'Michael, you promised.'

She is a woman of a certain age, committed to her work, unable to love anyone romantically other than the man now lost to her. She has no choice. This war has torn lives apart, changed the rules, and so they cling together, one damaged soul consoling another, the only possible hope being that a new life will come of this, one that she will love fiercely and protectively, nurture and cherish, and let no harm come to. She will make sure of it.

Ailsa rests her hand on her belly; she even knows the night it happens, she can feel it, somehow, the life begun inside her that coincides with the coming of a new calendar year; as she lies in her own bed in the dark, hearing church bells ringing out on every street corner, she whispers, hoping secretly that it is a daughter, *you will be strong, and loved, and beautiful, and you will have a happy life. You will learn and see great and wonderful things. I will take you to visit our friends in Holland, and you will meet many good people. You will grow up to know you can be anything you want to be, and I will love you with every part of my being.*

As she drifts into a deep sleep she is already thinking about a Montessori school, piano lessons, literature and art, a house filled with life and music and laughter, stimulation and love, with her mother, and Bridget, friendship from the women who come and go, up to the studio or to Flora's lively corsetless gatherings, the debate and creativity, the joy that is in the very fibre of her home now. No child could be more loved than this child will be.

Harl on Lime

Gertrude

London, October 1967

We have not long arrived home from the Biennale when he makes the announcement, right out of the blue. I have taken a long bubble bath and feel relaxed and warm, curled up on the sofa in my old quilted dressing gown, glad to be out of the night rain. It would appear a cosy marital scene if someone were looking into the lit room from across the street. Daniel has poured us each a glass of the French red we bought in Paris yesterday and I am imagining we will sit listening to jazz and talking over our favourite parts of the exhibition, then I will make us a light supper before bed. He is leaving for Aberdeen first thing in the morning so will want an early night.

I don't mind. I'm used to it. Anyway, I have a new hero. His name is Richard Rogers and he and his wife Su, both architects, had a scheme at the Biennale representing British Architecture. The entry was a simple, single storey, almost square house designed for his parents on a residential site opposite Wimbledon Common. His family sounds ideal: mother an artist, father a physician, Richard born in Florence and studied at the AA and Yale. He is associated with another architect, also on my radar, called Norman Foster. Richard has more charisma though, revealing the type of family I like to study, so I intend to concentrate on him.

The Rogers' design consists of five steel portal frames painted acid yellow, clad in white aluminium panels linked together with something called a neoprene jointing system. Two walls either end have full-height double glazed sealed units with sliding components, one of which is the front door. The interior is open plan and flexible, and the whole house is prefabricated and inspired by the famous Californian Case Study Houses. I loved it the moment I saw it, and have been talking about it all the way home. Daniel hated it of course. Too open, too industrial; *no stone you mean,* I laughed. Transparency does not appeal to Daniel. That is the point, I kept saying. No wet trades to slow it down. It uses factory components. It is flexible. It is like a hangar. It is brilliant. It is the future.

'I'm about to become a father.'

I stay calm. This is one of our rules of engagement. I've managed it for eighteen years, so I can do this. I know Daniel has other relationships, and our understanding is that we don't talk about these, or I become insanely jealous and then ill. This agreement is mutual, although I cannot imagine any way for me other than my exclusivity to Daniel. He used to say it often enough: *feel free to see other men; you've got your life, I've got mine.* I was devastated at first, knowing that meant he couldn't feel the same as I did, but he convinced me it made sense. I feebly tried to ape Simone de Beauvoir, and read *The Second Sex,* but I am too much of a romantic, and too insecure. Neither of us has married, although I always said that I would not mind if he did. I would not be jealous of that. Despite two proposals of marriage, the first to Susan, the second to a musician called Honor, which was a tricky time for me, he never went through with either. Daniel is married to his work, and his emotions are as impenetrable as his precious granite.

Another rule of engagement is that I wait, sometimes for as long as a year, for him to call to say he will be in London, for a conference, or to give a lecture perhaps, or passing through. He has expanded his father's granite business to include architecture and it is highly successful; he has made a name for himself as an expert on anything to do with stone: building, cleaning, mining, grinding, cutting, cladding, polishing, injecting, repairing. He is invited to speak at conferences in such places as Venice and Florence on crumbling masterpieces and climbs dangerous scaffolding to view tiny hairline cracks.

He gives very little away, and I have learned not to ask. Of course he cares, and when he is with me he is present, interested, loving. He does most of the talking, usually about himself, while I listen. I don't want to scare him off, or to ask him for more, but he knows I love him because I tell him often enough. His mother died recently, and I was tempted to tell him then how she forced me to leave, but it is so long ago and would serve no purpose now. Daniel and I could never have had more than we had while she was alive, and anyway he never asked for it.

'A baby. Gosh. Who with?' Even that could be too much to ask.

'She's called Jean. She works in advertising. It wasn't planned. We've agreed we should get married.'

'Daniel.' I take his hand. 'How do you feel about it?'

Wrong question. He shrugs, smiling. I look at him and think, *have I ruined you for life, since you were seventeen?* Was it a form of abuse? Daniel may not love me, but he needs me. His desire was shaped by a teacher seducing him before he was mature enough to deal with sexual feelings. After all these years, he still cannot say my first name.

I get up and go to the kitchen, prepare an omelette and try to think. I return and give him his plate and fork, then sit back down and look at him, really look at him. We've been here before, like an old tune, but this is a new verse.

'Well, this time please go through with it. You have a responsibility now. I take it she is young?'

'She's thirty.'

I am forty-five of course. I would no longer pose naked on a bed, although he has never mocked or criticised my appearance. He is too careful for that. He knows it is my Achilles' heel and wants to keep things the way they are. I try to stay slim but it is hard; I don't eat much but I drink. That is my downfall.

His hair is turning grey, but that doesn't matter. With his droopy moustache and sideburns, forty is an acceptable age to become a father.

'Daniel, you mustn't come here again. It is the only way this is going to work. This time it has to.' It is perhaps not what he wants me to say, but he agrees.

We go to bed and hold each other the way we always do and, as he is falling asleep, I say, 'do you still have the photographs?' Yes, he says lazily, but I'll destroy them.

I believe him. I also believe we will see each other again.

He is gone when I wake up. He leaves no footprint. He leaves no notes, no replies to my letters, no gifts. When I would have dark times and write at length, pouring out my turmoil about my early life, my troubles, my father, my mother who may or may not have cared for me, whose life I have no knowledge of, nor what happened to her, it was therapy for me, and he read them. I know he did. Sometimes we would talk about whatever the topic had been when I next saw him. But he never wrote back. It is how we were. I have no complaints. I allowed this. I gave him my best years and I would do it all over again. It has been the most agonising pain at times, and ecstatic joy at others. My self esteem is always low because I have had no influence over this. I am always waiting. Finally I have taken control, and he has responded as I knew he would.

I have been desired by a decent man. He will have his new family. I will stop waiting. I've wanted to say this for a while, as I've spiralled into drinking more than I should and hated my various dead end jobs. I will move, out of London perhaps, and commute. I will take up that part time lecturing post if I am offered it and see where that takes me. I will follow the career of this young architect Richard Rogers and try to get close, to see if I can work with him in some capacity. The materials library perhaps. It is not too late to turn my life around.

I recall angry words from long ago when I couldn't goad him into telling me his feelings, during the Honor years, when I mixed pills with too much drink and my downstairs neighbour took me to hospital, when he still didn't come. Telling him he had turned into the granite he so loves. Comparing our relationship to harl thrown onto wet limewash over stone, in a melodramatic speech I had prepared in the days I seethed in the recovery ward. Screaming down the phone about how he takes anything I throw at him, but he never lets me inside. *It will be me who ends this one day* I remember saying before I hung up. And indeed it seems that it is.

Lovely Greys

Ailsa

Glasgow, October 1922

My dear Ailsa

I am sorry I have not written for such a long time. So much has been happening here in the Biltstraat.

I have had a private sitting room created, somewhere to entertain, within the apartment. It was Frits' idea, can you believe, who finally accepts how much I dislike what our home stands for. I enclose a photograph for you. You will not believe who designed it for me? Gerrit Rietveld! He had designed a jewellery shop on Kalverstraat for one of Frits' clients, Cornelis Begeer, who was most enthusiastic about this young architect. When we went to see the result, I was so taken by the beautiful proportions and simplicity of the shop, I told Frits I should like Rietveld to design my room.

I was disappointed with his first attempt, so I showed him pictures of the Arts and Crafts interiors we saw in England and pointed out my objection to the vertical lines of the room here. He understood and came back with a completely different design. And it is not 'de Stijl.' I would not have known how to do this, but he visually reduced the room by partially covering the windows and lowering the ceiling and lighting. He wanted to put some of his furniture in, but it is too much for me. On the table I have a beautiful red tablecloth with soft blue dots and everything accentuates the horizontal. I have set up the room with my own simple furniture. It is beautiful Ailsa: all hues and shades of grey, in a simple unadorned space.

When An came she said she had no idea, went away and brought the artist Jacob Bendien, as he is a 'specialist in greys'! Rietveld too has brought people to see it. Architect Bruno Tait and the artist Paul Citroen have been. They call it 'the room with the lovely greys.'

Ailsa, at last I have found someone, apart from you, who understands me, and he has asked if I want to keep up with developments in his work. I have said that I do.

I mistakenly thought Frits' family were beginning to accept my modern ways, but they are saying the most absurd things. 'Surely as a woman, you could not really think this design is best.' I know they are thinking 'if your husband lets you decorate one of the rooms like that, with not a trace of luxury, whatever next?' They are already shocked at my break with the church, with the exception of one cousin who continues to visit me. This family will never understand me Ailsa. I wish you were still here.

She goes on in the letter to ask about Ailsa and to wish her well, before returning to another whole paragraph on Rietveld who, it seems, also understands her sensitivities about religion and society. He feels the same himself. They can talk for hours about the problems of their two religions, he a recently lapsed Calvinist, about family, home, hierarchy, and the position of women in society. Truus feels so alive in his company she says. He is of course from the artisan class, but this adds to the appeal. Out of all her values, the overriding one is austerity, and a desire for frugal simplicity in contrast to her life to date. Gerrit represents that very thing in his background and in his work. She hopes he sees her as more than a wealthy client on which to try out his experiments.

Ailsa remembers him well, and can see how he and Truus would spark off each other. Indeed, she saw a glimpse of it once, the night she first met Johan. She also remembers his wife, who Ailsa recalls was slightly older than him, a serious woman, and so many children, coming to Klaarhamer's studio. He was proud of his family and seemed contented then, not the troubled soul that Truus describes. Has Gerrit undergone some kind of epiphany, or is it the infectious personality of Truus, which Ailsa knows well, that has opened his eyes to alternative possibilities in life?

Anyway, thinks Ailsa, Truus is beginning to get her way at last. After her father died, Truus felt free to break with the Catholic Church. Her children now go to that Montessori school she advocated for so long. And now she has this room.

With regard to that, Ailsa and Truus have discussed modernity many times over the years. What if smaller homes with plain spaces could be built for everyone? Women, especially, would have less housework to do and be able to spend more time with their children. Families could live together in homes where those children would be allowed to play, set free by the lack of preciousness about restrictive furnishings and breakables, everything on show. Materials would be simpler, enabling standard sizes and easier construction. Costs could be reduced, and light and space would become the overriding features.

The new Sunlight homes Ailsa has been involved in are examples of this progress. Although she is only commissioned to design the kitchens, it is a start for her to make her way in residential design.

Truus had attended lectures on architecture during her time in Hanover, although not as many as intended. Given that she felt so liberated after London, she wasted much of the time at parties, as she readily admitted at the time. Still, she never ceases to be fired up by the changing world, the tide of fresh politics around women's rights and freedom to work, and from repressive tradition. The war in Europe allowed women to temporarily operate in a man's world but all that seems to have taken a step back now. Truus believes the war, with movement in or out of the country having been almost impossible, formed quite liberal ideas in the Netherlands which continue to resonate today. She ends the letter by saying she hopes Ailsa, who was of course part of that time, is able to continue to design in this new way back in Scotland.

Ailsa smiles. Since the baby arrived she has hardly had time to think about design, or women's rights. For the moment she will leave the former to Truus and the women who are working tirelessly in the attic, and the latter to her mother and the suffragettes. She simply feels blessed. The house has been further transformed, if that is possible, with a baby in it. It is a special time, and Ailsa had never known love could be so strong. Flora and Bridget between them show her how to deal with new tasks associated with motherhood. It is like learning a whole new craft: a wonderful and mysterious world of feeding, changing, comforting, bathing, playing and talking a new language.

The baby has a routine. When Michael comes that routine is upset, and he is already beginning to ask for more than his allotted time. Of course it is time with Ailsa he wants. He is not fooling anyone, Bridget has said to her, on more than one occasion. It is hard enough for Bridget to understand how her mistress could have chosen to have a baby out of wedlock, saying it must be the talk of the Shields and she hardly knows what to say when she meets other housekeepers while walking out with the pram. On such occasions Bridget says it is a private matter and she is not at liberty to discuss. She has on occasion mumbled something about a husband, an architect working in Holland, who comes and goes when business permits.

Ailsa knows that Bridget never approved of her arrangement with Michael, nor does she have time for him. She looked after her mistress throughout her confinement, bringing her own mother to attend as midwife to Ailsa and to administer the birth at Knowe Terrace. This kept the situation as private as possible, which Bridget advised. Ailsa named her perfect baby girl Gertrude, after Truus, with her dark curls and pale blue grey eyes, and she knows Bridget adores the baby, her little Trudi as they call her, as if her own flesh and blood.

Ailsa and Flora keep to their close circle of women friends and colleagues, all of them loyal, staunch supporters of women's rights, and far too discreet to ask who the father is. Michael comes on Sundays, when the women are not there, not to hide the fact, but as the most practical arrangement. Ailsa is respected, she is a professional woman who has made her own way in the world, the first female architect in Glasgow, despite her battles to be registered professionally as one. She is something of a heroine in local people's eyes. Her connections to the Netherlands and her war years there are vaguely romantic, enigmatic, and she is a patron of women who want the opportunity to work in the sphere of her own professional world. Not one of them is going to gossip or speak out of turn about Ailsa Bray.

Toughened Glass

Gertrude

London, April 1978

Head tilted back, I stare open mouthed at the balcony surrounding an atrium at the top of escalators, where office workers are actually standing, chatting, beside what appears to be an open ledge, but is in fact a clear *structural* glass balustrade, with no handrail to lean on, simply set into a floor channel around all four sides of the void. Square sheets of toughened frameless glass. I realise I am seeing the future, again. So clever of Norman Foster to beat the building regulators at their own game. *A handrail is stipulated only on a stair or ramp.*

I am as impressed with that baluster as with the groundbreaking solar glass curtain walling that curves around the undulating exterior of these Ipswich offices. *God is in the detail.* Glass. Light. If glass can be used in this way, who knows what this can mean for future homes. No longer restricted to windows, but entire walls, houses even, can be of structural solar glass without being cold or leaking like earlier attempts. And balconies don't need handrails.

I remain in awe until it is the appointed time to leave, when I reluctantly board the bus and headcount my charge. The stragglers climb sheepishly up the coach steps, dragged from a nearby hostelry, beery breath depressing and predictable as they pass my front seat beside the driver.

The tour of East Anglia kicked off this morning with Foster's revolutionary Sainsbury Centre for Visual Arts in Norwich, then on here to his much celebrated Willis Faber Dumas offices, and now the coach shudders into life to press on to Arup's Snape Maltings for a somewhat incongruous acoustics masterclass. The students feigned interest at the start but are now bored and don't see the significance. After all, I am coming to the end of my tenure and possibly sounding past my prime as I enthuse over the microphone at the front of the fifty-two seater. Even I can hear how ridiculous I will sound to them, orgasmic over a glass balustrade.

My legacy says it all, and they know it. I pride myself on my image, rarely seen without a navy blue jersey number and flat pumps, exactly as the great woman herself wears, draped flatteringly as only a Jean Muir can. My hair is regularly coloured, straightened and bobbed at a reputable salon, lips a classic Chanel red, weight kept below nine stone through determined lifelong abstinence from anything sweet, yet this manufactured designer image cloaks reality.

As the coach leaves Ipswich I resume my seat, even my own enthusiasm trailing off now, the students tired of pretending, yawning from the effects of the pints of Greene KIng they escaped to while I was gazing enraptured at glass. From the rear of the bus the final year adonis Jonno has taken up his acoustic guitar, his adoring peer group swaying and humming to his Neil Young repertoire, passing joints surreptitiously, long hair drooping over peasant shirts and bell bottoms, affecting peace and love. Meanwhile the first years towards the front distance themselves, their safety pins, studs and Doc Martens striking a pose as they glare with disdain through the windows. I expect my Jean Muir is lost on both camps.

This part of England is familiar to me and is becoming modernised, ancient buildings rubbing up against and reflected in plate glass. I smile to myself as I recall my foray into escaping London, once I knew Daniel was never coming back. I imagined him turning up at Richmond Avenue and I'd be gone. He wouldn't be able to find me. It was Suffolk I looked first and then Diss in Norfolk where I was tempted briefly to buy a disused windmill, but it was too bold a move for me, and belonged to a different life, not mine. Better to stay in London, an ordinary mortal rubbing up against the famous. Besides, there were no examples to follow in windmill conversion. And there was always the chance he would come back.

My grief after he'd gone lasted longer than it should have. It was like a bereavement; deep, dark depression that I could not lift myself from nor share with anyone. Eventually, after two years, when I accepted he really was never coming back, I shifted into a different gear. I had initiated the ending after all. Stupid, stupid. Even waiting, having no control, would be better than this. Or would it? Gradually I became who I am now, going through the motions, putting one foot in front of the other, breathing, giving people what they want. Always thinking of his return.

Gazing out at the flat countryside I reflect on my tired London routine. Most mornings I sneak an envious peak as I walk past, on my way from Islington, through the windows of Foster's design offices. By contrast I am heading to the dull design firm that employs me part time, my career having stumbled to its peak in the Festival of Britain era on the coattails of others.

Acceptable though that would be within my London peer group, if indeed I had one, my heyday was fortunate to be at the time of a suburban post war dream of modern living. We created semi open-plan interiors complemented by futuristic, bright organic patterned textiles, abstract art, curved edges. Ideal homes for the nuclear family where demobbed Dad played with the kids while Mum could keep an eye on his unpredictable mood and whisky consumption from the open kitchen or through a neat hatch. Nothing terribly earth shattering. You needed to be in America then for the real innovation.

I suppose we represented optimism, a sense of rebuilding and promoting the British nation as one of design and technology. Now when I look back it feels like papering over cracks. Teak veneered composite boards concealing floor to ceiling storage, doors without handles that sprung open with light pressure applied, all oh so clever. Lots of earthy colours to represent calm and containment.

Nothing like the world this new movement has created. Unafraid of exposure. Buildings turned inside out. Services on the outside. Primary colours. Naked structure. *High-tech* they are calling it. So obvious to do this. Logical. As bold as the early Modernists were after the First World War. Form following function. Less being more and so on. A continuation really. I knew it the day I saw the Rogers' house at the '67 Biennale. My generation, and the last war of course, were probably responsible for holding up years of design progress in Europe.

My only outlet is through part time lecturing at this second rate college, where I talk up early modernism: the Bauhaus, de Stijl, in the way my own college tutor Miss Burnett did. She admired the European schools, and I augment that with the work of the new Modernists: their influences, their approach to technology and the use of factory components. It is a sad reality that this is the nearest I will get to my idols, although I have tried: this and looking through their office windows, or hovering near them at public events. I am too old now anyway; even Richard Rogers is in his forties. I have followed his progress, a good disciple, for ten years now. He and Su divorced some years ago and he is now married to an American called Ruth (he calls her *Ruthie*). They lived in Paris for a few years and I lost track temporarily, but from there emerged his masterpiece: The Pompidou Centre, or *Beaubourg*, as *we* call it, his new culture and leisure centre, with its services on the outside, colour coded. He is back now in my sights, his bright self coloured shirts pleasing on the eye, his charismatic, clipped voice challenging the establishment.

My highlight of last year was visiting Beaubourg when it opened. I could have told them ten years ago that this man was a genius. Finally he is recognised: he won the competition. I wanted to take the students, but the recession has put paid to field trips abroad, so I went alone to Paris and spent a week exploring, touching every surface, every detail. They had to throw me out each night at closing time.

I am not what they call *top drawer* down here. Especially an industrial designer who has specialised in residential projects since the Fifties. And they are hardly cutting edge. I try, but capitulate easily if a client wants something traditional or eclectic. Of course they don't want exposed steel beams painted acid yellow, or minimalist open plan living with glass walls and concrete floors. They want a floral country house feel, or Harrods bronze and leather kitsch, and I give it to them. I take the easy route when it comes to other people. Give them what they want. They care more than I do. I simply go through the motions.

As I lingered outside Foster's office yesterday morning, *en passant*, I saw Norman himself with a small group of younger, equally tall and charismatic male associates and one woman, slim, cool in their black polo necks or white Oxford shirts, seated on Scandinavian moulded plastic chairs, each chair a different colour, around a white moulded plastic table like something off a spaceship, a core team discussing a working model of a building. I applied my tried and tested act of apparently waiting for someone, rooted to the spot, glancing at my wristwatch, a stance I have perfected somewhat over the years. I observed sidelong that each individual was animated when he or she spoke, long legs swinging under the table, hands working to shape ideas in the air, equal around that table. No neckties worn here. No private hierarchical boardroom with Norman at the head of the table, as my own bosses always do. No fiftysomething woman whose claim to fame is a bent plywood coffee table that managed briefly to reach the furniture department of Heals.

It has always been my way to covet others. Not only architects and designers, but also a certain type of family: the creative type where members ooze enthusiasm and positivity, talk animatedly on any subject to each other without cynicism, who foster talent and confidence in their young, encourage debate. Old money types especially, eccentric ones who don't judge. My downstairs neighbour Natasha is one of those.

The flat, on Richmond Avenue, is rented on a long lease, an unfurnished top floor and attic of a Georgian end terrace where I've lived for the past thirty years. I have seen them come and go, especially the indigenous residents, who thought I was mildly interesting when I moved in, a young Scotswoman working in design, but they have mostly died off. Now it is all middle class incomers, aspiring left wing politicians and theatrical types who intimidate yet fascinate me.

Meanwhile, downstairs and occupying the preferred ground floor and basement, the young Natasha slobs around, unkempt and fabulous with her tumbling ebony curls and kaftan, house a tip, always creating something quirky for her Royal College of Art MA furniture degree. She goes to weekend parties of her extended family, whom she once confirmed in passing is a well known acting dynasty, although it had to be coaxed, she wasn't boasting. I'd give anything to have belonged to one of those families, especially those with interesting women.

Her famous and beautiful Aunt Pippa, an actress who lives in the country and refuses to acknowledge British Summer Time so is always arriving at the wrong hour for appointments, gave me one of her latest litter of kittens. Of course I didn't actually meet Pippa. My choice. Natasha would have driven me out to Sussex but I made some pathetic excuse and instead Natasha delivered the kitten to me. In a way though it made me feel part of the family and I was thrilled by the association, until the feral cat ran away.

They don't have to be famous: any liberal, arty family will elicit the same reaction, even those I know personally, and I do know some, through the Barnsbury Residents' Association, whose excruciating meetings I attend purely to see who has moved into the area, whereupon I scan the previous Minutes for their address.

If it is the type I am interested in, I have on occasion walked out after dark to take a closer look at their house from the street. With the few who know me, I duck out of the way in broad daylight if I see them in the street or jogging round Thornhill Square. Why make them stop and waste their precious time on me? The ones who used to invite me to dinner, or parties, or some fundraising arts event, eventually stopped when I kept giving my apologies: illness and so on. I don't want it to be found out that I'm not one of them, not in fact the self assured persona that I project on the surface, or have them stuck talking to me when a more interesting person will be across the room and they are only being polite until they can join them.

Last year my covert *petite bourgeoisie* roots were no doubt evident to all when I whitewashed over the slogan 'FUCK THE JUBILEE' that had been spray painted in massive black letters overnight on our white stuccoed gable. The politically correct thing to do would have been to leave it there, as a statement of anarchy, given that we liberal Islington middle classes boycotted the Union Jack bedecked street party in nearby Chapel Market, but I simply could not allow myself to do so. Not as a Royalist, which I have no great feelings about either way, but as someone who would rather die than live with graffiti of any description. How prim I have become over the years.

My preferred association (hobby), is to glance sideways, once I alight the 73 bus on Caledonian Road on my way home after dark, to peer through brightly lit Georgian windows, where families I have researched sit at their colourful, checkered oilcloth covered Habitat tables. In their fashionably peeling townhouses, bunches of herbs and copper pots hanging from traditional clothes pulleys (the type that hang over every cooking range in Glasgow tenements, wet washing dripping into the soup pot, but here considered the height of fashion), the families talk and cook and drink wine and move among each other. In the dark street I glance in awe as fathers, home from work, sit laughing with children of various ages, listening to stories or sharing a joke, just hanging out together, agreeing requests for Saturday morning classes at the Anna Scher drama school at the top of the road. That is another thing I covet. Other people's fathers. Those gentle, kind ones who treasure their daughters and talk to them, encourage them, stroke their hair casually, are not suspicious or cynical, laugh with them not at them, welcoming their friends into the casual, haphazard home where no-one worries about mess. Their minds are on higher things.

The coach crunches to a halt in Aldeburgh. We trudge into the sumptuously converted barley store, the purpose of our visit to see first hand how the combination of natural brick and timber, ably combined for optimum reverberation and sound absorption or reflection, can inform our latest fictitious little project of church conversion to concert hall. I realise right away that this has been a step too far. The students know little about classical music and care even less, and have clearly not read up as requested on the science of acoustics. *Where do I think I'm teaching? The RCA?* I decide not to push my luck and therefore we glance around briefly then beat a hasty retreat back onto the coach. I shall cancel the arranged visit to the new Southbank next week and revise the project to something more fitting. A glass house perhaps.

As we head back to London in the gathering darkness we receive a final caterwauling of *After The Gold Rush* from the back seat, the metal stud brigade up front sinking deeper into their seats in horror. It would appear I'm not the only one who is past their prime. I root through my bag out of boredom, and it is then I remember the plain white envelope which I was too rushed to open this morning and shoved into my bag in haste. Assuming it is a circular from the bank, I open it halfheartedly.

It is from McFarlane and Murricane. Following my father's recent death there are contractual matters relating to my stepmother's continued residence at Knowe Terrace. Please could I make contact at my convenience to discuss.

I look at my reflection in the darkened window for a minute then begin to hum quietly to myself.

I was hoping for replacement
When the sun burst through the sky.
There was a band playing in my head
And I felt like getting high.

Fine Porcelain

Ailsa

Glasgow, September 1923

Ailsa hands Trudi to Bridget so that she can read the letter properly. She has to sit down, so shaken is she by its contents. The short note from Truus, arrived at breakfast this Friday morning, she expected to be the usual news of soirées and illustrious visitors to her private room, her talks with Gerrit about life and religion, the children, her visits to An and Reinder, with the latest scandalous happenings in the Harrensteins' household, and of course her marriage problems with Frits. The first line shakes Ailsa to the core. So emotional is she that Bridget thinks her mistresses' missing lover, or one of Ailsa's Dutch friends, must have died. When she is handed the letter and reads it for herself, she realises that the weeping is for joy.

135 Biltstraat

Johan is alive!

We today received news from Brussels that he is in a sanitorium near there, in the countryside. He has no memory and, without papers, his identity has been unknown all this time. We are going to visit him as soon as we can, but it will be you he wants to see Ailsa, I'm sure of it. We only discovered his whereabouts because, when his memory was jogged by something, he kept saying over and over,

'The Architectress' and 'Utrecht.'

Can you believe it?

Of course they did not understand this, but someone contacted the Kunstnijverheid here and they knew right away and contacted us.

Can you come? We will bring him here to convalesce and find specialist medical treatment through Reinder's contacts in Amsterdam…

Bridget needs read no further. 'It is wonderful news Miss Ailsa' she says. 'This will change everything.'

Ailsa must go to him. Nothing can stop her. She pulls herself together and tells her colleagues, when they arrive for work, that she has to go to Utrecht to visit a sick friend; she has received unexpected news. She makes the necessary arrangements to have the work overseen, which is straightforward now given how advanced her protégées have become. Lisa Mellor is already undergoing her Diploma and showing great promise. She can be put in charge of the office and liaise with Sunlight and Glasgow Corporation on the current projects and oversee them until Ailsa returns.

Flora tells her not to expect too much. Johan will be a changed and traumatised man. Bridget doesn't care. She knows enough from all she's been told about this Belgian to know he makes her mistress happy, and the baby will have a proper father. The lines will become blurred, they will go on to become a family, and the arrogant little man, the one she has the measure of, who she is sure she has seen by his limping gait in Pollokshields on days when he should not be here, watching for a glimpse of Ailsa, to discover her routines, to take over her life again, will be usurped.

She says some of this to Ailsa as they are sorting out clothes to pack the following day. Ailsa is so euphoric she just laughs at Bridget having it all worked out, running ahead of herself as usual, and hugs her. She knows her mother will always have this steadfast woman, a stoical companion to her through the years when Ailsa was separated from them, and now, whatever happens, she will be here. Bridget is family, and has a home at Knowe Terrace for life if she so chooses. The work to her annexe, to make it a proper flat over two floors, with heating pipes and her own kitchen and water closet, is all her own.

*

On Sunday morning Ailsa waits to see Michael, to explain the circumstances, and to say she will write soon about arrangements for him to see Trudi: once she knows the situation clearly, she will return. She will bring Johan if he is fit enough to travel. He can convalesce at Knowe Terrace and be fussed over by the women, or he can have total rest and isolation if he needs it.

It is Bridget's day off. She goes once a month to visit her elderly mother and check on her brother, but this morning she is reluctant to leave. Flora has a rally to attend in George Square, which she helped to organise, regarding the ongoing issue of universal suffrage for women, and Bridget thinks it is unwise for Ailsa to be alone.

'It will be fine Bridget' says Ailsa. 'Michael knows about Johan, and will understand. I don't know what is going to happen, but I will assure him that he can continue to see Trudi.'

The truth is she doesn't know what this means. She hasn't had time to process it. All she knows is that she has to go. Bridget and Flora have suggested she leave Trudi here this time, but Ailsa will not be parted from her little girl. At one year old, bright and inquisitive, Ailsa wants Johan to meet Trudi, to see for himself what has happened, but know that nothing has changed in her love for him. If he has trauma and memory loss, matters will need to be placed before him clearly. Once he meets this little one, he will love her as much as Ailsa does. She is part of their future.

Michael lets himself into the kitchen from the back lane, a habit he has developed on the Sundays that Bridget is away, as if the brief time he stayed here and the events of that time have permitted him rights to the house. This irks Ailsa, who usually finds him lurking silently in a doorway, unannounced. Ailsa has not mentioned this to Bridget, who would only say he wouldn't get away with it if she were here and offer to forfeit her days off.

It troubles Ailsa that Michael habitually dismisses Trudi on arrival, that his attention is focused on her rather than the baby. She is required to make reference to some detail, some small development in Trudi since his last visit, to get him to pay attention to his daughter. Today he sits at the dining table, having hardly noticed that Gertrude, as he will insist on calling her, has begun to crawl and is doing so now, happily, among her toys on the hearthrug. Ailsa hands him the letter. This seems the simplest way to explain. He reads it over twice, a look of horror spreading across his face.

'You cannot seriously agree to this Ailsa. You surely are not thinking of going back there?'

'I am. Of course I am. This is the news I have always held out for.'

'But......you have your.... business. And.... the child. Everything is different now.' He is stuttering, trying to make sense of what he is being told. 'I will not allow it!'

'You will not *allow* it? Michael, what are you talking about? You do not own me!'

Before she knows it, they have taken up their old adversarial positions.

'You will not take the child. I have rights.'

An old fashioned phrase enters her head. She remembers her mother saying it used to be common when a baby was born in the Highlands. *Is it a boy or a child?* She thinks, if Trudi were a boy Michael would have said, *You will not take my son.* A girl is an object to him.

'Her name is Trudi.'

She has forgiven Michael's lack of affection for the baby up to now, putting it down to male awkwardness, or his shell shock, or their unconventional arrangement, and has told herself that as her daughter grows he will find ways to take an interest, in the same way most women seem to do naturally following a birth. She has made excuses for him, when in her heart she knows how Frits was with his little ones from the start, openly devoted to each of them, despite his busy life. And other men too. When Gerrit Rietveld brought his children into Klaarhamer's studio, the little girl Bep, or each new baby as it arrived, his pride and love were evident. Michael lacks that connection, and comes on Sundays with an overriding interest, not in his baby, but in Ailsa. He is only now using Trudi as an excuse to stop her from leaving. It is about control.

His shouting makes Trudi begin to wail and she looks up imploringly at her mother, who sweeps her up and holds her close in order to pacify her. They exchange words, his angry, Ailsa's steady, measured. At that moment a loud noise, a motorcar exhaust backfiring, goes off on the street and Michael begins to shake. He is enraged. He is calling her terrible names now, saying she didn't *hold out* in every way, she was happy to be unfaithful to this Belgian lunatic soon enough. She is nothing but a *common whore*.

The first china teacup hits the fireplace where Ailsa is standing with Trudi in her arms. The crash of breaking crockery against marble makes the baby scream louder. Everything goes into slow motion then. Michael begins to pick up anything in his orbit. Plates and dishes are hurled unceremoniously towards the fire, cutlery at the walls. His rage, just below the surface, is not only from his war experience. This is Michael of old. He throws a saucer at the mirror behind Ailsa, missing her by only a few feet.

She panics. She has to remove Trudi immediately, frightened suddenly for them both. She must get past Michael to reach the door and moves that way, shielding Trudi with her hand. With horror she sees a tiny shard of fine porcelain must have rebounded and hit the baby's head, embedding itself in her hairline. The cut has started to bleed.

With horror she sees that Michael has the large knife from the carvery in his hand. At that moment he seems to hesitate, as though horrified by his own actions. This gives Ailsa enough time to run out into the hall and onto Knowe Terrace. Clutching Trudi to her, she looks wildly around for help. Everyone is at church, or at home. The street is empty. She knows it is really her that Michael wants to destroy. This way he is stopping short of that, but she cannot risk going back inside. He has lost all reason and was holding a carving knife, even if he did not actually brandish it.

Shielding the baby's head, she goes round to the back lane and runs upstairs to the attic by the back stairs. Trudi has stopped crying now, caught up in her mother's actions. With a pewter key that she keeps in her smock Ailsa locks the doors quietly from inside, knowing that he cannot climb these steep stairs anyway, and takes Trudi up and out onto the roof.

It is a beautiful Autumn morning, and completely silent. The trees across the gardens and squares of Pollokshields are turning copper, and the Campsies are silhouetted against a calm sky. Trudi is pacified now. Ailsa has removed the tiny porcelain shard, trying not to imagine the situation had it hit an inch lower, and presses a handkerchief to the wound to stem the bleeding. Trudi is distracted by the birds and by her mother's reassuring words as they sit, emotionally exhausted, on the chimney parapet wall. Here all is still, save for Ailsa's heartbeat.

After a while she risks going back down to the attic, where she can hear Flora calling her name. She unlocks the door and calls down to say they are safe, and to check that he has not harmed her mother. *Has he gone Mama?*

Later, when they are telling Bridget the story and clearing up the wreckage, cleaning Trudi's wound, and comforting Ailsa who is still in shock, she hears her mother saying that when she came home with two activist friends Michael was sitting smoking, on the floor of all places, among a pile of smashed crockery, but left then, limping past them in the dining room doorway, saying brusquely *your precious daughter has used me for the last time.*

Flora wants to call the police, but Bridget says it could delay Ailsa from leaving the country with Trudi, as a named father has rights.

Better, she says, to let him think they will report him, that they have witnesses, reputable witnesses in the form of Mrs. Forbes-Hamilton and Mrs. Laing, but that Ailsa and the baby should leave for Utrecht before he realises they have gone. He will lie low for a few days. They will ask Robin Asher to write him a letter, stating the evidence and naming reliable witnesses to his destruction of property if this were to go to a court of law, and the assault on the baby as the reason he is not to be given access to his daughter at this time.

Ailsa agrees. She is so buoyed by the thought of seeing Johan that she recovers quickly from this terrifying event. As she resumes her packing a single phrase is going round and round in her head, the last thing she said to him, over the noise, the destruction, although no doubt in his apoplectic state he could not hear her.

'Michael, you promised.'

Salmon Sky

Gertrude

Glasgow, July 1984

I let myself in with the house keys that have remained on my Islington keyring all these years: the cylinder and mortise ones, and the pewter. The locks haven't changed in over forty years. The inner key at first sticks in the rusty keeper, but turns eventually to reveal the familiar musty smell, the hall's cracked black and white ceramic tiled floor, diamond pattern around its border, chequerboard squares in the middle, evoking a smell of polish, long gone. I know every line, obsessed as a child, never allowing myself to step on the joints, one of many rituals, like rubbing doorknobs all over to leave an imaginary coating on them from my hand, or making sure my shoes touched each other beside my bed (getting up several times to check), or ensuring every part of a plate's surface was wiped equally by the tea towel when drying dishes as my father washed them in silence.

Some of these behaviours I still slip into from time to time, even now at sixty-one, but less often. As an adolescent, the urge was so strong even I thought I should seek help, but I would have been ridiculed. The frequency reduced over time and I learned to live with it. Perhaps everyone is the same. I never thought to check. Like my synaesthesia. I thought everyone saw numbers and letters in specific colours. Apparently they don't. Like dreaming. Not everyone dreams in colour I'm told. I'd love to take someone's place for a day, just to see how differently minds work. Did my mother see numbers in colour too?

My father died six years ago. When I heard, in a short letter from my solicitor, he had been dead for three months. I had to return to sign papers relating to Edith's sitting tenancy, so I went to stay for two nights. There was no sense of reunion, and I saw to my horror that, in the intervening years, Edith, by now a bent and wizened chain smoking hag, had further imprinted her tasteless brand of decor onto the house. A mix of even louder floral, and now tartan, carpets, each clashing loudly with its neighbour at a door threshold. Scalloped pelmets and cheap tie-back glass fibre curtains, reproduction nests of tables and ubiquitous glass animals, faux baroque telephone table and not a book in sight. At least when I specified vulgarity for clients, I tried to keep it consistent. The entire house reeked of cigarette smoke, years of seepage into every greasy fabric and surface.

The worst was the drawing room (lounge), originally the full width of the house across three tall windows (now hooded by the scalloped pelmets), which had been subdivided by a thin stud partition, ruining its classical proportions and symmetry, destroying the continuity of the elaborate egg and dart cornicing and high moulded skirting boards. Rooms must at one time have been sublet to tenants, crudely carved up and accessed via the common hallway, which thankfully remained intact. There were cheap locks on all the beautiful moulded panelled doors, even the dining room, which had served as one of a number of bedsits.

When Edith was sleeping I tiptoed up to the attic with the pewter key, relieved to find that it had been kept locked and not altered in any way. For reasons best known to himself he had preserved it, kept it from Edith, as if it didn't exist.

The whole district looked worn back then. Sandstone, once blonde, was now soot impregnated black, most of the large Victorian villas subdivided into bedsits, no longer fit for purpose as single-family dwellings. According to the monthly newsletter I receive via Margaret from a local pressure group, of which Margaret is a member, the Corporation had at one time wanted to raze the whole suburb to the ground and replace it with new homes. I supposed they would have had to let me know first if it reached Knowe Terrace. No doubt I'd have capitulated as usual and given them what they wanted in the cause of modernism and seen (or not seen, from London) the neglected, once magnificent houses bulldozed to the ground. Nothing but bad memories.

Later I was relieved I had never voiced an opinion on the topic, even to Margaret. It would have been the wrong one, and embarrassingly public. The dream of Sixties new build, streets in the sky, knocking down slum tenements and large dilapidated villas, creating zones for re-housing on a mass scale, had been halted at Pollokshields almost in time. The local campaign beat the planners. Most of the villas were reprieved, although a few were lost.

I read a recent article by Richard Rogers on his proposed conversion of two traditional nineteenth century townhouses in Chelsea that he and Ruth have bought, creating a cavernous modern interior behind a traditional façade, and saw that now the fashion is for faded grandeur to be revived. Gentrification they call it in London. Up here it will be called something else, but essentially the same thing.

I didn't ask Edith to vacate of course. We parted on civil terms. I gave her six years notice, calculated between us to be roughly when I would retire. I had a vague idea back then that I would restore it to its original state, then sell it. Edith, to her credit, kept to the bargain and left earlier this year to live with Janet in the village of Admaston, in Shropshire, at which point I had the house surveyed in absentia through my solicitor. She has let it fall into further disrepair. I didn't have the courage then to come and see it for myself. It was locked up after the essential repairs were undertaken through a management company, addressing the damp, dry rot and water ingress. Dry rot is rife at the moment apparently, spores creeping through the stonework to destroy the timbers of so many older buildings here, almost an epidemic. Something to do with the hundred year mark. Daniel would know.

I cannot imagine this house one hundred years ago. 1884, when it would have been new. Perhaps my mother was born around then. Try as I might, I cannot bring that time, or her, to life. I never have been able to. I cannot even conceive of our lives overlapping, or that she knew me. Growing inside her is a concept I can't relate to. I know people who are adopted must feel the same, but I often think that they, though by no means all, were wanted by their adoptive parents. That surely must make some difference.

I do have this house at least. I will live here with the ghosts of these strangers, Ailsa and Flora and Charles and, with the exception of her attic, I will tear it apart, with my bare hands if necessary, until all memory of my father and Edith are gone, in waking hours at least. I will make it as in my dream: white, with sunlight pouring through an open window. If the memories can be demolished along with the interior, then maybe I will stay.

I think that is what the Rogers have achieved in their new home, except I imagine theirs will be filled with people; family and friends, coming and going, across the open plan living area, which he likens to a *piazza*, drinking wine, chatting, laughing, eating Ruth's delicious food.

The task seems enormous, but I have the time. I also have the money, due to careful saving over the years, not for any specific reason, just because I could. It became a sort of hobby. I knew that one day I would come back here. I just couldn't imagine how. For a time I harboured a fantasy that Edith would die and my father would write a letter, saying how much he'd always loved me, how sorry he was, it was all my stepmother's fault. He would beg me to come home and look after him, which I would, and he would tell me endless stories about my real mother, about their life together at the start, before the war that ruined everything and changed him, when they were deeply in love. He would tell me how they met, produce boxes of photographs that have existed all this time, and lovingly describe every detail. Even what happened to Ailsa. He would even tell me that.

I have had my few pieces of furniture delivered from London, so my own bed is set up in the drawing room, what is left of it, beside the window, where I can breathe. As the evening sky turns salmon pink, I sit on the bed looking across at the horrendous Bovis flats that have been built in the grounds of The Knowe, obscuring it from view. I am in no position to judge, but it is a pity they are so ugly, with their tacked on 'Greek Thomson' decorative concrete arches planted above diminutive windows, not even structural arches. At least The Knowe villa has survived, along with its gatehouse, and the retaining wall with the stone Greek urn details.

Before I draw up proposals for permissions I will strip the house back to its original form. The partition across this room will be first to go; it is non-structural and can be attacked with a hammer, by me, gratifyingly. I will start tomorrow. Demolition work is therapeutic. I will hire a skip and fill it with musty chunks of broken and mildewed plasterboard and lengths of rotted timber. I will call a locksmith and have these Yale locks removed from all internal doors then offer the doors to a Victorian salvage company to dip and re-sell. I will drag every piece of Edith's tacky furniture into the hall, pitch old mattresses over the bannister onto the black and white tiles below, pile up the lampshades, baroque side tables, box up the glass animals, everything will go. I will get a man to come and carry down the cheap utility wardrobes and chests of drawers, and take the whole lot away to the Barras market, then lift the mismatched filthy carpets and dispose of them.

The kitchen is original, with the pulley and the Belfast sink I remember standing in to be washed, that my mother stood in, and the range housing the back boiler. I will leave all that for now, and later offer it to the salvage people. Victoriana is in vogue. When the place is stripped bare, I will get Rentokil in, and check that all traces of dry rot have been eradicated. Wet rot and damp one can deal with, but that stuff can eat away until everything crumbles, its mushroom spores spreading across stone to colonise the next unsuspecting piece of dry timber.

As I drift into sleep I dream about the white room with the corner open to the sky, and of clouds forming shapes in the breeze. Daniel is there, studying the wall structure, and as he turns he becomes Richard Rogers, who looks right through me as he crosses the room to speak with another woman.

Bleached Oak

Ailsa

Utrecht, October 1923

Ailsa is aware that Truus' life has been turned upside down even more than her own. This past year has been distressing for the whole family, with Frits being sick for so long. Always a robust man, full of life, now so diminished. For this to be happening at the same time as Johan is recovering his own health, gradually regaining his memory, his frail body starting to return to its former strength, has made it all the more poignant for Ailsa. Her available time when not with Trudi or working is divided between supporting Truus through this crisis and making her daily visits to counsel Johan.

The weekday routine starts with taking Trudi to kindergarten, who sings to herself on the back of the bicycle as she snuggles contentedly into her mother's back. After dropping her off and waving goodbye, Ailsa returns to the apartment on Annastraat to work through the morning, before visiting Johan in the early afternoon. She is assisting Klaarhamer with a row of small single storey residences in Oog in Al on the west side of Utrecht and also signs off the work that Lisa sends from Glasgow. The business at Knowe Terrace is expanding, with the women having found a niche market in kitchen design, providing layouts now for more contractors and the expanding work for Sunlight, and Lisa is nearly qualified. They may need to take on another apprentice.

In the afternoon Ailsa collects Trudi and together they buy food for supper at the open air market on the canal, spending their evenings at the apartment or visiting Truus and the family. It is a simple existence filled with routines and rituals and suits Ailsa for now. She needs this time to recover from the trauma of what happened with Michael and the shock of Johan's emotional state and physical change, which far exceeded what she was expecting. So ecstatic had she been at the news that he was alive, her mind had blocked any negative thoughts of what she might confront in Utrecht.

When she arrived nearly a year ago and discovered Johan in such a dark place, it had devastated her. At first she did not recognise him. He had gone from the gentle giant she knew to a thin, emaciated shadow of the man he once was, and she had to rush from the doorway of his hospital room to weep outside in the corridor, in order that he would not see her anguish.

It later emerged through painstaking research and letter writing by Ailsa to the Belgian authorities, building on the channels of communication opened by Frits, that Johan had witnessed the murder of his parents, had been forced to watch a mass execution of academics at Leuven University before he was taken prisoner, to then be tortured and starved almost to death by the Germans. He remembered none of this when questioned, cautiously, by the doctors, who did not wish to trigger the memory too suddenly. Ailsa was told by her contacts that Johan had escaped and joined the Belgian resistance, hiding out and fighting in France for a time, and by all accounts had buried deep inside everything that had gone before, even his life in Utrecht. No-one knew his identity. When he was badly injured in a shell explosion he was moved to a sanitorium near Brussels, but the explosion meant he had lost all memory, long and short term. He had no papers and for four years this tall, gentle, ravaged man, who could barely speak but demonstrated, unprompted, that he could draw complex architectural sketches, remained a mystery. He helped the sanitorium with repairs to the building, using the technical knowledge he remembered perfectly, and seemed content to stay there. That place became his life.

Then one day, prompted by the sight of a young nurse with her vivid red hair tumbling down the back of a cape as she cycled past, late for duty so had not yet pinned up her hair under her starched cap, Johan uttered the words that led to his reunion with his old friends. He was transferred to Utrecht under the guardianship of the Schröders, whom he did not recognise, but he knew Ailsa the moment he saw her in his hospital room, said the word again, *Architectress,* and smiled. This was seen by doctors as an indication of his likely recovery.

Ailsa went to sit with him every afternoon, taking along drawings and photographs of work they had undertaken a decade earlier with Klaarhamer. She was patient, she didn't take her daughter, who stayed to play with little Hanneke in the afternoons until the time she started kindergarten and Han started school; it was thought it would confuse him to see that the only person he remembered now has a child.

After this past year of slowly regaining strength and fragments of memory, he seems responsive at last, so finally Ailsa took Trudi with her last month. Johan didn't ask who the child was, but was won over immediately by her, as were the nurses and the other staff. The funny little girl made everyone laugh with her English words and her confidence. They brought colouring pencils and Trudi drew pictures for him, of Johan with his big beard and his denim hospital boilersuit, which made him laugh too, and of Mummie with a mass of red curls riding her bicycle with herself on the back.

Johan responds well to anything visual, and draws all the time. It is evident he has not lost his ability to create. In fact Ailsa was asked months ago to help nurse him through the medium of art therapy. She drew visual images of her journey back and forth from Scotland. He seemed to remember her arriving on boats, of leaving on boats, that she would go away to another country, but that she always came back to him. He trusts her, she knows that, and she hopes one day he will remember he had loved her too.

So today Ailsa has finally been allowed by the doctors to take him out for a few hours. She wants him to visit his old apartment on Annastraat, where she has been living with Trudi, to see if he remembers their time there. He miraculously knows to find the key under the Delft tile, which makes them both laugh. They sit in the weak October sun at the square bleached oak table and drink tea. She watches him closely, imagines the mechanics of his brain begin to click with vague recollections, looking around, at people passing outside the window, the drawing table and even the simple wood and canvas chair she tells him he designed and built. He nods and smiles, as if he feels a good association, a sensation, a hazy memory of good times.

Everyone is terrified of the day, which will surely come soon, when the memory of his parents' execution will return. The doctors want to be there when this happens, because Johan's reaction is going to be unpredictable. That single event seems to be at the root of his trauma.

Ailsa is not trained to cope with this occurrence, so has been advised to avoid certain triggers.

Sitting in the apartment he starts to remember he left Utrecht for an important reason, that he had to leave the Architectress, still his name for her when he is trying to remember. *Yes,* says Ailsa, encouraged, without thinking, *you did, you went to Leuven.* She realises her mistake and moves on quickly from the mention of his home town. *You sent me messages through others who came, to say you would be back soon.* He nods slowly, as if he can remember this. She holds her breath, frightened of what might come next. He stands and crosses to her side of the table, takes her face in his big hands, strokes her hair and lifts her gently from her chair, holding her head against his chest. They stay like this for a long time, familiarity washing over them, before Ailsa leads him slowly through the double doors to the bedroom, where they lie together for the first time in almost ten years, in the pale afternoon light. They are changed, physically and mentally, but in that moment the years melt away. They find each other again, and it is just as before. She knows now it will not be long.

After a time they dress and lock up the apartment, walk past the church out to the main street then take the trolleybus back, holding hands thoughtfully, quietly, aware a corner has been turned.

Johan seems ready to fall into a deep sleep when he is back in his hospital room so she leaves him and goes to collect Trudi from kindergarten. On the way she thinks about the future. Soon she will have to tell Johan about how she felt she was running out of time, but never of hope; that in her grief she took the decision to have a child without him, with a man she didn't love. She hopes he will understand.

He was never a possessive man. He has a simple, clear outlook on life, pragmatic, generous. He will accept this, she is sure. She is far more worried about how he will take the horrific realisation of his enforced witnessing of something no person should be made to endure.

Ailsa and Trudi call in at 135 Biltstraat on the way home, entering by the back way through the gardens. It is unusually quiet for the time of day. The children are normally playing out at this time as their supper is prepared and Trudi always runs to join in the game. Ailsa lets herself in and calls out *hallo* in the silent passage. The housemaid comes from the kitchen to meet her.

Frits died today.

Clockwork Orange

Gertrude

Glasgow, July 1984

The morning feels fresh and optimistic. I have slept well, and prepared
my task. I will go into town to Catanis and buy tools. Throwing open
the storm doors to greet the world, I pick up a pile of dusty circulars
and mail that has gathered behind the door since Edith left and no
doubt from before that. I carry it into the dining room and sit in my
father's chair at the head of the table, the one with the arms. The
symbolism is not lost on me. I am allowed to open the post, to sit
facing the window, to be the one in control. Discarding the junk, I pick
out one or two items that look like bills, and notice one on blue airmail
paper, handwritten in spidery handwriting. It is addressed to T. Bray.
Perhaps a mistake. There is no T. Bray to my knowledge. I open it out
of necessity.

Prins Hendriklaan, 50

Utrecht.

2 July, 1984

Dear Trudi

*This will have to be my last attempt to contact you. I have tried over the years, but
my letters were always returned unopened, I assume by your father, and latterly not
even returned.*

You may not remember me, but I was a good friend of your mother, since we met in London before WW1. I don't even know if you are at Knowe Terrace, which is unlikely, but if this does reach you by some means, I would be most grateful if you, or a representative, could contact me at this address at the earliest opportunity.

I am in possession of items belonging to Ailsa which by right are yours and, once I clear the house, which I am currently in the process of doing, I will not be in a position to keep them.

I hope to hear from you.

Yours

Truus Schröder

Trudi? Does she mean me? I've never been called that, or any derivative of Gertrude, although I vaguely remember a man in Aberdeen calling me Gerda. This is another, like Hilda. And why Bray? Who is this person Truus Schröder? The name is familiar to me. I check the address again. Prins Hendriklaan 50, Utrecht. For a moment I imagine she has written to the wrong address, until I re-read the missive and see she mentions Knowe Terrace as if she is familiar with it, and Ailsa by name. My mother had a friend in Holland? In London? Yes of course, the photograph I have is from London.

For the first time, someone who knew my mother, who has items belonging to her!

If I am Trudi, then she knew me too and must have called me by that name. How can this be? Letters returned unopened? He did that. My mind is reeling with this new information. The woman must be in her nineties at least, perhaps going into a care home and has to dispose of all but essential items.

There is no telephone number on the letter, so all I can do is reply in writing, which I set about doing immediately. The demolition work can wait. I dress and dash to the newsagents on Albert Drive and purchase an airmail letter, then write an apologetic note, rushed, short, assuring her that I knew nothing of the past correspondence. I finish by saying that I will visit as soon as possible, thanking her over and over. In fact I am already mentally travelling. My head is in turmoil. I do not intend to wait for a reply. I cannot let this woman go. I rush to Maxwell Drive to post the letter then catch the Subway into town to book a ticket to Utrecht, wherever that is.

As the newly launched Clockwork Orange dips into the old tunnel, with its familiar smell, hurtling down under the Clyde towards town, my thoughts sway with the sideways rhythm, the noise and sense of theatre, strangers facing one another, imagining each other's lives against the background screech and thunderous rattle. I consider the possibilities. Could she be a crank? Why is her name familiar? Another thought niggles at the back of my mind, not for the first time. A thought so powerful I have hardly ever dared admit it even to myself. Did my mother leave us, leave the attic, leave my father because of his abuse, leave me, and move to Holland? Had she been alive all the time I was growing up?

Blank Canvas

Ailsa

Utrecht, February 1924

'You see I'd left my husband on three occasions because I disagreed with him so strongly about the children's upbringing. Each time they were looked after by a housemaid, but still I thought it was horrible for them. And after my husband died and I had full custody of the children I thought a lot about how we should live together. So when Rietveld had made a sketch of the rooms, I asked, 'Can those walls go too?' To which he answered, 'With pleasure, away with those walls!' I can still hear myself asking, can those walls go, and that's how we ended up with the one large space.'

Truus Schröder-Schräder, Interview, 1982, aged 94

Ailsa and Truus are walking arms linked along the Bilt following an evening visit to the hospital. The ground is icy underfoot and they are holding each other for balance in the darkness between the street lamps as they cross the wide street from the central reservation of the tramcar stop. Johan has finally been given the all clear, and they are in optimistic mood. Good nourishment and months of the best psychiatric treatment have uncovered the basis of his deep trauma and allowed it to surface and be addressed. Today the doctors have finally said he can leave and return as an outpatient. He is over the worst now. For a time, when he remembered the horrors in Leuven, he was in danger of regressing, but he gradually chose to accept it and somehow found a way to live with it like so many others do post trauma. His memory is still patchy, and Ailsa has learned how to coax him gently when he needs to talk, and let him be when he goes inside himself for periods of time. His hatred for the perpetrators will never leave him, Ailsa knows, but he has contained it.

Gerrit is coming over this evening to show Truus the altered design of a house he is preparing for her, and she is full of anticipation. Little Trudi is sleeping over tonight and will be following Hanneke everywhere she goes, toddling after her in the nursery, copying her movements, such is her adoration of the six year old. Binnert is a mature boy now, the little man of the house, and his sister Marjan is not far behind him. Both are coming out of their shells again. The housemaid will have allowed, on Truus' instructions, for the children to stay up to see their mothers before bedtime. This simple act is a novelty still for Truus.

The contrast of freedom afforded her family now is beginning to show in the children's behaviour: no longer expected to be silent, out of sight, doing their homework in another room like they used to, even before their father was sick, while their parents entertained or dined together in private, or went out for a whole evening to some social engagement on behalf of Frits' business. Now they run to Truus constantly, telling her about their day, showing her their books and drawings, chattering and laughing. The older two first, then the little one, followed by Trudi toddling along behind when she is there. Ailsa notices that Truus often smiles as if in wonder at the children's newfound freedom and has told Ailsa how much she loves the time she can now spend with them, even when it is relentless, and certainly not usual for a woman of her class. It is as if Truus wants to make up for the difficult years when she had sometimes left for periods of time. Ailsa remembers some of those bad times, but she was not around for all of them.

As they climb the mansion's grand stair, Ailsa wonders how much longer the family will remain here now that the paperwork is in order. She has always had mixed feelings about this apartment. Of course it is beautiful, one cannot deny that, especially the central hall with the rooms off it, and the domed rooflight above, with so much light. Yet she knows Truus longs to leave this behind, with its mixed memories and stifling ostentation.

Truus knew once the reality of her situation was clear, they all knew, that she wanted to get out of the oppressive home, her late husband's taste almost exclusively throughout, with the exception of her private room. She had imagined herself and the children renting something for a while that perhaps Gerrit could remodel, moving to Amsterdam after a few years when school changes would make it easier. There she would be near An, and to be close to her sister is the most important thing for Truus, especially now. Ailsa hadn't minded. She would see her often enough, and anyway, these days her own life is filled with Trudi and Johan.

An's own marriage, to Reiner Harrenstein, a left wing doctor in Amsterdam, the first Dutch paediatrician, is unconventional to say the least. It seems that An may have brought the much debated concept of free love into the mix, being more than close to Jacob Bendien, an artist who is living with them, but this is pure speculation. An's life, with so many friends dropping in to her home regularly, bringing unconventional ideas about life and art, chimes with Truus. She has always wanted to live like her sister, but never had the opportunity until now. As the wife of a prominent lawyer, Truus had come to realise this would be an impossibility, and gradually the expectations had become unbearable. She was never going to fit that convention, nor to find common ground with her husband's family or associates.

When Frits died after that long illness, after thirteen years of marriage, some of them difficult, Truus told Ailsa that she realises she now has the chance to live life on her own terms. She had loved Frits very much at the start, he was charming and handsome, so dashing, he had swept her off her feet, and she would do it all again she says. When he became bedridden and sick, she had felt guilty for all the times she had railed against his conventional rules. Some of it early on in their marriage she had taken in good humour, but when he started telling her that An was a bad influence and that he disapproved of her influence and consequently the way the children were being raised, Truus couldn't bear it. An hardly ever came to the house in recent years. She was surprised when she saw the grey room for the first time, pleasantly surprised, but it had been there for some time and Truus had not told her much about it. Truus had left on several occasions to stay with An, but always came back for the children. Now she has full custody, she can decide for herself where and how she lives. Her ideals of frugality, freedom of thought and independence can finally be brought to bear.

It appears that, following a discussion with Gerrit, where Truus had said she could not find anywhere at all that she wanted to live and for him to renovate, he had said, *well, then you must build a house!* Truus was not in favour of this idea at first due to her planned future relocation to Amsterdam, but then Gerrit had said, *well, then you will sell it,* and thus had won her over. His clear, practical, positive approach is something Truus obviously values very much at this difficult time and their closeness is no surprise to Ailsa.

Gerrit and Truus had agreed to set off in separate directions over a weekend to look for a potential site. The small plot of filthy brown scrubland on the edge of town had been a surprise to Truus when she found it at first because it was not what she had been looking for at all, yet she had immediately felt it a distinct possibility. Then, when she met up again with Gerrit to compare notes on the following Monday, they realised they had each favoured this same piece of land at the end of a row of unremarkable new houses. It sits on the edge of town, a rural plot that adjoins a plain gable end, a blank canvas, facing outwards towards open farmland, meadows and canals, sitting there as if its back could be turned not only on the town but also on convention, as if to say, *put the rules behind you, this is where you can build a house to be happy in,* and she knew then it was meant to be. And of course, Gerrit, his wife and six children live in Utrecht, so it is practical for consultation purposes, as there is no-one else Truus trusts to design a house for her.

Truus first met Gerrit before the war. Ailsa remembers it well. They had hit it off instantly, each sharing the same disdain for the overly elaborate furniture her husband favoured. Although a furniture maker like his father, Gerrit had a completely different outlook on design. They were not to meet again for eight years until eventually he designed the grey room for Truus in the family apartment, where she could receive guests, and she and Gerrit grew inseparable in terms of ideas exchange. Still, having a room of her own was exactly that: a temporary escape from her real life. It had amused her that it shocked her husband's family and their social group so much, having no embellishment to it, and she had enjoyed receiving her own visitors for a while, including Gerrit, but it was no long term solution for a woman in a stifling marriage.

Tonight Gerrit is bringing sketches for the new house from the model they discussed, having lightened the form of the structure at Truus' request. She told Ailsa today she can hardly believe this is really happening: a house of her own, of her dreams even, for her and the children, to her own specification. As usual, she laughed, Ger will talk about the design, hopefully a departure from the original block form he had presented last time, the outside of the building to be more influenced by the interior, and lighter, more transparent, at her request. Also as usual, Truus said, I will listen patiently, then ask if something or other is possible based on how I want to live, as openly as possible, with the children, and with all the nature that surrounds it.

For Truus, who never realised her own ambition to train as an architect, it is all about how to live, not the design itself, and she is bursting with creativity. Ailsa stays out of the process because she wants her friend to have this time at last. She is like water bursting through a dyke. All that imagination, suppressed for so many years, is now pouring out as a torrent of ideas. Gerrit is a practical and easy going man, not precious at all, and he will try to accommodate any idea from Truus. *Well, I am the client*, Truus says to Ailsa at the top of the stairs, *and I know what I want, or at least I know what I don't want! This!*

Whenever Truus is describing her brief for the new home, Ailsa thinks back to a conversation they had during her early years here about open plan living. The two women have always spoken at length about how women and children might live openly, ideas Truus had partly developed from conversations and debates she'd had with An's circle of friends over the years, members of the Communist Party mostly, and other writers and intellectuals who talked passionately about overturning the rules of the *bourgeoisie*. They had ignited Truus' imagination with views on women's rights, even though nearly all of the ones who spoke were men, most of whom had a wife somewhere, either sitting beside them or back at home with children. Back then An was vocal in her opinions, more able than Truus to constructively criticise and challenge the methods discussed. Gradually Truus had drawn on her own skills learned through her travels and education and, although shy and introverted compared to her sister, could hold her own in any session. She knew she was probably seen as a hypocrite, living as she did within the confines of the *bourgeoisie* herself, married to a wealthy lawyer who was part of the establishment they all despised, but they also knew she was deeply unhappy in that life, and mostly stayed for the children back then.

Ailsa has listened to Truus' thoughts over the past few years on how things might change within a family structure, about open plan living without hierarchy or pointless decoration, and has always been in agreement with the rationale. In the conversation they often have about this, Ailsa always recalls a moment of inspiration they both had when they babysat for a woman in the Cotswolds, back when they first met and were staying in Chipping Campden as part of their Arts and Crafts tour. The woman was one of the artisan group working out there, who lived independently with her child on a large attic floor above the workshop and studios. She and her small daughter had seemed free somehow in that space. No separation between them, no walls or barriers, and that had seemed to Ailsa and Truus a good way to live closely with a child: to include that child in one's life, in conversation and social interaction. Such a contrast to their own childhood experiences. Ailsa had added that perhaps the fact that no man lived there was also a contributing factor. She had admitted to Truus that night how much her own life had changed after her father died, how her mother had seemed to blossom and become someone she hardly recognised, and they had become more like sisters.

In the few commissions that Ailsa has managed to assist with, for residences in Utrecht, she tries to suggest as much open plan design as possible, with labour saving kitchens in the main living space, so that the woman can be near her children, but not every client is prepared to live this way. The man of the house always wants separation, private space and the need to shut a door on children when he wishes to speak to his wife over dinner or socialise with other adults.

Truus has found herself in a unique position. In this way, Ailsa needs to think carefully about her own future. Could Johan agree to living separately from her and Trudi, but remain as lovers? Is such an arrangement even thinkable for a man?

'Mummie! Mummie! Mummie!' All four at once tonight, warm cheeks against their cold faces. 'Gerrit is here! He has been letting us play with his toys.' They sound thrilled. Gerrit will have treated them as little equals, explaining to them patiently how his models work in practice; how he assembles a piece of furniture from flat planes of wood, like parts of a kit.

'His toys are chairs and tables and even a house!' exclaims Han, who at six is learning how much she loves to create. Baby Trudi looks up at Hanneke with her big grey eyes like saucers, filled with admiration, as Han carries her to Ailsa.

'Did you know that Gerrit's toys are little scale models of real objects, that the house will become life size. For us. We are going to build it to live in. What do you think of that?' says Truus.

For Truus this project is playful but also very serious. Her children are in effect going to grow up in a kind of laboratory, an environment where they will be stimulated to live and think differently, a house that is going meet the requirements of an independent, modern woman and her family.

Once the children are worn out from creating fantasy furniture with pieces of modelling wood and have gone off happily to bed, Ailsa sits by herself, gazing out to the dark back garden, musing again about her future with Johan. Would he come to Glasgow with her? Should she live here? Trudi is settled here now. Flora is not so well, and is talking of going back to Applecross to live with Aunt Catherine, saying it is what she always knew she would do one day, the activities she has been involved in now becoming increasingly taxing. Ailsa thinks her mother hopes that Knowe Terrace will be lived in by her daughter and granddaughter, but in truth Ailsa is happiest here, far away from Michael, and where her best work has been so far. There is a saying here. 'Anyone who comes to live in Utrecht never leaves Utrecht', which she can understand.

As she is considering the possibilities, the conversation across the room at the table over the working model and revised sketches floats in and out of her consciousness.

'Could we make the side of the house that faces Prins Hendriklaan look like its neighbours in scale, then have another feel round the corner…...an entrance from the garden, then round again an open side looking onto the fields?' Truus is saying, followed by 'I don't want to live downstairs!! I want to be upstairs, nearer the sky! I have never lived on the ground floor. Too dark.'

She hears Gerrit affirm this. 'Perfect. That is good. The views will be magnificent. Downstairs we will have the kitchen, library, study, maid's room. That sort of thing.'

Truus continues. '…and I'd like the upstairs rooms to be close to each other so the children can be near. They have missed so much. I want them to join in when they are older, and be part of the main space. I want us all to be together. They should be part of the visits from our friends, and learn from the discussions we will be having, you know, with Ailsa and Johan, An's friends, the de Stijl people, visitors from outside Utrecht. '

'And I don't want a grand bedroom for me. Just enough space to sleep. I want as much of the upper floor as possible to be used for living.'

He sketches out upstairs bedrooms, a living space, a bathroom. They work from the plan, not the elevations. 'The exterior will be whatever it will be', says Truus. She asks can each room have access to a balcony or at least an open outlook. Where the sun hits the space and at what time of day is critical.

But as the layout takes shape, it is clear that Truus is still not sure. She doesn't like the separation.

'Can the walls go?'

'With pleasure, away with those walls!!' laughs Gerrit, scribbling out the lines with his heavy pencil.

'I want each of the children to have their own washing and cooking areas with electrical outlets in their spaces. To be independent. And I'd like them to do their homework, all of us together, so it becomes a central activity. Can we make a shelf, like a desk, along the wall?'

'Of course.' Gerrit looks concerned about some aspect of the new layout.

'You know, we will never get building consent for this open plan living, because there is a lavatory.' He thinks. 'But we could call it an attic.'

Ailsa smiles to herself. This man finds a solution to any problem. She sees Gerrit and Truus look at each other in this moment, as if a light has been switched on. A shared understanding of something. They nod, smiling together as he draws the layout.

After a while Truus turns her thoughts to the downstairs level and is making suggestions. 'You want a garage?' exclaims Gerrit.

'Yes. One day soon everyone will have a car. You can't have those things all sitting on the street. And we need a study, for when quiet time is required. The kitchen can be downstairs, and we can have a hoist to carry food to upstairs.'

Gerrit is sketching an overlay to the upper floor, rooms around a central core connecting both levels.

'Ah yes!' says Truus. 'You have put a lightwell in the centre. Like here, but neater. More compact. That is perfect.'

Truus told Ailsa earlier that tonight she is going to suggest to Gerrit that he include an office for himself in the house plans. *This will mean he can save money* she said. Truus knows the positive effect he has on her children and so much wants him to be part of their cultural development. She is unabashed about this, although certain his wife will object. But Truus holds the purse strings. She knows this will be a risk, but as his patron she feels she has the right to suggest it, especially if they are going to keep working together. Ailsa is wondering which of the downstairs rooms will be designated as his office once Truus makes the suggestion. Of course. The garage. For now there is no motor car, if indeed there ever will be.

Really, thinks Ailsa, her friend wants the best of both worlds, and why not. Now independently financially, Truus does not want to marry again, as she has experienced all she ever wants of that confining institution. She does however want the input of a male role model for her children, and Gerrit fulfils this. He seems more alive with her children than with his own, from what little Ailsa has seen. Years before, when Gerrit would bring in each of his babies to the studio and show them off proudly, he was besotted, especially with his eldest daughter Bep. He is different now. Life, and Truus, have changed him. Still the same outgoing personality, living for the moment, but his views have changed radically. He has denounced his religion, like Truus, and is far more sceptical about institutions, or even on a personal level the influence he is having on his own children. He said recently to Ailsa, 'they will be what they will be.' Gerrit is such a free spirit, so quick, so talented, and becoming well known in Utrecht for his work. The more he takes on, the less time he will spend with his children, thinks Ailsa, simply because he is so driven, not because he is a disinterested father. He will go where the work takes him. And like all such men, he has a devoted wife who will pick up the pieces.

Ailsa has taken a new apartment for herself and Trudi. It is office premises on the Oudegracht, but the size of it means they can live over, where it has a kitchen and bathroom off a large open space to live and sleep. Her very own attic, understated but perfect for her needs. When Johan leaves hospital it will be to go to his old apartment on Annastraat, so they can start as they mean to go on. He has dealt with the worst: the pain of his memory returning fully, and recalling the horror of his parents' death. He has confronted it, and come to terms.

Also, he has understood Trudi's place in Ailsa's life. He may have lost ten years of his own, but he has been carefully counselled to understand that other people's lives had moved on during that time, and things happened. He has grown to love Trudi as Ailsa does. It is time now for her to decide where to live, here or Glasgow, and Johan must decide for himself. Her heart says here but she cannot be sure. There are responsibilities to consider.

Ailsa knows it is time for her to emerge from the shadow of Klaarhamer, who is becoming something of a recluse himself these days, having never recovered from being snubbed by the de Stijl group. She will always be indebted to him, but now wants to be recognised in her own right. She plans to focus on social housing. She is already searching out commissions on her own, to work on with Johan when he is ready.

She intends to write to Lisa with an idea she has been formulating, on the back of something she has read. In 1920, in the wake of war and the suffrage movement, the Women's Pioneer Housing in England raised funds to buy large houses and convert them to low rent homes. Many women had lost a partner in the war and had to work to support themselves but no landlord would let a room to a working woman. Meanwhile the shortage of domestic servants had hit the value of large houses designed to function on the back of cheap labour and, in once wealthy central London, hundreds of large houses are lying empty. Ailsa is thinking about such a possibility here: there must be women in the Netherlands who want to work and remain single. Maybe not having been part of the war means there are not the same number of widows, but in other ways this country likes to be seen as progressive, and women here have the vote, so change is coming.

Ailsa has thought a great deal about this since she started the work for new housing in Glasgow, which Lisa now oversees. Although Ailsa remains fully involved and signs off the design work, she would like to take the business a step further and try out her ideas in the Netherlands. She is about to submit an entry for a competition for new housing on Laan van Minsweerd, close to where Truus' house will be, and in her proposal she is playing with the idea of designating apartments exclusively for women, adding this to her supporting statement. She has other ideas too: central heating and common laundry facilities with a standardised kitchen in each apartment, a concierge to take in deliveries when women are out at work, and for the entire set of building components to be prefabricated and mounted on site, inspired by the Sunlight model. Ailsa cannot help but think this is the way of the future, and dares to imagine that, should she win the competition, it would also resolve the decision about where to live. She would need to remain in Utrecht to oversee the build.

Looking out into the blackness of the gardens at the back of the Biltstraat apartment, she makes a decision. She will focus on the competition submission and leave the rest to fate.

Open Corner

Gertrude

Utrecht, July 1984

In my haste I do not make the connection. I'm assuming Bridget had said this name, Truus Schröder, when I was a child, hence its familiarity. My decision to travel by hired car and ferry is based on the possibility that the items being held may be bulky, and will not be able to be taken on a flight from Amsterdam. I have worked myself into a state where I believe this old lady could die at any moment and I will not be able to ask her the vital questions from which I need answers. Yet despite this imperative, I have chosen not to fly.

I pack lightly, taking only flat shoes and an anorak along with light summer clothing. As I drive down the east coast to Newcastle, past Edinburgh on the lorry laden A1, inside I feel more like a child than a sixty three year old retiree. The concept of *mother* has resurfaced in my consciousness but, for the first time, not in connection with life at Knowe Terrace or a photograph in London. Here is a new connection, outwith these associations, which extends to a mystery woman in the Netherlands.

As I settle into my cabin and lean back against the bulkhead, familiar detailing of laminated inbuilt shelving and coved skirting upstand from my work with Austin, I wish I could go and relax in the lounge bar and have a large glass of red wine, soak up the ambience of holidaymakers and parties of students enjoying themselves on the outward leg of their journey, but it is not worth the risk. I stretch out instead on my berth and dare to hope. All I wanted when I was young was for someone to sit with me for a day and tell me about my mother, when I was old enough to understand, give me some kind of insight into the woman she was, other than my father's version. I feel like one of those adopted children heading to meet their birth family for the first time. When I am feeling really sorry for myself I still tell myself my situation was worse. *All you ever think about is yourself.*

I travelled extensively at one time across the Continent, through work, attending trade fairs, or with Daniel for some spurious purpose or other, and several times on holiday alone to Italy by train, but never to here. The Netherlands is somewhere I always felt drawn to, but kept putting off.

*

Only as I walk past substantial residences that border a delightful park, Wilhelminapark, consulting the free hotel city map which I picked up after parking and checking in, following an hour's drive from Amsterdam to Utrecht along a wide, flat motorway; only as I walk to the last section of this long street, Prins Hendriklaan, glad of my flat shoes, and see the last house, number 50, on the left, before an ugly motorway flyover, does it hit me. This? This is the house? I know this house, this little gem of a residence shimmering white against the adjoining traditional dark brick apartments with their Dutch roofs, from books and design studies. Suddenly I connect the name Truus Schröder, not to Bridget's stories from childhood, but to this house, one that I used to show students: The Rietveld Schröder House. Gerrit Rietveld's masterpiece of De Stijl as architecture. Truus Schröder, his client and muse. This woman, this famous woman who inspired this house, where she lived as a widow with her children and presumably still lives, knew my mother?

Another sensation hits me. One of déjà vu. This is the house from my dream, the white house with the open corner.

White House

Ailsa

Utrecht, October 1924

'You strew ideas wherever you go. People say I have many, but you have far more. I simply come and sweep them up. And they're not petty ideas; they all have a purpose. How they are to be realised doesn't interest you a bit; and that should be none of your concern indeed. We must keep working together.'

Ailsa is recalling the words Gerrit penned recently in a dedication to Truus. The house is almost finished and through this tender message he is telling her that she is more than a muse, more than a client; she is as much a creator as he is.

Ailsa and Johan are discussing this as they cycle side by side through the new Wilhelminapark, towards Prins Hendriklaan, on the edge of town. Trudi is holding on behind Ailsa, her arms wrapped around her mother's waist. It is another crisp, late autumn morning. Lack of rain since the summer has allowed the building work to be completed on time.

'Truus has insisted on moving in before the inside is finished, to try it out. She wants to experience it to iron out any snags.'

'Really? It is cold already at night. They should stay at the Biltstraat until it is heated properly.' Johan hates the cold now.

'I know. There will still be damp plaster. It will be a while before it dries out. But Truus won't wait. They have Biltstraat until the end of the year so that is an option if it is freezes. But she is impatient.'

'And no wonder. Gerrit has excelled himself with this project.'

'Yes, his first house but, as I say, I think it was Truus' influence that makes it unique. She pushed him you know. I saw it, Johan, when you were still in hospital. He took on all of her ideas about the lifestyle she wants and incorporated these into the design. I think of it as *their* design, and I think he does too. He has credited her as co-designer.'

In fact Ailsa knows this to be the truth. She witnessed the early discussions and the brief set by Truus, how she hadn't been happy with the first design, and took Gerrit to the edges of his imagination. He is a genius though, no question. Proportion is everything to him, and he has created this masterpiece in perfect proportion. Form in perfect harmony with space and light.

'It is the same with his chairs. He always has to go through the stage of a block form first, before paring them back. The house was the same process. Not a mass with holes punched through it like most houses.'

Ailsa has studied the drawings and been on site previously. She cannot wait to see the final realisation. It is not so much a house with walls, more a house with horizontal and vertical planes overlapping and intersecting the spaces between. The outside appears to be part of the inside, no separation between nature and indoor living. Ailsa wishes she possessed half his imagination, or perhaps a client like Truus, which is the real rarity. Still, she has a new client of her own, as of this morning. For the moment however Ailsa has decided to keep this information to herself.

When the planning permission was granted back in July, they had a little party because they could almost not believe it! It was the way Gerrit had been able to suggest a pitched roof simply by showing the gable wall and roof profile of the adjoining building behind. He didn't cheat, not at all, but Truus decided that perhaps the authorities thought the proposal had this same roof profile when in fact it is completely flat. Very clever. Too late now. It is stamped and approved.

Work began on site the same week, before some bureaucrat at head office could change his mind. Gerrit has no time for rules. It is part of his charm. Nothing poses a problem for him. He lives for the moment, views life through his senses, and does not care if this house lasts for a few years and no more, serving a purpose. It will be inexpensive and suit the frugal lifestyle that Truus craves.

Ailsa is proud of this choice her friend is making for herself and her three children. No-one else, even with the societal advantages that Truus has, would take this bold step and no doubt incur the criticism of Utrecht society that will be the fallout. For every supporter there will be a detractor, not least from Frits' family, who will surely pour scorn on this house as they did with the grey room at Biltstraat. But she knows too that Truus wants to prompt such a reaction. This house is propaganda for her. All those years ago, when Truus and Ailsa first talked about lifestyle for those who could not afford paid help, how women could be freed from endless housework to live simply, to have time for their children, this small house will be the embodiment of that.

Compared to life in Glasgow, and the drive for new housing there, more to do with women working and having equality in the workplace therefore requiring labour saving homes, this is, for Truus, more about the position of women in the family, in the home, not outside the home. It is bourgeois family life that is the focus here, but that is what Truus knows, and Ailsa appreciates this. The house could not be replicated, of course, not like the apartments Ailsa designed for the competition, but it does stand as a model for a *style* of living, and it will provoke. It may be one woman's propaganda, but can only add to the wider debate of state support for single mothers, birth control, the woman's position in the family as independent and respected.

Today is Ailsa's first visit to the house since it received its completion certificate, to celebrate over a makeshift lunch on site. As they approach the end of the road at the edge of town and the open fields, she is stunned by what she sees on the left, like a phoenix risen from the ashes. It is perfect, a small rectangular house with such dignity, such presence, on what was a piece of wasteland at the gable end of new brick apartments. Slim vertical slices of smooth white rendering are suspended in mid air, with fine steel sections appearing to hold them hanging there, with such a lightness of touch, as they intersect. Only those in the know, like Ailsa and Johan, would appreciate these vertical planes are rendered brickwork. They appear as if concrete, but that had proved too expensive for the build. Gerrit made that concession in his ever practical way.

Johan lifts Trudi from Ailsa's bike rack and onto his shoulders. She wraps her plump arms around his neck. The two of them are inseparable these days. He is going to film the house today and Trudi wants to join in. An and her Amsterdam circle have got hold of Soviet films that are banned in the Netherlands: an experimental art medium and vehicle for social progression. Inspired by the medium, Johan is keen to develop a skill for architectural documentation with overlaid commentary. The act of filming his friends' work is helping to ease him back into the world, to be part of that world without feeling pressure to participate fully if he is anxious, which still happens from time to time. He hides behind the hefty camera he has acquired from Reiner and talks from there. It is great fun and they intend to take the camera to Scotland next summer, to capture Ailsa's Glasgow and Flora's breathtaking surroundings of Applecross. Trudi loves the whole concept and they have promised she can appear in the film today. He will later use the phonograph and movie projector borrowed from the Harrensteins to edit the film and add a voiceover that Ailsa has agreed to record in her clear Glasgow voice, describing the design and philosophy in a script yet to be written but one that will be approved by Gerrit and Truus.

All three stand in awe of the building from a vantage point at the edge of the field as they prop the bicycles against the shed that sits outside the gate. Truus waves down to them from an open corner, where it appears for all the world as if no window exists.

'Look at her, Johan' laughs Ailsa. 'She looks so happy. I wonder if you could capture that *joie de vivre* in your film, show how the house brings that out in Truus.'

Ailsa waves up. Johan lifts Trudi down and takes the heavy camera from his backpack and checks that the celluloid reel is tightly wound. He suggests that Ailsa walk over with Trudi to the gate and he will film them. As he begins, Ailsa and little Trudi walk hand in hand through the gate, Trudi toddling up the path to the main door. They turn and wave back to Johan. Trudi laughs, Ailsa picks her up and swings her round. He follows closely behind, capturing every movement in the viewfinder.

The proportion of the whole is indeed a masterpiece. A pristine white structure sitting proudly against its darker neighbour, perfectly in harmony yet totally different. Defiant. The proportion of width to height in every direction is a thing of beauty. The house sits solidly, yet it is light, ephemeral. Gerrit does not care about longevity. If this house lasts for twenty years he will be happy enough. He favours mass production, inexpensive materials, a short life span for a dwelling. But this perfect little house deserves to last a lifetime. It is truly original. He has in this instance a client who, like him, favours frugal simplicity, but who demanded her architect meet her brief for how a modern woman with children may choose to live. He has fulfilled that brief to perfection.

In this semi-rural setting, Johan looks through the lens as he pans the camera around. Beside the kitchen window there is a sign on a post. A grocer's boy or mailman arriving will see the message 'goods to be delivered here', and a speaking tube enabling him to talk to upstairs if no-one is in the downstairs kitchen. He will be able to open the window himself to leave the agreed goods or parcel on a sealed shelf, secured from inside with shutters that can be opened later from inside. Ailsa smiles but is not surprised at this level of detail. Trudi shouts *Ha-llo* into the tube and Truus answers, which makes the little one jump, then giggle helplessly. Ailsa kisses her daughter and smiles at Johan, who is beside them now, filming all the while. Ailsa's red hair in the breeze he could film all day long.

The ground floor is four simple rooms forming a rectangle, a fairly traditional layout, orderly, off a narrow central hall fitted with an open coat and shoe cupboard, cleverly positioned over a drying radiator, and at the half landing above four steps, a built-in shelf for a telephone, with drawers, and a bench. There is no possible indication here of what lies above except for a winding stair leading off in a tight space behind an open sliding door. To the right of the downstairs hall is the kitchen, which Ailsa knows is going to house a service lift to take food and items to the first floor dining area, and the long window with the tradesmens' shelf they saw outside. The tops of the internal walls have glass panels, giving a sense of continuity from one room to the next. There is a maid's room behind the kitchen.

'This would make a good dark room. Truus has no intention of having a live-in maid' says Ailsa, teasing, knowing Johan is desperate for the use of a dark room.

The third downstairs room, facing onto Prins Hendriklaan, has been designated as a future garage, but in fact this is for Gerrit to use as his studio meantime. The fourth room to complete the downstairs is a study, facing the gate where they came in. Each room has a door to outside. It is very clever. They return to the half landing in the hall and locate the tightly angled staircase leading to the first floor.

To climb this is to enter a different world. Never could Ailsa have imagined the sense of pure space and brilliant natural light as she emerges in the centre of the upper floor. This core, the rectangle through the centre of the house, was inspired by the Biltstraat apartment. Light falls from above. A raised rectangular glass tower on the flat roof cascades light down the stairs, tiny by comparison to the mansion, but serving the same delightful function. The stair enclosure can be open or closed to separate the upper floor. Ailsa is impressed with how they have made what was labelled the *attic* on the drawings into a living space that she understands will be able to be totally open or sectioned off into separate rooms with sliding partitions.

Only a woman can live like this is her first thought. Ailsa feels strongly about this theory; she always has. A man imposes territory, however well meaning. He changes the dynamics. Even Gerrit would. She looks around the space. It is ingenious. It is also cold.

'Don't worry, we have a heater. At night when we shiver we sit round it' Truus calls from the open corner. Clearly that is going to be her favourite part of the house. The corner seems to have no visible support. It appears open to the sky when the large framed panes of glass are opened out. Gerrit has cleverly set the support structure back from the corner. The influence of his furniture is everywhere: crossed over joints, intersecting planes, balconies that seem to hang in mid air on the three sides of the house, facing either towards the polder or onto the street. It is simply a series of elements held in space.

Ailsa crosses the room and embraces her friend. 'It is lovely Truus, just lovely.'

'It is lovely to be in at last and in the thick of it' replies Truus, ever practical, and Ailsa sees new joy in her expression, like she has finally found home. A workbench sits in the room, still being used by day. 'Because the house has a lot of glass, I'm going to have shutters made, or blinds. I've asked van de Groenekan to come and measure up.'

Even for Truus this house feels exposed, thinks Ailsa. She was used to the Biltstraat security, even if she despised it.

'We are installing industrial radiators but they are not ready yet. Expensive, but at least they are plain, not like those decorative radiators that everyone has' says Truus. 'I tell you, the way it's going those radiators are going to cost more than the house. And they are coiled tubular pipes. Not even square! The de Stijl people will not approve.'

The de Stijl group is indeed all over the project, hoping to be involved in the colour application.

'I'm not the slightest bit interested in the movement or these de Stijl men, apart from Gerrit of course! Ah, here he is.'

Gerrit arrives back with the children, Truus' three and two of his own. His eldest girl, Bep, is growing fast and is protective of Wen, his youngest. She carries him and glares disdainfully around the space. Wen is the same age as Trudi, and Ailsa hopes they will become friends as he is a sensitive little boy. Gerrit has brought food, which he distributes on the floor. The younger children go to play in the part that will be the children's bedrooms, which for now makes a good playground. Binnert and Marjan sit with the adults, happy to join in the discussion. Bep could too, but she prefers to hang back with the little ones. She is unsure of this other woman in her father's life.

'There are going to be areas of colour applied to the floor here' says Truus, pointing to where they are sitting 'and to certain elements outside. I am going to leave that to Gerrit, as we cannot agree, and I don't really care.'

'One thing is for sure' concurs Gerrit. 'I don't want de Stijl involved. I will decide the colour, determined by functions and by my senses, not by some colour code according to van Doesburg.'

Ailsa is thinking how Gerrit designed what is now being called his Red Blue chair back in 1918 but only added colour to it last year to appease the group. Colour is really not his priority.

'We are happy to use the de Stijl colour palette' says Truus. 'red, blue, grey, yellow, black and white, and the sliding partitions will determine where each colour goes.'

'Ah, the sliding partitions!' sighs Gerrit.

'Gerrit is not happy about those, nor the tracks on the floor,' says Truus. 'Not happy at all, are you? There will be wooden partitions sliding and retracting, with primary coloured tracks in the ceiling too. What is wrong with that?'

'Too much fuss' he says. 'All that slide, pivot, click, locking mechanism.'

Truus explains the rationale good-humouredly to her guests.

'They will be used to separate off rooms for the children. Binnert will have his own room with these windows looking out across the polder and Marjan and Han will share a room over there with the windows facing Prins Hendriklaan. Their divans will become couches scattered with cushions during the day, and we can open the whole space like this for family gatherings or to entertain, or just for ourselves.'

'Why don't you just put curtains around the sleeping areas for the children' says Gerrit. 'That's what I'd do.'

'No, no. It is not only about privacy to sleep. Each area, for the children, has its own basin, gas ring and storage. I want the children to learn to be independent and yet have the choice to be part of the whole. Curtains indeed! Gerrit, this idea will be like assembling a kit of parts, nothing heavy, immoveable, or immobile, but a modular framework, multi-purpose. Everything you love!'

Ailsa moves the subject on. 'And typical of you Truus, you have given yourself the minimum area for your own bedroom.'

'That's what I wanted. To keep as much space for the purpose of living. I know. It is barely more than the size of a bed, but the end opens onto the outside balcony with a view over the fields, so really that's an extension of the room. I love it. Go and see, Johan.'

He sees that Truus has designed a built-in wash basin and clothes storage in her little bedroom.

'Truus, do you remember when we babysat for the woman in the attic, in Chipping Campden, and how we thought it was such a great way to live?' asks Ailsa.

'Yes, I still go back to that as my inspiration. That's the reason I didn't want walls. She lived there so openly with that child. These children here, all of our children, will grow up feeling part of it all, part of our discussions. They will absorb things we cannot imagine, and never be made to feel they must be *seen and not heard*. And if they're tired or busy, they slide their partitions and can be alone. The children will flourish in this environment. I will remind you all of this in twenty years time when the proof will be there for all to see!'

'It is much more than that though' says Johan. 'You have taken the complexity of domestic life, and given the children the opportunity for self-sufficiency.'

'Yes. I thought about this a lot' says Truus. 'It is deliberate. A freedom of choice, even these sliding partitions, the furnishings. It will be a 'stage' for our relationships and, like Japanese folding rituals, I believe these activities are liberating. I want to promote a new openness in families, a new truth different to the bourgeois, respectable hierarchy our generation has always known. Happy, playful, with a sense of discovery, not sombre like other houses. Like the Biltstraat for example.'

'It has a certain discipline about it nevertheless' ventures Johan. 'One could almost say moralistic.'

'Yes, but an environment free of repressive traditions and rules that prevent expression. That is what children need' says Truus. Not to mention some adults, thinks Ailsa, Michael fleetingly entering her mind.

Truss has spread a tablecloth out on the floor and they are sitting in a rough circle on cushions. Ailsa passes round the plates and they call the young ones over to eat. Bep hangs back and Truus tries to include her by talking to her directly.

'When I was a little girl, Bep' she says, 'my father would take me and my sister on long walks around Arnhem and we would discuss the beautiful old farmhouses there. I think that gave me the love of architecture. Then in 1901, I went to boarding school. I was very lonely. But it was a beautiful old house. Inside there was a big, white marble hall adjoining a conservatory and a grand oak staircase. There were tall windows looking out onto a beautiful garden at the front with wild gardens at the back. It was very comforting, and there was a rather kind nun, who helped me feel better.'

'Are you Catholic?' asks Bep pointedly, wrinkling her nose. She will know this already from her mother. She may as well be saying *are you from Mars?*

'I was, yes, back then, but I was probably already questioning it. That religion leaves no room for doubt. All those rules. I found it too hard to live with so many. My sister and I both felt that way.'

'Do you not believe in God now?' Bep is trying to test her.

'Well, I believe in the power of nature, and of art. A frugal life, and of course, the power of work. I believe that each one of us can find his or her own way, individually, and should not be led by rules, or covet what others have. For me, I prefer not to have too many possessions, and I don't care what others have. I am not addicted to wanting more and more things. The people who always want whatever the next new thing is, or whatever their neighbour has, are never content.'

'But we like clothes, and books, and to decorate our house' says Marjan.

'In my opinion three quarters of possessions are not needed and mainly for show. All that caring about possessions takes the fun out of life. I only want simple clothes, and few of them. No excess in anything: food, drink, furniture. Wouldn't you like us to live so that we could leave at any moment and go on an adventure?'

'What about all the things we have at Biltstraat?' asks Binnert.

'All I want to bring from the Biltstraat is the piano, and the bathtub.'

Ailsa knows Truus is trying to break it to the children that she has no intention of hanging onto their father's things.

'What will we sit on Mummie?' asks little Han.

'We will design and build the furniture we need and any necessary freestanding pieces. We will decide together. In order to experience a space one has to occupy it. One needs to feel where the sun comes in, the view out, the interior space, how we use it. When a piece of furniture is placed in a room, it alters the space. One can do it consciously or unconsciously. In most cases, the conscious intention is to make a pleasant interior, where one can sit back and enjoy it. But architecture has only one goal. To realise space. We must live in the space first, then decide.'

'But people like to have things around them' says Bep.

'Yes, but when a person gets home from work, or school, tired, it is rest that he or she needs, and recreation, to revive the senses. That person may put on some music. This is what we call a *sensory action*. Space can also offer this. Space speaks to our senses and activates them. Interior architecture is '*space art*.' There is no need for a frilly curtain here, a decorative pelmet there, or a fussy lamp on that desk or table. It's too much, unless it has a purpose.'

Bep looks at her, frowning. 'In my own opinion' adds Truus.

After the lively lunch discussion, which the older children participate in as much as the adults, giving their considered opinions about design, with Binnert saying he still thinks he will use the downstairs room to study, Gerrit carries Wen down with Johan to show them his new studio. Truus allows the older children to climb up the ladder onto the flat roof to look at the view so long as they don't go to the ledge and only lean against the adjoining gable wall. The two women are alone for a moment except for Trudi.

'I'm still convinced only a woman can live this way' says Ailsa, sharing her earlier thoughts. 'A man would change it, put boundaries around it, create rules. He would want his wife to himself more.'

Truus agrees. 'Imagine what Frits would say about it!'

'Don't worry, his family will say plenty on his behalf.'

Truus simply shrugs at this and smiles mischievously. She goes to climb the pull down ladder to the flat roof to check on the children as it is their first time up there. Ailsa stays behind, holding her daughter, gazing out over the meadows. The vast sky and white clouds form the animal shapes they love to guess at, passing in the breeze, currently Trudi's favourite game. Ailsa marvels at what has been created here. She believes she is witnessing history. It is like nothing before. How lucky she feels to be part of it, for Trudi to grow up in this life, with Hanneke and the other children, and to become whatever she wants.

There is another reason for Ailsa's musing. This morning she received a letter informing her that she has won the competition for the design of the new apartment blocks. The judging panel found her ideas highly innovative, not only in the use of prefabricated components, but also in the designation of a portion of the apartments for single women.

She has kept the news to herself for now. Tonight she will tell Johan over a romantic dinner, and hope that he is ready to consider becoming her business partner. Today is about Truus and Gerrit, and the new house on Prins Hendriklaan. She will tell them next week, but doesn't want to steal the limelight today, when they are so excited about the completion of this project.

As she stands with Trudi, in the stillness, on this day, in this home of the future with her dear friends, holding her beloved daughter up to the open corner and pointing to the shapes in the clouds, making Trudi laugh, kissing her, this moment exuding a sense of pure joy, Ailsa makes up her mind. She will put down roots in Utrecht permanently. She loves her life here and can think of nothing more she could possibly want. She has everything she needs. Even the battle for professional recognition no longer worries her. It too will come in time for women. The competition is an indication. They are taking a risk on a woman. Johan is better, Mama is happy to be going home to Applecross, Bridget will look after Knowe Terrace, which Ailsa has decided to convert wholesale into an architectural office. She can oversee it from here. She will set about formalising the business with two offices: Utrecht and Glasgow. Where else would she choose to live and raise her daughter? It is no choice at all. She stays like this for a long time, at peace. Trudi seems to pick up on her mood and copies her.

After a while she snuggles into Trudi's neck and whispers 'I love you my little Truitje. We are going to have a wonderful life.' She whirls her around in the air, dancing with both their arms out, laughing as they spin across the room. Trudi screams with delight as Ailsa stands her on the workbench and beckons for her to jump, hands outstretched. Trudi jumps into her arms.

Johan is back upstairs and has been capturing this intimate scene through his lens without them knowing, forgetting that it is the house he is meant to be filming, so enraptured is he by this woman and her love for her daughter. The house serves as a backdrop to that, enriching its essence with playful light and shade. He knows this is going to be his best work yet. It will show a woman and her child embracing the future and a new attitude to living.

Small Miracle

Gertrude

Utrecht, July 1984

At first I stand and gawp like any tourist, at its very presence, as though witnessing a craft touched down from outer space, boldly taken root in the landscape, sent to deliver a vision of the future, even now, decades on.

From the memory of my lecture notes I recall it was built in the Twenties, yet it is as if new. A small garden sits neatly bordering the property with fine, black steel section between white timber posts and gates. One gate leads to a side door, the other is round the front where the garden faces the ugly motorway flyover. The gleaming white house is as fresh as when it was built. Even the primary colours on simple features: the yellow steel stanchion, the red post beside the main door, are painted as if yesterday. I turn the corner and open the front gate on its well-oiled hinges, walk up the short path and press the bell.

A young woman opens the door almost immediately, as if she might have been standing behind it. I explain who I am and show her the letter. She is polite, as if expecting me, and shows me into a hallway. I see it has a few steps up to a half landing with a sliding door off that must lead to the upper level. We enter a room on the left: a compact study. There is a glass strip at the top of the wall and I can see the ceiling of the hall through it, cleverly giving the impression of one continuous space. In contrast to the exterior, inside looks tired and scuffed, cluttered with books and papers, much in need of a fresh coat of paint, if not a complete refurbishment.

The young woman, friendly but studious in her demeanour and appearance, is saying she needs to explain a few things about Mrs. Schröder before introducing me, as if it is her job to do so. I realise now she wasn't expecting me personally, but that this is a regular occurrence. They call unexpectedly she says, professionals mostly, or architectural students, ring the doorbell speculatively, at which point she intercepts them. To her I will appear like any one of a stream of bespectacled middle-aged disciples of de Stijl. We sit on two hardbacked chairs either side of a desk beside a window that faces the gate where I came in.

'Mrs. Schröder is always happy to show visitors round, but she tires easily now. Since she broke her hip the second time she doesn't try to use the stairs, so remains on the upper floor the whole time. She walks around for fifteen minutes each day for exercise. That is her world now, up there. You will find she wants to talk about the house, and especially about Rietveld. It is her purpose in life, and she will want to show you around exactly as she does with any visitor.'

From the letter I showed her, which perhaps she herself posted, she will know my reason for being here, but no doubt assumes that I know where I fit in, from some back story that I will know already. I decide to make it sound like I know more than I do.

'That's fine. No problem. What age is Mrs. Schroder now?'

'Ninety four last August.'

I should be patient, she is saying, and let Truus Schröder go at her own pace, go through her well rehearsed routine, before asking for the items I have come to collect. She cannot know I am here to uncover a far greater truth.

'Are you her granddaughter?' I ask. She seems protective, concerned for the old lady's welfare.

'No. I am a lodger. But we have an agreement that I also act as carer. I occupy these ground floor rooms. I am on call at night, or if I am away, I ensure someone else stays over. We have a signal if she needs help.'

She doesn't tell me what the signal is.

'I'm writing a thesis on the literary works of de Stijl movement founder Theo van Doesburg, and it is a privilege for me to live here, close to his world. Anyway, the ground floor has been let out many times over the years to lodgers, sometimes three at once, even refugees during the war. Each of the four downstairs rooms has its own door to outside, so it works well. The house has undergone many changes since 1924. Even the windows were blown out during the second world war. And at one time it was a Montessori school, but only for a year.'

'The outside looks new' I say. 'Just as one remembers from old photographs.' At least I recognise it, I tell myself. I know this house professionally. Many wouldn't. That is worth something.

'Yes. It was restored ten years ago and a smaller garden created within a reduced boundary. It used to extend into surrounding fields. The motorway flyover ruined all that in the Sixties. The house has been bequeathed to the city, but any interior restoration is considered too disruptive for Mrs. Schröder. Perhaps one day that will happen. I don't think anyone else will live in it anyway. She's lived here for sixty years. Rietveld said no one else could live in it but her.'

I am dreading the young woman asking my mother's connection, for which I would have no answer and be embarrassed. I realise she may, at this point, know more than I do. For all I know my mother was here at some point; even recently, I dare to think. There are so many facts about Ailsa I don't know. If the old lady has items belonging to her, which are rightly mine, she must of course be dead. I know this, rationally. But at the moment all bets are off. I'm still reeling with shock at the iconic place I have found myself in, and how an Edwardian Glaswegian got to know this famous and unconventional Dutchwoman.

Fortunately she doesn't ask. She does not see my inner child. She sees a middle-aged Scotswoman with a loose connection, like others before me. I must look impatient to get on with my quest, because she says,

'Wait here. I will go up and see if she is feeling up to a visitor now, or if you should come back later.'

I hear her footfall on the steps in the hall, then up more stairs, presumably behind the door. Low voices murmur above my head. Within minutes the young woman is back, and smiles, more welcoming now.

'Truus is very happy you are here. She has been resting, so asks if you can wait half an hour or so until she is ready for you. Do you have time to wait?'

'Of course. I have all the time in the world.'

'Tea?'

We sip our tea which she has carried from a kitchen across the hall, and after a minute she fills the silence with her own rehearsed talk, the one for waiting visitors, in excellent English with a disarming Dutch accent. She is calling her landlady by her first name now.

'In many ways Truus has spent her life ensuring the recognition of Rietveld and the preservation of his work, of the man himself, with the help of discarded notes, newspaper clippings, books, interviews and conversations with people who knew him. Her own contribution is always secondary. It feels a little strange to feminists like myself, and no doubt to your generation, but that has been her life. She was in every sense a feminist in her day, highly unconventional for the time, but nevertheless she lives for his memory.

'This house for her was like a laboratory. And she was from a higher class than him. I think of them like John and Yoko. Rietveld was talented, a genius even, but essentially his interiors were conventionally modern. She changed that in him. Pushed him further. One phrase about him is that he 'regulated light for the sake of joy.' For her, it was all about a new approach to living. She wasn't interested in de Stijl. It was once said that the Rietveld Schröder house was a three-dimensional Mondrian. Truus did not like that at all.'

'Were they an actual couple? Lovers?' She made the John and Yoko comparison after all.

She hesitates. 'It has never been stated explicitly. But yes, despite his wife and six children, they were, for more than thirty years. They rejected bourgeois notions of respectability. Rietveld had his design studio here before he took on larger premises on the Oudegracht.

When his wife died he moved in here with Truus until he died, in this house, the day after his seventy sixth birthday.

'He never thought this was his best work, but she remained convinced. He always looked ahead, to the next thing. He wasn't interested in keeping hold of things - papers, sketches and so on. Not her though. She saved everything. She told me she used to retrieve them from the bin! She was so convinced of his legacy even from an early stage.'

She shows me a book with an inscription.

'I looked for a little book for you, my dear Truusje, and the first thing I saw in the shop window struck me because of the title - I know nothing about the author or the subject, but (now that I've known you for more than half of your life) the title exactly reflects the tremendous appreciation I feel for you as an individual and for that honest, intense attitude to life of yours that you bring to each and every situation with such insatiable fervour. Regardless whom you meet, you always discover a small miracle in each. With regards to you, dear Truus, the word 'small' merely guarantees the absence of my personal exaggeration.'

The dedication is in The Small Miracle by Paul Gallico, which he bought for her 70th birthday.

'They designed a number of houses together, which Truus funded. She escorted him on his business trips abroad and kept records. Because she was unable to produce technical drawings herself, and had little knowledge of structure or materials, she took correspondence courses, but she was ashamed of her ignorance and did these under a false name. She did write articles and give lectures on design though.

'After the children left she rented the lower rooms out. Her bedroom upstairs was converted into a kitchen, which you will see when you go up. For one year she rented it out and lived in a flat designed by her and Rietveld on the Erasmus Avenue over there. She had bought the piece of land opposite when building on the polder was relaxed, so she could determine what she looked onto.'

She points towards the motorway viaduct.

'For part of that year, the house was a Montessori kindergarten, but she wasn't happy and soon returned. But then it got worse. The municipality decided in 1963 to extend the ring road right past the house. Rietveld wanted to demolish the house then. She felt the same, but decided to keep the house anyway.

'Shortly after that decision, Rietveld died. For years, Truus has made efforts to preserve the house for the future. The Rietveld Schröderhuis Foundation was her initiative, along with her children. It has been agreed that after her death the house will be managed by the Centraal Museum. On her ninetieth birthday she was awarded a knighthood in the Order of Orange-Nassau, for services to the city.

'She is a special woman. A strong personality with pronounced ideas. Somebody who has spent her life promoting simplicity and independence.'

This is all really, really interesting, but...

There is a rhythmical tapping from above. A walking stick perhaps. This must be the signal. Crude but effective.

'She is ready for you now.'

The impact is profound, such brilliant light in contrast to the ground floor. Emerging from the darkness onto the first floor is like climbing onto the upper deck of a ship. I arrive at a landing which has a rooflight above. There is clutter everywhere, boxes and papers, furniture. At first I do not see her but then there is a movement. Sitting hunched over by a window, beside a door out to a balcony, is an old woman sorting through papers.

She looks up and the first thing I register is her smile, then her grey hair pulled back into a bun, laughing eyes, immediate warmth. She is struggling to stand on seeing my arrival at the top of the stairs, and reaches for a stick, then leans on furniture and boxes to navigate her way. This space of no more than eight metres in each direction is her world. I go to help her. I want so badly to touch her. She is stooped over, back hunched, as though at one time she has been taller. She looks up and cups my face in her weathered hands, nodding. *Hallo again, kleintje. Let me look at you.* She takes in my features, tactile in her familiarity, leaning onto my shoulder now with one hand.

Ah, you have your mother's eyes.

She gestures towards a chair. *You have not come here to look at the house. Please, sit down.* The young woman downstairs underestimated her.

I realise, somewhat bizarrely, that I am probably sitting in the original Red Blue chair designed by Rietveld in 1918, not a copy.

She holds my hand and wipes away a tear.

You look so like Ailsa. I miss her still.

So she is dead. It is too soon to tell this delightful old lady that I know nothing. I want to hear her first. Like a detective I will start with an open question. Classic interview technique. Learned at the feet of my father, literally. We sit close, holding hands. 'You met her first in London?'

'Ah yes. London was my first liberated time. I felt like I was in a new world. Ailsa had been my sister's pen friend, and it was arranged that she would come and stay with the family I was with for a time. We had similar interests. Art, and so on. Then Ailsa introduced me to Arts and Crafts and I never looked back.'

The white attic in Knowe Terrace.

'I went on to Germany after that, but that time in England made me see the world differently. Then after I married, it was a difficult time. I was not happy. I was afraid to leave as it would hurt my father, whom I loved a lot. Ailsa was a great friend to me then.'

She talks as if I know more than I do, making assumptions. I desperately want to ask questions, but don't want to interrupt her flow. We have time, so long as she doesn't tire. She refers randomly to events, slipping in references to 'Ailsa', or 'your mother', and 'you.' I feel like I'm part of a surrealist stage play. Her narrative drifts back and forth, so I let it, to build a picture. Inevitably it is mostly about this house, or her lover, whom she oddly refers to by his surname, Rietveld.

'I've lived here for sixty years. I suppose I kind of got stuck. It became my life, telling people about this house. The kitchenette you see over there was originally my bedroom. I sleep in the girls' divan area now, here, where we are sitting.

'You see, the old world was brown, and de Stijl wanted to make a white one. A modern one. I wasn't intentionally trying to create something modern. I was more interested in where the sun rises and sets. For me, contact with the outside world was very important. I wanted the new house to be a place where people could exchange ideas. But contact with the outside world for me also meant contact with nature, especially with the sky. Light and air mean so much to me. I like to see a lot of trees and greenery. It's really all about the sky and the light.'

She continues, some of which I was told downstairs.

'Rietveld was so upset when they built the motorway. It destroyed the house for him. He wanted to demolish it, but we kept it. The house never lost its joy. Rietveld thought it too complicated when it was new. He worried about details but later when he lived here he said, 'it's really quite a nice house.' People came to stare. They thought it would collapse like a house of cards; that the planes of the exterior walls would separate.

'I just wanted to make propaganda and have an exchange of ideas. A declaration of how a modern woman can live her life.

'I have read a lot, all my life. Now I get tired, I just read poems, or this book here.' She shows me a blue book filled with Rietveld's texts. She smiles. 'What I call 'my bible.' Yes, that Catholic education never leaves you completely.

'After the restoration I loved to sit outside again on the blue bench like I used to. It made me very happy. Like being young again. The same bench that once looked onto meadows and canals. But I can't get down the stairs now. Living in the Rietveld Schröderhuis has been wonderful. It's different every day.

'It required a certain discipline though. Unnecessary clutter or things that were not in the right place affected the space and that bothered me. Therefore, I taught myself to be 'neat'. As you can see that didn't last. That's life!'

We gaze wordlessly at the clutter covering every surface, including a painted floor of different colours, now scuffed and faded.

'Later I thought the colour layout was too busy. There were drawbacks, but it was too late to change. The children were told to jump over the white bit at the top of stairs when they came home from school if I had cleaned it. I hated making them do that but they told me years later that they loved it! I was not a strict mother. The house inevitably became untidy.

'The partitions can be closed or half closed. I still close them at night. It is a ritual. I like rituals.'

I'm thinking about my dream. The Japanese screen.

'This storage unit came later. It's like a Rubik's Cube with these boxes sliding, don't you think. We stored the film projector in it. It housed a gramophone too. I must not forget. I have a film for you.'

She has a film for me? Another mental note.

'The sliding screens and built in furniture were my idea, and the sloping shelf facing the fields for the children to do their homework.

'There was no contract. This was not a business arrangement. We made the house together. Maybe you can say that the inside was more me and the outside was more Rietveld but, you know, the outside was designed from the inside, so it's not possible to separate it. But what does it matter? On the birth of a child we don't ask who made which part.

'With the exception of An and Ailsa, there was nobody who really understood me. Even a cousin who was the only Schröder family member to visit his Aunt Truus after I broke with Catholicism, even he did not understand the grey room on the Biltstraat. 'It looks like a kitchen, Aunt Truus,' he said.

She is distracted now, speaking of things I don't understand. Biltstraat? Grey room?

'Back in our old apartment, which you were in a lot but you probably don't remember, Kurt Schwitters, the artist, came after my husband died, and gave a Dadaist recital. It was great fun. You were there that night with your mother, and Johan.'

My mother was at a Dadaist evening? Where was my father in all of this? Hardly his cup of tea. And who is Johan? The mystery man from Knowe Terrace?

'You children were at the top of the stairs with the maid, listening to Schwitters booming out his Dadaist poems. You all loved it but the maid said it was 'more than shocking.' Do you remember any of that?'

'I don't, but I did teach Dada in art history classes. Perhaps some of it went in' I say.

I don't mean this. I am convinced she is speaking about someone else, and any minute now we will both realise it.

'You are an art teacher? I knew you would be artistic, like Hanneke, my daughter. You did everything that she did. Drawing, making little models. She was a bit older than you of course.'

'I'm actually an interior designer...' I trail off. I don't want to talk about me.

I'm going to interject.

'Did I spend a lot of time with Hanneke?'

'Oh yes. You followed her everywhere. I think if you had grown up here, as we wanted, you would have followed a similar path. Anyway, it sounds like you did.'

As we wanted? As who wanted?

'All of Rietveld's children ended up in something to do with the arts. They were more troubled though, with dyslexia, and having such a famous father of course.'

'What did Hanneke go on to do?'

'She is an architect. She teaches interior design too, in Richmond, Virginia. She has lived over there, in New York too, for twenty years. She worked with Rietveld a lot over the years too, on a number of projects, right from when she was a teenager. She wants to come home now though, to help with the restoration of the house. Han says this house is 'an original, new attitude to life given physical form."

She gets up slowly and, seeming to take forever, moves cautiously across to an old projector with a reel of film already set up in it.

'This belongs to you. Not the projector, but the film. I also have photos, sketchbooks and so on. You can watch this film while I rest. After, I will tell you more about the early days. I expect it was very hard for you growing up without her. Your mother.'

Hard? That's an understatement.

But where was she all my life? Did Ailsa hand me over to my father so she could live a bohemian life abroad? I've read of such mothers, especially in the Twenties and Thirties. What am I about to see in this film? My mother like an F. Scott Fitzgerald heroine, sipping champagne in a feather boa with her lover Johan, spending decadent weekends in Paris, while I languished back in Glasgow, unloved? I am uneasy now. Is this what my father meant? Do I even want to see this film? *Your mammy was a lovely person hen.* Bridget's words. But that could have meant anything. Lovely as in *glamorous*?

The projector is already positioned to face a white wall in the space that Truus tells me used to be her son Binnert's room. She closes the surrounding partition and pulls down a window blind.

'You will see yourself sitting next to Han in the film, having a picnic. We are all there, sitting on the floor' she laughs.

'You know, Han went on to become one of the first female architects in the Netherlands, like your mother was in Glasgow, but much later. Your mother understood space. She learned so much from her training here during the war. I always remember her in here on New Year's Day, you too; we moved in properly that day, the first of January 1925. My sister and her husband came, and her friend Jacob. We had such a lovely party, the first one in this house. It was just as I'd imagined for so long, all of us together, in such a beautiful space.'

The projector begins to whir and a grainy black and white moving image flickers into life. Truus is showing me how to switch it off when the film ends. But I'm not listening.

I'm sorry. Did you just say that my mother was an **architect?**

Crimson Tulips

Ailsa

Utrecht, 10 July 1925

It is the freshest morning yet this year, promising heat, the Friday of Trudi's kindergarten party to mark the end of term. The canal water sparkles like diamonds as laden narrowboats wend their way through the old quarter. Both upper and lower levels of the Oudegracht are bustling, the early housewives on the upper wharf waving their greetings across the little bridges, barrows of brightly coloured tulips being set up by the market traders, and workers on the flat barges stopping off at the cellars along the wharf-basement, discharging their wares in rapid exchange. Shouts echo up the steps and down the herringbone brick side streets. Everywhere is fresh and cool in this early hour before the heat takes over.

Ailsa smiles to herself as she watches from the open top floor window, listening to the sounds below and taking in the sights and smells from her seat at the table as she encourages Trudi to finish her breakfast, satisfied that she made the right decision to remain in Utrecht, this special place in her heart. Johan is well again, and the commission for new apartments they have taken on together, the competition, on Laan van Minsweerd, close to Truus' house, affords an opportunity to provide solutions: radical fittings, homes for single women, and innovative building techniques. Flat roofs too are becoming desirable, and this aspect, on the edge of town facing meadows and lush polder, is ideal for social housing.

Ailsa and Johan have each kept their separate apartments as agreed, but they work out of her premises. Living above the studio, Trudi and Ailsa have all they need in the two reception rooms. Back in Glasgow, Knowe Terrace has been officially converted to office use, with Bridget in her annexe keeping a managerial eye over the whole operation, servicing the requirements of Lisa and her staff. There are five women now, the house fully equipped with as many drawing boards, meeting room furniture, library shelves and plan chests. The dining room is now a crèche. Bridget has the kitchen and annexe as her domain, with Papa's study as her sitting room.

Ailsa registered the change of use for the property when Flora moved back to Applecross at Christmas, happy to spend her twilight years with Catherine in the cottage beside the schoolhouse where they grew up. Ailsa is looking forward to taking Trudi there this summer, Johan too, so he can finally meet Flora, whose health is not good these days. Ailsa misses her mother a great deal, but they write every week. They will stay first in Knowe Terrace, in the attic flat, which has been retained as a separate apartment for Ailsa's use. She will use the time to sit down with Lisa. The two women correspond regularly and mutually agree any major business and design decisions but this visit will allow them to look over the work in progress together. Ailsa plans to make this trip each summer, combining it with an annual holiday in Applecross.

Meanwhile Truus is taking the children to Switzerland, leaving Gerrit to execute the contentious colour application to the upper level of her new house. He is resisting advice from the de Stijl group, who still think they know best about colour. Gerrit is less bothered about de Stijl principles and more about how the colours he wants, for instance a pale yellow to *reflect the blond hair of a Dutch girl,* or the greys he is adamant about in terms of tone, and where he wants primaries and neutrals to go to reflect the function of each space. The sliding partition positions are integral to that. Truus is getting out of it, as she says, as she couldn't care less about the colour. Ailsa hopes she will not live to regret it.

The only apprehension Ailsa has about the trip to Glasgow is Michael. She can never fully forget about him. Domiciling herself and Trudi in the Netherlands has been about lifestyle and work, Johan too of course, and Truus, but she knows that having the North Sea between her and the man who, the last time she saw him, became deranged and a threat to his own daughter, is part of it. Now that Trudi is almost three, and settled, Ailsa does not want him to put that at risk. Nevertheless, although she will be careful not to encounter him, she will refuse to hide if it comes to it. She wants to show Johan her home city in all its splendour, take him along the Clyde to where her father built his business, wander at leisure around the Victorian mercantile architecture, through the west end to the University. She will show him her beloved Pollokshields, and the School of Art, then they will take Trudi for tea and cakes at Miss Cranston's.

As the holiday has drawn nearer, Ailsa has been having nightmares about Michael. In these he is berating her, following her at a slow but relentless pace, his walking stick tapping rhythmically on the ground, always close behind her. She woke in a sweat last night only to find that the sound of his walking stick was a tree branch tapping against the glass. This has not been helped by the fact that there is a man in Utrecht who has the same unfortunate gait as Michael. She has seen him several times, always just out of reach, rounding a corner or turning into one of the side streets off the Oudegracht. Lack of sleep and an overly vivid imagination are the cause of this *déjà vu* brought about by the imminent return to Glasgow, she has decided, and so she has not mentioned it to Johan or even to Truus.

Ailsa drops Trudi off at the kindergarten on her way to the site, where she is meeting Johan with the structural engineer later. They are walking this morning, as Trudi has a box of cakes, baked last night, to take for the party. Ailsa realises with annoyance that she has left a vital drawing back at the studio that is essential to the meeting so, once the usual blowing of kisses and waving goodbye with Trudi in the doorway is over, takes the quickest route back, along Hamburgerstraat. There is that man again, disappearing onto Korte Nieuwstraat. She shakes her head to clear it and goes up to the studio to pick up the drawing and retrieve her bicycle from outside. As she looks across the canal from behind the glass, she sees the man staring directly back at her from behind a barrow of crimson tulips.

It is Michael.

Pink Geraniums

Gertrude

Glasgow, September 1985

'Some people turn barns into houses. We have turned two houses into a barn.'
Richard Rogers

The call, from the Chairwoman of the local heritage group, surprises me, given that I have spent months trying to win this group over in support of my planning application, without success. Perhaps the article, on Richard Rogers' recent and far more controversial Chelsea family home, which I posted to her, patiently explaining once again the rationale, has done the trick. Not only am I to speak to the committee but also to give an illustrated talk to all members. I expect their vanity at being seen to be open minded, at least in association with one of the elite, combined with their natural curiosity, has swung it. I aim to convince them of the merits of the Knowe Terrace design, that how we live our lives has changed beyond recognition since these nineteenth century houses were built, and thus the way we use the space in our homes has changed accordingly.

By the time the evening event comes around, I have carefully put together a full carousel of slides selected to flatter, not patronise, their knowledge, yet with enough balance of visual and technical to demonstrate expertise beyond what they will be familiar with.

I sense my new confidence as I dress for the event. All my life I have operated on the periphery of groups such as this, not committing to joining, which I never could; rather I remained slightly apart, so no-one discovered my sense of inadequacy, my false persona drawn from those I sought to emulate. Here no-one knows me except Margaret. I am a blank canvas.

I slip into the silk Issey Miyake, the one I ordered through House of Fraser after seeing it on the beautiful Czech architect Eva Jiřičná, in a Sunday supplement, being interviewed about her high-tech suspended steel and glass staircase in the new Joseph store. My clothes receive interested looks in Glasgow I've noticed, where in London I was forever running to keep up. I look at my reflection. I have settled into a shape and weight that suits my age. My hair is its natural peppered grey with dark curls left untamed. I put on my oversized square framed glasses and assess the final impression. Shades of grey. Here they wear their bright Hermes scarves and colourful Jaeger sweaters as a kind of uniform. My London years allowed me to hover close enough, and for long enough, alongside the great and the good of the design world, literally, at my professional body's events and suchlike, so I do know how to dress with taste.

I joined that society of course, out of necessity, an associate who did not associate. Happy to manoeuvre into position near the likes of Jean Muir and Gordon Russell, Terence Conran, even Richard himself once, with one of those too many cheap house wines in hand, cripplingly unable to make small talk, pretending to be searching someone out who had yet to arrive. I would smile at everyone and no-one, not able to overhear actual conversations but close enough to mentally bank styles and mannerisms for later use, before repairing to hide in the powder room prior to an unremarked drunken escape to the nearest Tube station.

I can make out Margaret waiting to intercept me at the arched entrance to the Scots renaissance style Burgh Halls, designed by Henry Clifford, a revered local venue on the edge of Maxwell Park whose ownership is in limbo at present between the Social Work Department and a new Charitable Trust hoping to take over and avoid a catastrophic public sale. Its deep red rock-faced ashlar is glistening from the short but heavy shower that preceded my walk from Knowe Terrace over the brow of Leslie Road, down Newark Drive and through the park, where memories of walks with Bridget to feed the ducks can still make my heart ache. I have learned to push away the thoughts that will come next and threaten to engulf me, by concentrating on the moment. As I wave and approach the hall, darker memories do start to flood in as I see the road beyond, of my father creeping behind me in his car, following my every move, but I force myself to push these away too, my self-esteem much required for the task ahead. The evening sun has returned and will shortly be setting behind the limes that line the perimeter of the park, gold already and promising autumn on a cool September breeze. A rainbow has appeared beyond the boating pond, which I will take as a good omen. I focus on the beauty of all this.

Margaret has her white hair cut short these days, expensively I can tell. She was the mature one even when we were sixteen, an old soul, always looking out for me, never judging. Tonight she looks more nervous than I feel, hands twisting together or fidgeting with the string of pearls draped over a pale blue cashmere twinset, greeting members as they pass. The Craigholme former pupils have always intimidated her, and she has spent the best part of her life seeking their approval, a fact she doesn't hide from me and I try to understand. Perhaps in her own way she has lived a life not dissimilar to mine: coveting others who fit in with such ease.

Despite the years apart and very different lives, we kept up contact through letters and phone calls to share life events, Margaret as wife and mother, me as neither, and we share the same sense of humour. Margaret married her pilot after the war, settled into the expected West Pollokshields way of life, raising two well mannered and spirited children who attended the same private schools as their parents, whilst running her comfortable and spacious villa in the Avenues. They recently downsized to one of the socially desirable and now listed H.E. Clifford tenement flats in the prestigious Terregles Avenue. Her husband David, a *decent man*, progressed in his law career and is now retired. Margaret was of course brought up to this life, with its code of practice (weekly cleaning lady, theatre, bridge, golf, art club), loved by the already middle-aged parents when she was growing up, who she in turn cared for in their declining years. Such decent people, her mother and father, non-judgemental, intellectuals and Fabians, so kind to me in their home that I never wanted to leave. They treated me as equal, and Margaret and I were trusted, respected, in that safe, unpretentious house.

Margaret is happy enough I think, her outlet in groups such as this, dinner parties, coffee mornings and local gossip, her two holidays per year with David a combination of sun and culture. If she has struggled emotionally, or secretly longed to rebel, or indeed has rebelled, I am not aware of it, as she is fiercely loyal to her somewhat smug husband. It was never a life I could have had of course.

We embrace and share a private joke about the former pupils I am about to encounter, then she ushers me through to the main hall. I am pounced on by the Chairwoman, who I vaguely recall was Head Girl, her glee reminiscent of a tricoteuse at the guillotine, as the assembled members drink wine (I am now teetotal) and chatter among themselves, until it is time to take to the podium. Margaret never leaves my side, knowing instinctively that work is my saviour in social situations, and introduces me as a diversion to the young technician who has kindly set up my slide carousel and the film reel in separate projectors.

The lights dim and a sea of middle aged wives and their dutiful husbands take to their seats, quietening gradually, coughing expectantly, as the stained glass windows with their masonic symbolism all around us diffuse the dying glow of sunset. This accidental combination gives a theatrical sense of gravitas to the proceedings.

This I can do. I sit where I've been told, to the left of the podium. Public speaking ceased to be a problem some years ago, at least when I have something to impart that I believe in. Head Girl begins with an update on the ongoing battle with the council over the Burgh Halls, then reads my résumé word for word from a sheet of paper as though I am a stranger to these parts, which irks me, as it is meant to do. I scan the audience. I am aware that some will be women with whom I went to school briefly, as unrecognisable to me as I am to them, unless we re-introduce ourselves and possibly recall earlier facial features, now buried, lined or plumped with extra or sun ravaged flesh, or if I see a familiar name on the attendance sheet. Still, this feels like a test.

I left this city forty five years ago, and will be something of a curiosity, as perhaps I was even then, the girl with the odd name from Knowe Terrace back from England. Margaret and I were thrown together: she the compensatory child born after both of her older brothers, whom she never met, were obliterated in the trenches before her birth; I the oddball surviving in a house without love. Her parents, in their late forties by the time she went to school, cherished her but were so consumed by grief that she spent her childhood listening to stories about her brothers and the waste of war, as though that had been her parents' real life, not this one with her. She too was a misfit among the Craigholme girls, with their complacency and sense of entitlement, and thus we sought each other out and have remained friends since.

I begin by showing recent extensions to nineteenth century houses in other cities, notably San Francisco and London.

'These extensions are variations on a theme but the architectural approach has lessons for Pollokshields, the properties being built in the same era as the villas and townhouses here. Similar problems exist for old properties in any city and it is these that I want to address.'

My theme is developing now as the carousel clicks round on its turntable: how we inhabit structures built for the demands of a different time, the original houses expressing a lifestyle that relied upon domestic help. I explain how the rooms concerning these uses were suppressed to the rear of the house while the set pieces of the reception rooms dominated the front.

'Today's family is more relaxed, more open, more likely to enjoy an open kitchen space with easy access to a rear garden. The house to be converted can act as a solid base from which to add light through contemporary materials and structure".

I focus in on materials: glass, steel, even weathered wood. 'These complement the sandstone-built houses and age with dignity. The result does not clash, nor is it a pastiche of an earlier style, but adds something richer. The façade remains intact, the streetscape undisturbed. What occurs when one enters such a residence is to experience light and space that these contemporary materials and technology allow.'

I move on to show Richard and Ruth Rogers' newly converted Georgian home in Chelsea, the *pièce de résistance*. Hidden behind the Georgian façade of a smart London stucco rendered brick terrace, with tall uniform windows hosting pink geraniums in outside boxes, lies a dramatic contemporary living space: industrial staircase, bright colour, natural light, double height. Richard calls it a *piazza*, no doubt a nod to his birthplace of Florence. I take pride in throwing in anecdotal information that only a devoted follower such as myself would have.

Even I have never seen a space quite so minimal, so devoid of the detritus of living. Nowhere in the photographs of the open plan living and kitchen space can be seen the usual kitchen utensils, piles of newspapers, scatter cushions, plants, vases of flowers, carpets, ornaments. *No clutter.* One imagines a room off this space jammed full with the Rogers' family possessions, the *stuff* one gathers over a lifetime, but perhaps not. It differs too in its high-tech style, adopting elements of his Pompidou Centre. For my audience, thinking of their three piece suites, their oak dining furniture, that coveted teak sideboard, the lace covered side tables, a piano bedecked with family photographs, the ubiquitous table lamps, the best china in a glass cabinet, kettles, jars, magazines, book collections, this must seem like an impossibility, certainly not practical. Their lifestyle and habit of filling a room with collected objects represents personal status embodied in materialism.

Even the more discerning ones, or perhaps especially these, who will have the more modern Scandinavian or Habitat influenced homes, will be wondering where on earth Richard and Ruth have hidden their kitchen jars, spice racks, candles, floor cushions and rag rugs. They will also reassure themselves that these essential items have been shut in a room out of sight for the camera. Who can live like this? No-one. There are a few books, and one (one!) piece of wall art: a mural, a single column of Andy Warhol's Mao Tse-tung portraits.

Only now do I present my own project. The façade is retained, so from Knowe Terrace one would register no change to the streetscape. Inside however, the entire first floor is removed, the deep open space with set back mezzanine and steel staircase interconnecting the two levels. The glass to the rear onto a raised decking level outside can slide open or closed according to the time of day and the season. The kitchen is almost part of the outdoors. Everywhere is space and light, design that reflects how we live today. Open, transparent family life, minimalist, easily maintained, joyous.

I sum up by showing slides of famous houses around the world, each ahead of their time, to illustrate how progress is always controversial and takes time to bed in. I finish with the Rietveld Schröder House. Imagine, I say, how this design was received by the city of Utrecht in 1924, when everywhere was heavy, dark brickwork, grandiose mansions with decorative cornicing and ornate plasterwork detail. The last slide is a grainy black and white image of its interior taken in 1925.

As it clicks off and the glare of the projector fills the retractable screen. I thank the audience and sit down, indicating Head Girl may take over. The room breaks into spontaneous applause.

There are questions from the floor, but I am sensing the mood to be one of support. Members try to outperform one another, as always in these situations, to trade superior knowledge. There are a few difficult questions, but nothing I can't deflect. I have done my homework. At the end of the day it comes down to taste. There will always be those who would wish to preserve a traditional interior at any cost, for the sake of history, yet the arguments around societal and lifestyle change are compelling. We end on an upbeat note with another round of applause as Margaret presents me with an Interflora bouquet.

They top up their wine, light each other's cigarettes and the chatter begins. I am introduced to one or two of Margaret's more enlightened friends and the evening closes pleasantly enough. Head Girl will rally her troops to ensure no more letters of objection wing their way to the council planning department.

I make my excuses, promising Margaret that I will be round to hers in the morning for coffee and a debrief, and gladly step outside into the cool air. In the gathering dusk I breathe deeply then turn to begin the short walk over the hill past the converted villas back to Knowe

Terrace. There is a young woman outside smoking. She introduces herself as Claire Mathieson. We shake hands awkwardly around my bouquet and her cigarette. She is local but works term-time in Aberdeen, a lecturer at the Scott Sutherland School of Architecture. She found my talk inspirational. The ideas I put forward apply to the granite city equally. Do I know Aberdeen? And, if it is not too impertinent, would I consider giving this same talk to her students next term, expenses paid?

I have found my place in the world. My own. Could it be she is inviting me because I gave an interesting talk on a valid architectural advance? Or is it perhaps because I have uncovered the life I was meant to have and some sense of self worth?

Most likely, it will simply be that, before I clicked off the slide projector with the last image of the Rietveld Schröder House, almost casually I said the line I had prepared: *I lived in this house as a small child, in 1925, when it was first built, with the Schröder family. This is me on the left.*

The final black and white image was the one of me with Han, standing in front of the table at the open corner window, my chubby face serious in contrast to hers. Smiling bravely, Hanneke has her arm thrown protectively around my shoulder. It must be winter because there are no leaves on the trees outside. We are looking diagonally across the room, directly into the lens. The photographer, Johan probably, must be beside the stairwell. A middle-aged woman is standing to the side, almost out of shot, nearest to me. I am holding myself stiffly in a little double-breasted coat, buttoned up tightly, and wearing a hat. Truus told me this photograph was taken on the day I left, as a keepsake. The woman is Bridget, who has come to take me home.

Lush Polder

Ailsa

Utrecht, 10 July 1925

A jolt passes through her. Michael, unmistakable in his small wire rimmed glasses and stuffy pompous suit, conspicuous here where the men dress casually for work in summer, usually light poplar or linen. He is staring directly at Ailsa from across the canal. Instinctively she tugs the mesh curtains closed across the window with one frantic movement.

When she looks again he is gone. Her heart is pounding, with fear but anger too. She would have more respect, feel less threatened, if he knocked at her door and was open about his presence. But that is not Michael's style. He will intercept her now when she leaves, for he knows she has seen him. How long has he been following her? Days at least. And Trudi: he must know where her kindergarten is on Herenstraat. Trudi will be safe. The teachers would not let her go with a stranger, even if he says he is her father. Anyway, they assume Johan is her father as he picks her up often and they know him.

She paces the studio, trying to think how best to manage this intrusion, no, this *intimidation*. She must get to the site, find Johan. She tries to remain calm but her breathing is rapid and her mind is confused. Why is he here? How did he know to find her? Then the realisation hits her. The papers to register the new business and branch office at Knowe Terrace include her address here on the Oudegracht as head office. He has no doubt been scrutinising her tax returns over a period of time, then seen the Glasgow business registered here, indicating that Utrecht is her permanent residence. He has come all this way, and for what? To use his daughter as an excuse? He never cared about her before. He surely will not pretend to start now.

Of course she knows that he will. Why did she not report the violent incident to the police at the time, when they had evidence, that day when Michael lost all reason? The letter from Robin Asher would still be relevant, but it would not stand up in court. Michael will claim he has every right to see his daughter, perhaps even demand that she return to Scotland. Why did she allow his name on the birth certificate? For misguided reasons of propriety. If Frits were alive, she thinks, he would know what to do. She must find Johan. Of course. Michael will have seen a Johan Peeters registered as a partner in the business. That is unquestionably what has tipped him over the edge and brought him here.

She locks up hastily and decides to take the route along the canalside through the Museumquarter towards Laan van Minsweerd for the scheduled site visit. She pushes her bicycle over the first bridge. If she cycles she can move faster than Michael. His leg has not improved in the past two years by the look of him. She mounts and pedals as fast as she can. She will be too early for Johan but at least the foreman and his three apprentices will be there. Michael will not make a scene in front of the men. He is too much of a coward. All she has to do is wait for Johan to arrive. If Michael has been following her for days he will know where the site is, for she is there on a daily basis at the moment, overseeing this stage of construction.

The men are not there when she arrives. The site is deserted. Felix will have suggested they go somewhere cool to eat an early lunch seeing as they start work before most people are up and about. Perhaps they are across in the fields taking shade behind one of the water pumps. It is calm, except for insects buzzing, and an oppressive heat already beginning to hang over the exposed site. Ailsa does not feel safe enough from Michael to wait inside, where tools lie around and could, at a moment's notice, become weapons of rage. She climbs the scaffolding ladder on the front of the apartments, deft from years spent on building sites, and instinctively moves back from the edge. The scaffold stands proud of the flat roof by enough height to act as a guard rail. She positions herself where she has a vantage point but is protected by the shade and bulk of the raised central core section. The form is similar to Truus' house nearby, with this same small raised structure, head height, over the central portion and forming a stairwell rooflight. From here she can see in both directions, including Truus' house on the next block, and to the polder in front, its stretches of water dotted with windmills in the distance. Johan is not due to arrive for half an hour, so she will simply wait.

When she hears the rattle of the scaffold ladder she breathes a sigh of relief. It will be Felix back from his dinner break, or Johan arrived early with the engineer. If it is Johan she will tell him and they will go together to pick up Trudi, then arrange to meet with a family lawyer. She looks over and recoils in horror. Like the tortoise in Trudi's story book, slow, deliberate, unrelenting, as in her own nightmare, Michael is patiently scaling the scaffold ladder. He drags his bad leg up each metal rung with some difficulty, using one hand to propel the inert knee, but he is managing the ascent, half way up already. He looks up to see her glancing over.

'Ailsa' he says calmly, reasonably. 'I only want to talk.'

She will not, cannot, reply, but has no escape. He has her trapped.

'Ailsa, I have come all this way, surely you will not refuse to *speak* to me. I have papers for you to sign and suggestions for how you can best manage your taxes and property.' He sounds measured, rational, like Michael can so easily sound. My God, she thinks. He will never give up. He has brought documents by hand that could have been mailed to her by a clerk in the tax office.

' How is Gertrude?' He is panting, hot and indignant at having to climb to her.

The very sound of the name no one apart from Michael has ever used for her daughter takes Ailsa back to that day when he lost control. She moves away from the scaffold as he continues to climb. The heat is making her lightheaded, the buzzing insects now a cacophony in her head. She looks down, distraught, through the square rooflight aperture in the centre, thinking she will be able to open it and reach the ladder that clips on, as in Truus' house, where they climb up to sit while the children play on the flat roof. She imagines she can hear children's voices below, Trudi laughing at something Han has just said. But no ladder is there, and no children. The voices are coming from a nearby school where pupils are having their playtime. This is not Truus' house. This is the municipal apartment block that is only half finished. She backs away, dizzy with the thought of Michael's presence. She will sit for a moment against the gable wall and face him down. He cannot hurt her there and she can keep him talking until the men get here.

Michael's head and shoulders appear over the edge, framed by a cloudless sky and open fields behind him. He is not as crippled as he would have people believe, she thinks. He is clearly angry from the effort, trying with difficulty to step over the parapet, waving papers at her from the ladder and mumbling something about Knowe Terrace.

'..if you will not discuss your tax affairs I cannot be responsible for the outcome...'

In that moment, when he realises her look of repulsion is for him, his face twists into the expression she remembers: the one of utter disdain for all women, barely below the surface.

'...these people here are a laughing stock; this man, this lunatic...he has turned you into his harlot. He is using you. No decent man would...'

Ailsa knows Michael's tipping point and he has reached it. His rage takes over and he loses all sense of perspective. She knows he will use every ounce of strength to pull himself over the parapet by the guardrail. On the baking flat roof she can see a hammer and chisel, both within his reach, and within hers. She will get to them and drop them through the rooflight aperture out of harm's way. But she cannot move, cannot bring herself any closer to him. She is frozen to the spot. Her legs are shaking now, uncontrollably.

'... it's not good for the child....'

Even as she backs up to the gable wall, even then, in the searing midday heat, the relentless noise filling her head, louder now, like a chant, drugging her, making her flushed, as though she might faint at any moment; even as her foot reaches an edge where no scaffolding has been erected, she still does not make the connection. Only then, when there is nothing to lean against, no gable wall, only a void, as she tries in vain to grab onto anything, does she think for the second time *this is not Truus' house*. There is no gable wall at its back. It is detached on four sides. She knows this. She is here every day. She designed it. How could she have been confused? Why did she think she was at Prins Hendriklaan, a hundred metres away? Even at the moment when it is too late and there is nothing, nothing to grab onto or lean against, even as she walks backwards, *as if in a trance* witnesses will say later, and lands with a crack at the rear of the apartment building, she is thinking this.

*

A crowd gathers, within minutes, out of nowhere. People come running from neighbouring houses and apartments adjacent to the back of the site, and from side streets. Three women, who were chatting from nearby apartment windows opened wide in the heat, saw a woman fall. She seemed to lose her footing, they tell the policeman who arrives, blowing his whistle. *The woman must have expected a guard rail to be there like the other three sides, but the men had not finished erecting it when they went for their lunch. Or else she wasn't in her right mind. She seemed to walk backwards as if in a trance.* No one else was on site. This apartment building stands isolated, facing open meadows. *The workmen were not there. We saw them leave earlier and go off towards the cafe on Prins Hendriklaan.*

Others, including Felix and the men, back from their break, hear the commotion and look, as people will, shaking their heads as they stare, unable to lift their eyes from the blood spreading over sprawled crimson hair, black blood baked already, in the searing heat, onto the brick paviors. The ambulance arrives and they are asked to please move back, make room. The small crowd shuffles onto Pieter Saenredamstraat. Felix is speaking with the policeman, clearly upset. He cannot understand.

The women, arms folded and muttering with authority to the group of bystanders, are tutting and head-shaking now. They have seen her up there before. *A building site is no place for a woman.*

No-one pays attention to the insignificant little man in the brown suit with the walking stick, one of the many who saw nothing. He mingles easily with the crowd, shaking his head, nodding silently along with them as if part of the conversation, even though he cannot understand a word. No-one gives him a second thought. A local office worker out for his lunchtime walk probably, and a cripple, poor man. Only Ailsa, from where she lies, unable to move or to speak, fading in and out of consciousness, sees the scuffed brogues, the pressed turn ups of pinstriped trousers, the brass tip of a walking stick tap-tap-tapping on the hard ground. As he turns to leave, anonymous in the dispersing crowd, as she tries to move her lips or lift a hand to point but cannot seem to manage either, before the blackness descends and envelops her, forcing her to surrender to its finality, she has only one thought.

Trudi. He must not take Trudi.

Polished Twilight

Gertrude

Aberdeen, November 1985

He turns up the lapels of the signature black overcoat and brushes back silver hair with his right hand; same old reflex. Through the damp fog that blankets this polished grey city at twilight, carried in on the wind from the North Sea, he appears to shiver. To the world tonight, Daniel Ogilvie cuts a tall, purposeful figure, monochrome against the wet and marbled granite façades, as I watch him forge his way along Schoolhill.

It was here we first connected, on Schoolhill. As his young art mistress during his final school year, fresh from my own studies, I found him witty, and listened intently as he showed off to his friends. He was different to the other boys. My talk, in one of the loveliest Victorian galleries in the country, was unimportant, irrelevant; as I recall my mouth moved to words about surrealism or whatever the lesson was. He made *me* feel surreal. I was open, transparent, as I tried to draw him to me. I chose him, picked him out, even then. Does he think of that occasion too, whenever he passes the gallery?

He has stayed too long in this city. The hard rock quarried here for centuries, sharp cornered streetscapes hewn by his forefathers, has settled in him and kept him a willing prisoner. Now oil is the new mistress, and a hundred stone quarries, manmade holes, lie neglected and filled with water.

He chose the easier route. Unlike the quarrymen who chipped away at the sharp rock with their blocking hammers, patient, slow, enduring, his own grandfather one of that number, Daniel plundered the granite in a different way. Renowned for his architectural knowledge, Daniel's crisp postmodern designs are a testimony to his love affair with this cold, glittering material.

I smile at the irony reflected in the geology of where we have made our lives: mine the clay of the lowlands and sandstone of the central belt: multi-layered, sedimentary, yielding, Daniel's the igneous crust of the earth's surface: impenetrable.

It was easy enough to find him. After delivering my talk to the architectural students, I asked in the Faculty office what time Dr. Ogilvie would be arriving this evening. I don't have long to wait. Now, seeing him, I am unsure whether or not to approach him. Do I really want to stir up old feelings, old memories. Will he even recognise me?

I follow him at a distance into the building and watch as he shares a joke with a janitor on the front desk, who takes a briefcase from him to keep while he goes up to deliver his lecture. After he leaves, I sit in the lobby and write a note. If he wants to see me, he can. If not, I will be on the train in the morning and nothing will be lost. I ask the janitor if he would mind giving this note to Dr. Ogilvie when he returns.

*

The tentative knock at my hotel door comes around nine o'clock and startles me. I have been lost in thought about another note and a missed encounter of forty years ago, a different knock on another door.

Sitting at the sealed window, high up in this contemporary city centre chain hotel, I have been trying to recall that young woman from forty years ago who capitulated and left too easily, without a fight, in shame, and donning a familiar cloak of guilt.

I walk across the soft carpet and open the door.

'Hello Daniel.'

'Hi. This is a surprise.' He steps nervously into the room. We look at each other for what feels like a long time after I close the door, each assessing two decades of wear and tear on the other, too unfamiliar now to embrace in a hotel bedroom.

'Sit down' I say, smiling, gesturing toward the window.

He takes off his overcoat and shakes the droplets of water from the surface before draping it over the back of a chair. He is wearing an expensive black cashmere polo neck sweater and dark brown thick cord jeans with sand coloured desert boots. He smells of success. Someone keeps him looking stylish. He must still be married. We sit at the window, facing each other in two tub chairs across a low table.

'Drink?'

He looks around for my open bottle, wine maybe.

'I don't drink now. But I can get you something from the mini bar.'

He seems glad of a gin and tonic. I pour a fruit juice to keep him company and sit, tucking my legs under me in the chair.

'It's changed. The city I mean. Aberdeen's rich now' I say, gesturing towards the twinkling lights, easing us into familiar territory.

'How did you know where I'd be?' A nervous hand through the hair.

'It wasn't difficult. I knew you taught part time for your old department. I read an article by you in the AJ that mentioned it. I was here today to give a give a guest lecture to the students myself actually. Do you know Claire Mathieson? I met her in Glasgow recently and she invited me to speak.' *Relax, I didn't come for you.* The silver hair suits him, and I see he wears it slightly longer, so the part that flops is the same length as the back. He is stylish for an older man, slimmer than last time, more his original shape. Perhaps he jogs, or follows a better diet.

'Are you still married?'

He is. His daughter Lucy wants to study geology, work in the oil industry, in engineering, probably seismology and tectonics. He is immensely proud of her. A wonderful, crazy teenager. He has been a good father I can tell. The kind that stroked her hair when she was little and told her she could be anything she wanted to be, so long as it suited the Ogilvie lineage.

I realise he's anxious. He can't stop talking, about himself, his daughter, his work. Every time I go to say something about myself he turns the topic back to himself. I watch his mouth move, words of no relevance, jokes even, and think to myself, *you have no idea. I could be just some old friend you happened to bump into. You don't know how it was, for years.*

I want to tell him the whole story. But I don't. I don't say any of it, because reality is dawning on me. I almost want to laugh. Even now I was about to try to make myself more interesting for Daniel. It was why I came.

Well, no more. He is diminishing before my eyes. I see clearly now the technique he had of talking up his own life, making jokes about mine with just enough empathy for me to believe he cared. Until, after years of this, I believed I had no life. My life became one of waiting for his. My own fault, waiting for a man to love me who never would.

In my dreams though, all these years, it was a different man. I'm not sure who, but not this one. I'd overlooked all his shortcomings to create an illusion.

He is still talking, about his latest holiday, his big new house, his recent award, his achievements. All designed to impress. He never was the torn, complex character I thought I had shaped. I was just convenient. He wanted it all. I thought he must love me but didn't say so because of Jane or Susan or Honor or Jean, and because we lived at opposite ends of the country. But it was none of those things.

He's just a man I used to know: shallow, materialistic, terrified to show his emotions. A man who didn't reply to letters, not because he was complicated, anguished, but because he wasn't interested. It's easy to sound interested when you're post-coital in bed with a glass of wine bought and served by the woman beside you. A man who visited when it was convenient for him. When he wanted to take pornographic photographs. When he wanted to save on a hotel bill. Who knows.

I gave my life to this man. Of course he never asked me to.

I catch him looking at his watch. I make excuses about an early start. I want him to go now.

'I'm moving to Utrecht' I say at the door.

'Utrecht? Odd place. Why there?' he asks without conviction.

'Oh. I met someone.'

Inscape

Trudi

Glasgow, September 1986

I pull the lion's head knocker for the last time and the storm door thuds closed. Then I put the keys back through the letterbox as advised. The other set is with the estate agent, including the pewter one, which now fits the lock on a new bathroom. My few pieces have been shipped on ahead by a removal firm that covers the Netherlands: an Eileen Gray table, a Marcel Breuer chair, the cracked leather Corbusier chaise, a few limited-edition prints, some boxes.

Behind this retained façade, with the same tall window openings, a set of three on each floor, arched ones at the top, with its Greek Thomson inspired chimney stacks, is an unrecognisable interior. Cavernous, filled with light and double height windows, one set tall and above those a set of arched ones; white walls and a study mezzanine with a structural glass balustrade, looking up to a glass roof and down to an open space accessed by steel and glass stairs, the kitchen and living areas seamlessly connected. Sleeping areas are down below, cool and dark. A landscaped garden and decking can be seen at the back beyond a fully glazed wall with sliding doors. In time this too will be altered. Such is the transient nature of domestic architecture, which is as it should be. The new family will move in today and then their own experiment will begin. All traces of the previous ones have gone from this particular laboratory.

Perhaps every family conducts life in a laboratory. Experiments with varied elements and mixed results. It can be the patriarchal caricatures designed for an exhibition in the 1940s and for nuclear families in 1950s Homes For The Future. It can be this Thatcher government's belief in what it calls *family values,* here in 1980s Britain, outlawing anyone who is different. It can be controlling and misogynistic, producing one willing to compromise almost anything in search of love.

A child will flourish in a laboratory nurtured by any combination of a man and a woman, or two women, or two men; or one independent woman, or one man, or an extended group. Blood, or not. Young, or old. Married, or not. To succeed the experiment needs only love. Perhaps one day the stigma will go, and the law will change. Ailsa Bray made one mistake: putting a man's name on a birth certificate out of a sense of propriety.

Truus told me everything, once she knew I'd been told nothing at all: about my mother's work; about the fatal fall, which no-one understood as Ailsa was always so careful; how Truus fought my father, whom she never met, for custody, as it would be what Ailsa would have wanted. In the end she lost, as did Johan Peeters, who my father cited as having suffered a mental breakdown. As next of kin my father had rights; he even changed my name. My grandmother never recovered and died shortly after Ailsa. Once he won custody he sent Bridget to fetch me. He refused to go to the Netherlands himself, refused to meet with the individuals he considered to have been a bad influence, refused to set foot in the country.

He would have seen Ailsa's obituary in the Glasgow Herald. Bridget believed his motive for getting me back was Knowe Terrace. He somehow believed it to be his rightful place of residence, as head of the household. The first thing he did was to close a women's drawing office that my mother had established there, specialising in social housing. Truus found Bridget impressive she said. They wrote to each other for a year or two, about me mostly, until Bridget left us. *Bridget, ze was formidabel!! Ze never trust your father.*

I got to know Truus before she died in April last year. Having an older woman in my life was something I'd not had since Bridget. It was cathartic. Now the interior of the Schröder House is to be renovated, restored to the original and, I hope, opened to the public. I'm with Rietveld on this. I don't think anyone else should live in it; a laboratory frozen in time.

I press my forehead against the cool cabin window of the new KLM Airbus and look down at the clouds, at the shapes forming, then close my eyes.

A woman is smiling, looking up and pointing at the sky from the open corner window of a white room. I watch her face. We dance. She laughs. I look into her eyes, hold her hand, touch her red hair, throw my arms around her neck. I hear her voice in a recording that offers a narrative, a new attitude to life given physical form. The room brims with light and love. She beckons me with her outstretched arms, and I jump.

Epilogue

Centraal Museum, Utrecht, 2018

Rietveld Schröder Archive   (iPad digital collection)

This early black and white home footage, filmed in October 1924 by Belgian architect Johan Peeters, better known in his role as leader with resistance fighters the Belgian Army of Partisans in World War II, and who died in action, is unique in that it shows the Rietveld Schröder House at the point when Mrs. Schröder and her children were in the process of moving in. They can be seen here with friends, including Rietveld and two of his children. They took up permanent residence on 1 January 1925. The blinds, sliding partitions and built-in furniture are yet to be installed, and the floor remains monotone. The distinctive colour palette would be applied to the floor and central core in the summer of 1925.

The two people featured in the film are Scottish architect, Ailsa Bray, a close friend of Truus Schröder, and her young daughter Trudi. The voiceover is that of Ailsa Bray, who died in 1925 after falling from the roof of an apartment block under construction, which she had designed with Peeters, nearby on Laan van Minsweerd (see postscript).

Trudi Bray died on 10 July 2017 in Utrecht, where she had lived since 1986. She was a longtime supporter of the Centraal Museum and donated this film in 1990 as part of the exhibition Rietveld Schröder House: The Luxury of Frugality. She has also donated her apartment on Koningslaan to the Museum, currently under renovation, for use by visiting researchers.

Postscript

In 2010 Trudi Bray campaigned to have a posthumous case brought against her late father, Michael O'Neill, of Glasgow, Scotland. Although her mother's death on 10 July 1925 was recorded as accidental, her daughter uncovered shipping passenger lists while researching her family history online that placed her father as a passenger on a ship which sailed from Leith to Rotterdam on 5 July 1925, and again on its return voyage on 11 July 1925. She was convinced he was connected in some way to her mother's death. Michael O'Neill had said in an interview in 1925 in Glasgow that he had never visited the Netherlands. It was however ruled that there was insufficient evidence, and no witnesses still living, to merit revisiting the original verdict of accidental death.

Gerrit Rietveld is buried at the Soestbergen cemetery. On his grave is a simple granite stone designed by two of his sons. Rietveld was originally buried in Bilthoven and shared the grave with Truus Schröder. At the request of his daughters Rietveld was, in 1995, reburied at Soestbergen and his wife's name put on the stone.

Trudi and Ailsa Bray are buried together in Bilthoven Cemetery.

A Note on Sources

While Truus Schröder, Gerrit Rietveld, Piet Klaarhamer and other people who actually lived appear in this book as fictional characters, I have tried to incorporate as accurately as possible the outward particulars and events of their lives as they have been documented. In some instances, I adapted real situations to fit the narrative. For example, Truus Schröder did stay with a family in London around 1909 and called it her "first liberated time". She did come to appreciate English Arts and Crafts during that stay. The woman who so inspired her by living in an open attic space with her child was probably in the Netherlands and not in Chipping Campden, but she did exist. The architect Richard Rogers' house in Chelsea and other references to his architecture are as described, but the pen left on a podium is fictional. Throughout the novel, events, quotes and details are based as accurately as possible on researched and accredited published information and interviews, except for interwoven conversations and scenes with the characters of Ailsa Bray, Gertrude O'Neill/Trudi Bray, Johan Peeters, Michael O'Neill and others associated with them, who are all fictional and have no relation to an actual person, living or dead.

Acknowledgements

I would like to thank the following:

Pollokshields Heritage

Jaap Oosterhoff and Natalie Dubois of Centraal Museum, Utrecht

Alice T. Friedmann for *Women and the Making of the Modern House*

Corrie Nagtegaal for *Tr. Schröder-Schräder Bewoonster van het Rietveld Schroderhuis*

Paul Overy for *De Stijl*

Bertus Mulder for *Gerrit Thomas Rietveld LIFE THOUGHT WORK*

Paul Overy, Lenneke Buller, Frank den Outsten, Bertus Mulder for *The Rietveld Schröder House*

Ida van Zijl for *60 + 20: The History of the Rietveld Schröder House*

Jan McCredie, Linda Megson, William Morrison, Joy Hugill, Ken Porter, Sean McNamara, Tracey Macdonald McNamara and Martin McNamara.